Pride Publishing books by Rae Marks

Hart Consulting
Sweet Hart
Dash
Savage

I0691672

Hart Consulting

SAVAGE

RAE MARKS

Savage
ISBN # 978-1-80250-994-6
©Copyright Rae Marks 2022
Cover Art by Erin Dameron-Hill ©Copyright November 2022
Interior text design by Claire Siemaszkiewicz
Pride Publishing

SAVAGE

Chapter One

Mase

"He's gonna kill you," Wade grumbled over the phone.

"He's gonna have to make me first," Mase said as he pulled up flights.

"He's an operator of the highest caliber. He'll probably feel it when you land at the same airport he did."

Mase rolled his eyes. There was no way Jazz would 'feel' when he landed. Then again, Mase felt it when Jazz entered a room. It was like the air changed. In the beginning, he'd tried to ignore it, but over the past decade, it had become a part of him. He was a sucker for Jazz.

"I'm plenty angry at him, too," Mase said. "I just might kill him for doing something so monumentally stupid."

Jazz wouldn't see Mase until he wanted Jazz to. And, at some point, Mase would want that. Jazz would learn he couldn't just go rogue at any time without being detected.

"Fuck," Max yelled as something crashed.

"Don't throw that keyboard. It belongs to Hart Consulting," Wade chided.

"I can afford to replace it," Max said.

"I have no doubt, but that would mean you'll have to use a regular keyboard until it arrives, so let's just respect HC property."

A scraping sound followed by the clackety-clack of typing meant Max had made up with his computer and was once again working to find Jazz with his mad hacker skills.

"I can't find him. Why can't I find him? I have better facial recognition software than the government does," Max mumbled.

"Only because you took theirs and made it better," Wade reminded him.

"Why start from scratch when you can improve on what's already there?"

"If it's so stellar, why can't you locate Jazz?" Mase asked.

There was a sigh and more typing on the other end of the line. Mase had three tabs open on his laptop, each ready to book a flight to a different city.

Jazz was already in the air, headed to some unknown destination. They were stuck trying to figure out which flight he'd boarded.

"This is ridiculous," Max said. "You can't wear a hat or a hood through security, so why can't I find him?"

Mase could tell that it was more of an ego thing than a general frustration on Max's part. Max never missed.

He didn't screw up when it came to computers. He was a genius with both hardware and software, and Hart Consulting was lucky to have him.

Max had never been in the military, but he still had a call sign. His name was S.I.N. Some buddies in college had called him a Super Intel Nerd and the name had stuck and shortened to 'Sin'.

The description fit Max, but the acronym didn't. Mase only ever thought of him as Max, because if he looked at Max, his thoughts were more protective than sinful. Max was cute as a button...in a grumpy kitten sort of way. Sure, he was a good-looking kid—but he was still a kid.

He looked about sixteen, not twenty-four. And he was one of Mase's kid brother's best friends. Mase still couldn't believe that his younger brothers had sought him out after all these years. He shifted in the pleather airport seat as he thought about how much pressure Nick was applying to get Mase to go see their father.

"Is there another way to find him?" Wade asked.

"Of course there is, but I still need to figure out how he slipped past my facial recognition software. If it's a flaw in the program, I need to know and adjust for it."

"Fret over your precious program later," Mase said. "For now, find Jazz so I can get on a plane."

Mase kept his voice low. He was already at the airport, bag in hand, ready to chase after Jazz. No one was close enough to hear what he was saying, but he was still paranoid. It came with the job.

"Fine," Max sighed. "Let me follow his coordinates for a minute or two. I'll match the trajectory with tail numbers of planes and find out where he's going. If we didn't have a GPS tracker on him, this wouldn't be possible, so when you do see him, ask him how he slips past airport security cams."

And Mase sent a thought of thanks to Dee, Jazz's grandma. They'd all been worried about his erratic behavior over the past two months. Dee had helped them plant GPS trackers in items Jazz almost always had with him.

Mase would do everything he could to keep Dee's name out of it, but he'd have to give up at least one of the trackers when he confronted Jazz. And there would *definitely* be a confrontation.

He'd give up the disk they'd placed in his wallet first. It was something any of them could have put there. Max had tagged each tracker. Currently, Jazz had two of the trackers on him, the one in his wallet and the one in the watch that had been his grandfather's.

They'd put a third tracker in his favorite knife and a fourth in the knife that had been his grandfather's, but Jazz had left both of those behind. It would have been hard to get them through airport security.

"Is it some CIA trick?" Max asked.

"What?"

"Dodging my facial rec program."

"I'll ask him if I ever find out where he's going," Mase said.

"Yeah, yeah. Almost there… Got it. He's on a flight headed to Bush Intercontinental in Houston."

"Fuck," Mase said as he clicked on the tab with the flight to Houston.

"Houston's bad?" Max asked.

"Martin Coleman lives in Texas, so not a good sign. Okay, flight's booked. I'm out for at least forty-eight hours."

"You're risking your cover, too," Wade warned.

"My job is to follow around Bernard. That's exactly what I'm doing."

Jazz was supposed to be undercover as a high-level French drug and human trafficker named Lucien Bernard. Mase had been rising in the ranks of a Ukrainian drug and human trafficking ring. Their covers were intersecting for the moment.

"We'll make it work if we need to." Wade sighed. "Texas is a believable place for you both to travel. I need you back by Wednesday, though, because Jazz has that meeting with Campbell, the lawyer from San Francisco, though I'd prefer to have you back by Tuesday. Double-D is coming in to go over financials, and since you're Stateside…"

"I'll be back. In fact, both Jazz and I will hopefully return long before Tuesday. I need to go catch my flight. We'll talk when I touch down."

Mase disconnected the call and got in line for the security checkpoint. Being back on American soil was great—and yet it wasn't. Wade wanted him to jump into a role he'd neglected three years before when he'd moved to Ukraine.

Hart Consulting had originally started as a joke. While he was being investigated for sedition, Mase started investigating the men accusing him, namely his commanding officer and teammates.

It hadn't initially worked out as he'd planned. Mase had been discharged, and two of the three men who'd testified against him were still in the army. But he'd done such a good job investigating his commanding officer that Captain Banning had been court-martialed and was still in jail. The assholes who had accused Mase of sexually harassing them were still serving their country.

Mase was no longer bitter, because he'd found his calling. The army had offered financial security when he'd had none. But Hart Consulting was his, and he was making a difference exactly where he wanted to.

He'd been cleared of most of the charges, though he hadn't received an offer to return to service. He could probably thank Major General Moore for that.

Mase shook thoughts of Blake and his father out of his head. Coming back to the US had his past bombarding him. It seemed Jazz was facing the same issues.

* * * *

Jazz was going to land soon. He could get in a hell of a lot of trouble before Mase touched down.

"Nervous flyer?" The woman next to him on the plane asked.

Realizing his knee was bouncing, Mase took a deep breath. He was an operator. He could be patient for the length of a mid-haul flight.

"Just in a hurry to get where I'm going," he said.

"Where *are* you going?"

The woman leaned forward and tilted her head to the side. She was young, beautiful and sultry, but Mase's mind was on Jazz.

"Meeting a buddy of mine so I can try to keep him out of trouble for the weekend," Mase said.

"That's too bad. I thought maybe you were looking for trouble."

She smiled. She was sexy, but Mase wished he'd brought headphones so he could block her out.

"No, ma'am," he said. "My wife would kill me if I got into any of that."

The flirtatious light in her eyes died at the word 'wife', and Mase was glad. If she'd continued to flirt, it would have made her so much less attractive.

Another time, another place, if he were going to meet anyone else, maybe Mase would have considered her offer of trouble, but he was going to find Jazz.

"Is your friend as cute as you?" she asked.

Mase raised his brows at how quickly she'd moved on.

She shrugged. "You already said he's looking for trouble."

"I'm afraid you're a little too feminine for him." Mase winked.

"Oh. Well then, I hope he doesn't find trouble." She lowered her voice. "Many Texans can be very closed-minded about certain things."

"That's why I'm flying out last minute...to make sure he doesn't do anything stupid."

She nodded, and after a moment of awkward silence, changed the subject. But Mase's mind stayed on Jazz. It was not a coincidence he was flying to Texas after going AWOL.

There had been a change in Jazz since the incident a few months before. That night had been pure torture. It was the first time in three years they'd been in the same room together, and everything had gone to hell.

Even two months later, Mase started to break out into a sweat when he remembered walking into that hotel room to find Jazz unconscious on the bed.

After ten years, Mase had given up hope that what he felt for Jazz would diminish. He did his best to hold himself back, but that had been impossible when Jazz had been calling his name.

The things he'd mumbled had been just enough to twist Mase's guts but not quite detailed enough to let him know what he needed to do about it. Jazz had told him the man in question was untouchable.

Mase hadn't realized why until Max had helped them put the pieces together. *Martin Coleman*. US Congressman Martin Coleman had gone to college and been in the Reserve Officer Training Corps with Jazz. And Martin Coleman had been at the gala that night. He also happened to live in Houston when he wasn't representing the great state of Texas in Congress.

Jazz had only been sixteen when he'd started college, so it didn't take a genius to figure out that the much older Martin had taken advantage of him in a way that had deeply affected Jazz—and was still affecting him to this day.

Mase's phone pinged—then it pinged again...and again. He was getting messages from Wade and Max. Jazz was at Martin Coleman's home. Max was working on accessing the security feed. He would remove any evidence of Jazz's presence.

Mase sat forward in his seat, only to lean back. Leaning forward again, he looked around until he realized he was looking for a quicker way to get to Jazz, and that just wasn't possible.

Jazz was on his own with no backup. He hadn't even told them where he was going, probably because they would have tied him down to stop him from making such a crazy decision. Mase didn't even try to stop his foot from bouncing on the floor of the plane. Jazz was the one person who could throw him into a tailspin.

"Your friend already find some trouble?" his seat partner asked.

"You could say that."

And there wasn't a damn thing Mase could do to stop the backlash that was sure to come.

Chapter Two

Jazz

Fuck.

Hands trembling, Jazz hid behind a curtain and tried to silently steady his breaths. It was like some bad spy movie. He thought he'd be in and out before anyone was the wiser. It was just his luck Marty would come home before Jazz was able to sneak out.

He hadn't seen Marty in more than fifteen years. Just the sound of his voice had Jazz's insides quivering with remnants of the panic that sixteen-year-old Jazz had felt.

His mind kept trying to trick him into believing he was still in danger. Jazz closed his eyes and kept repeating, *I can kill him with my bare hands*, over and over again. He wasn't the defenseless teenager he'd been when he'd met Marty.

Even those thoughts didn't calm his racing heart, so Jazz thought of the one thing that always brought him peace — Mase.

His breaths came easier when he remembered that Mase was safe and currently back in Virginia, waiting for him. He was probably pissed as a hornet that Jazz had disappeared for a few days. The thought made Jazz smile. Mase had always been protective of him...too protective.

After what had happened with Marty, Jazz had been determined to stand up for himself, to defend himself. It had taken a few years for him to build the confidence in his abilities, but he had, and though there were still a few fears that lingered, they only affected his personal life.

"I don't have time for this, Dad," Marty said.

"There are rumors floating around DC that you're a faggot." Marty's father, Charles, sneered the last word.

"There are rumors like that about many people in DC."

"Most times they're true and we all know it, but people are only willing to ignore it for so long. You need to keep it in your pants."

"They're just rumors. I haven't even been seeing anyone recently."

"And it'd better damn well stay that way. I won't be able to pull you out of this mess, Marty. This isn't something I can take care of, like the mess you made back in college. That Trent boy was haunting you for years."

"Kevin wasn't haunting me. He was just worried something would surface about the private parties we had."

"Private parties," Charles scoffed. "Orgies. Gay orgies."

Jazz reminded himself to breathe. Was that what Marty had told his father? An orgy implied consent. That was in no way what had happened.

"Yeah, well. I don't do that anymore."

"And moving forward, you will only be having sex with Laureen," Charles said.

"It doesn't work like that. I won't want her just because no one else is available."

"Then I guess you'll be gettin' real familiar with your hand. I mean it, Marty. No queer bullshit. If I hear a whiff of anything, I'll be backing away from you, and I won't endorse you in the next election."

"You're one to talk. You can't keep it in your pants. How many girls have I helped you pay off in the last five years?"

"This is Texas, son. All I have to do is bow my head, act humble and I'll push right on through. Being horny is a lot different than being a faggot."

Jazz stiffened every time Charles Coleman used that word. It shouldn't surprise him—and, in reality, it didn't. But to call your own son that name was too much. And yet Jazz couldn't bring himself to feel any sympathy for Marty.

"I have everything under control, Dad."

"And by that, you'd better mean you won't be caught with your pants around your ankles in some airport bathroom like any of those other pansies. You're a spoiled little shit who has always had me to take care of things, but I won't be able to help you fix this if you fuck it up. I took care of that Trent boy, but I can't—"

"I never asked you to...take care of Kevin. I wish you would have left him alone."

"He was developing a case of bad conscience. What were you going to do, Marty?"

"I told you I'd take care of it."

Kevin Trent had committed suicide two years before. Jazz had made sure to keep tabs on both Marty and Kevin. Had Kevin felt guilty? The bigger question was, did that change the situation in any way? Could Jazz forgive either man? He shook his head. If guilt had ultimately killed Kevin, then that had nothing to do with Jazz.

"And yet you didn't get him to keep his mouth shut," Charles said. "He was sure that boy disappeared after leaving the army and was determined to find him and make sure he was okay."

"Yeah, well, even you weren't able to find out where he was." Marty stepped closer to the curtain.

His proximity brought sweat to Jazz's brow. He wasn't ready to face Marty. The very thought took him back to his sixteen-year-old self.

When the panic started to rise inside him, Jazz realized that coming to Texas had been a bad idea. None of his team knew where he was. If anything were to happen...

He took a slow, quiet breath. He could kill Marty with his bare hands, he reminded himself again. Even someone with a gun aimed at him could be defeated with Krav Maga. He wasn't a defenseless teenager anymore.

"Jasper Thibodeaux is dead. He doesn't have a driver's license, a cell phone number, any open lines of credit or any social media. The man probably ended up the same as Kevin."

"There's more than one Jasper Thibodeaux," Marty said.

"There's not more than one Jasper Woodrow Thibodeaux who graduated from Rice University in the last twenty years. You don't think my people can find whatever information exists on him?"

Jazz stiffened at the sound of his name. He had plenty of driver's licenses, just none with his own name. That had been his choice, to leave the trail of his real identity cold. Now he was glad he had, though he'd have to pick that back up soon if he was going to leave the CIA.

He shook that thought away. Now was not the time. His current assignment could still last a few years, and he wasn't sure they'd let him transition like they had Sam.

Jazz realized that this part of his trip might have been wasted. If they thought he was dead, then who had drugged him? What would they do if he stepped out from behind the curtain, alive and well?

"Well, if that's true, then the only proof of my indiscretions is gone with him. I have to get back to the golf course. I only came home to pick up this document to show Henry Crane." Marty said.

And with that, they left the room and the house. Jazz pulled his hood up over his head, slipped out of the same window he'd come in and jumped the fence.

As he made his way back to the hotel to change, Jazz went over the conversation in his head. He'd been so sure Marty had been the one to drug him.

He needed to get Max and his handler on this, but he didn't want either to know where he was, so the request would have to wait. He had one more meeting before he could even consider heading home.

As he changed for his next appointment, Jazz considered the man he was meeting. Remy Dupree had plenty of connections in Washington, but Jazz had never met the man. He wasn't sure Remy even knew what he looked like, so he couldn't have been the one to set up the drugged drink in DC.

"You're getting paranoid again," Jazz told his reflection.

That had worked to his advantage since he'd gone undercover, but now he was taking risks he knew he shouldn't be taking. He shouldn't be in Texas under a sloppily-thrown-together alias.

Maybe part of him had known it wasn't Marty, and that was why he hadn't asked Wade to send someone from HC to plant the bugs in Marty's home and offices.

They all knew about Marty now. Jazz's loose lips had taken care of that. By the time the drugs had worked their way through his system, Wade, Mase and Sam had been demanding to know what his connection was to Martin Coleman.

He'd kept it vague, but the look on Mase's face had said more than any words could. He knew. Jazz hadn't told him, even while he'd been drugged, and yet he'd figured it out. Mase knew better than anyone else in the world that the aftereffects of what had happened back then still plagued Jazz.

The shame of it ate him up from the inside out. The humiliation made him want to curl up and hide, but he didn't have that luxury. Maybe that was why it was so easy for him to step into someone else's shoes and pretend to be Lucien Bernard.

Jazz changed from his tactical pants and hoodie into jeans and a T-shirt. He wasn't dressing up for Remy Dupree. He pulled his hair into a man bun then rubbed his palm along his newly shaven jaw. The trimmed beard he kept would grow back in just a few days, before he needed to be Lucien again. Still, it was strange to see so much skin on his face.

Chapter Three

Mase

As soon as Mase stepped off the jetway, he put in his Bluetooth and pressed dial. His stride ate up the walkway. He weaved around meandering travelers as the call rang through.

"He left Coleman's house without incident," Wade said as soon as they went through security protocol.

Mase breathed a sigh of relief.

"Technically," Max corrected.

"What does 'technically' mean?" Mase demanded.

"It means Max doesn't know when to be discriminating in his intel. Coleman and his father came to the house while Jazz was there, but they didn't notice anything and left a few minutes before Jazz lit out of there."

"And Max has destroyed all evidence?"

"Wasn't much to get rid of. He's good."

"He better damn well be, taking a risk like this," Wade grumbled.

Mase's biggest issue with this whole thing was that once again Jazz was trying to go it alone. He never opened up, never let anyone in. Even Dee was worried about how much he kept bottled inside that brain of his.

"Yeah, well, he made the mistake of using my devices. I have them all online and recording. They caught the whole conversation between Martin and Charles Coleman."

"Wade," Mase said, knowing Wade had already listened to it.

"Charles Coleman hasn't been able to track Jazz. They think he's dead."

So they were back at square one when it came to finding out who had drugged Jazz. Max hadn't been able to get enough for even a partial facial recognition.

"Max, you followed our blond friend through all the hotel security footage?"

"Yep."

"What about external?"

"There are some holes in the hotel's security cams. I wasn't able to follow him to the outside of the building."

"What about checking timing? Seeing what time he left?"

"It was dark outside by that time, so facial recognition wouldn't work because his face was too pixilated. There were also two blond men who left in a span close to when he would have made it to the front door. They were both wearing tuxedos."

"I know you have a lot on your plate, but just...please go back and see if you're able to find out what kind of car any of them drove or even which direction they were headed."

"One got in a car registered as a ride-share by the owner. I'm working on hacking the ride-share system to see who the client was. The other smoked a cigarette before talking to a woman and heading back toward the hotel with her, but I didn't catch them on the security cameras, so they didn't actually go back inside."

"See what you can find about the ride-share," Mase said. "And Wade, you may be practicing discretion, but we will have a discussion about Martin Coleman's conversation."

"I know, Savage," Wade said. "I had no doubt. Max will text you the car rental reservation. Jazz is currently at what we assume is his hotel. We'll send you the coordinates."

As soon as he disconnected, Mase's phone began to ping. He made his way to the car rental agency. He was on his way within fifteen minutes, but it wasn't fast enough.

Jazz was on the move again. Mase had wanted to corner him in his hotel and hopefully talk some sense into him. Instead, he followed the little dot on the app Max had sent him to trace Jazz.

When the dot stopped, Mase got as close as he could before pulling into a parking spot in downtown Houston. Jazz's locator pointed him to a tall building of mirrored glass.

Just as he was about to call Max, he got a text telling him that Jazz was on the twelfth floor. Mase shook his head. Max was a genius.

Floors eight through sixteen were law offices. Mase took a suit jacket out of his carryon and pulled it over his blue shirt and black jeans. It wasn't a suit, but it would have to do. Mase didn't have a gun, but he wasn't too concerned.

What were the chances of a shootout in a law firm? Then again, it was Texas. He had a Taser, a knife and zip-ties tucked in his pockets, so those would have to do.

On the twelfth floor, Mase wandered around. He didn't want to look lost, so he paced around a little, getting the lay of the land.

"Can I help you?"

Mase turned to see a cute blonde woman in a bright purple pantsuit. She gave him a warm, open smile.

"I'm just stretching my legs," he said. "I can't stand sitting in meetings too long."

She nodded in understanding. If he knew what alias Jazz was using, he might ask her where he was. Instead, he pulled his phone out as if to check the time.

"If you need any refreshments, just let me know," she moved past him into a little alcove outside the door of an office.

Mase heard raised voices, one of them he recognized. He was moving before he realized it.

"Sir," the woman in the purple suit called to him as he approached the door. "Sir, you can't go in there. That's a private meeting. It could be about confidential material."

He threw the door open and found Jazz arguing with the man behind the desk. Jazz turned toward the door and his look of anger turned venomous when he saw Mase.

"What the hell are you doing here?" Jazz demanded.

"Watching your back, like I always do." Mase stepped into the room. When he went to shut the door, the woman in the purple suit stepped forward and asked Mase to leave.

"It's fine, Kelly. Please shut the door on your way out," the lawyer said. "I'm borrowing this office while I'm in town, for fuck's sake. Can you two please keep your voices down?"

"It was raised voices that led me to your office," Mase said.

"How long have you been tailing me?" Jazz demanded.

"We'll get into semantics later. Are you done here?" Mase asked.

"No. I need to make sure my sperm donor gets the message."

"I wasn't looking for you on behalf of my father," the lawyer said. "I was looking for you on behalf of my mother."

Mase stepped back as if he'd received a blow. Jazz had a half-brother? How long had Jazz known? He kept every piece of himself locked up tight. Maybe he'd known all along.

"I have no interest in meeting her or you or anyone else related to *him*," Jazz said.

The lawyer's jaw clenched, but he sat back down in his chair. After a moment, he took a deep breath and placed his hands on his desk.

"Technically, my mother is no longer related to *him*, but that's neither here nor there —"

"They're divorced?" Jazz asked.

"Yes. I'm surprised you aren't aware."

"I have no idea what's happened to him. I stopped caring once my mother died."

Mase's head was spinning. He'd known Jazz's mother had died when he was young, but he hadn't known there was a father who could have taken Jazz in. Jazz always referred to him as 'the sperm donor', so Mase assumed that his mom hadn't even known the man's name. And if the lawyer was his half-brother, they seemed alarmingly close in age.

Again, the lawyer's jaw worked as if he were holding back some vitriol he wanted to spew. Jazz raised an eyebrow as if to egg him on.

"That's not exactly true now, is it? Or you wouldn't have weaseled money from him when you were still a kid."

"I never took any money from him."

"Maybe not directly, but your grandmother did."

"No. We lived off my grandfather's pension until I went into the military, and it was no bounty, especially with all the medical bills we had when *Pépère* died."

"I don't know what stories your grandmother told, but that money came from our family trust."

Chapter Four

Jazz

Jazz opened his mouth to deny it, but two things ran through his mind — the first being that he had known *Mémère* had had to fight to get *Pépère's* pension transferred after his grandfather had died.

The second thing that ran through Jazz's mind was something he'd almost blocked out. The reason *Mémère* had needed to fight for the pension had been a sore spot.

The oil company *Pépère* had worked for had wanted to drop him from the insurance once he'd exhausted his leave options but *Mémère* had found an attorney to send a letter and the company had let them keep his insurance, especially since the physical strain of his job had contributed to his heart issues.

With his *Pépère* in the hospital, Jazz had been scared about losing the only family he had left. Then the unthinkable happened. A social worker came to visit their house to do a welfare check.

He'd known his father was a lawyer, so he'd tracked him down. Jazz remembered waiting for his father in the parking garage of his office in Houston. He'd been angry and scared. He'd used the only weapon he felt he had.

"*Do you know who I am?*" Jazz had asked.

"*Why would I know who you are?*" Lance Dupree had said as he'd pushed by him.

"*Maybe because Marie Thibodeaux was my mom, Mr. Dupree?*"

The man had stopped dead and turned to face him. He'd squinted as he looked Jazz over. He hadn't said anything for a moment.

"*Do you know?*" Jazz had demanded.

"*Know what?*"

"*Do you know how she died? When she died?*"

The man had swallowed and given one nod.

"*Good. I hope you rot in hell for what you did to a sixteen-year-old girl then tossed her aside when she got too old for you.*"

Lance had stepped menacingly closer and whispered low, "*You'd better be careful about the accusations you make, Cajun.*"

Jazz had laughed. "*You think I'm afraid of you, Mr. D.A.? You forget I have your blood running through my veins.*"

"*There's no proof of that.*"

"*That's what you always told her.*"

Lance had stepped back as if he'd been slapped.

"*That's right. I was there. I heard every word. Every insult, every threat. I could probably sue you for wrongful death.*"

The man had had the gall to roll his eyes. "*I wasn't even there.*"

"You're a lawyer. Don't you know that someone can be convicted, at least in a civil case, of being liable for the death of someone even if they didn't hold the razor?"

Lance had paled but hadn't responded.

"Bet you expected me to be some backwater hayseed. Well, I'm not. I'm here to make a deal with you."

"What kind of deal?"

"My grandfather's in the hospital."

"What's that got to do with me? I didn't put him there."

"No, but my mother's dead. My grandparents are all I have left. If they die, I'll become a ward of the state...at least until I tell them my father's alive and well and living it in a big mansion in Houston. You always said my mom couldn't prove anything, but the state will sure as hell be willing to pay for a paternity test."

Lance had licked his lips. "What do you want from me?"

"I don't want a thing from you. I wish it were you who died, and she who lived. You can rot in hell. As far as I'm concerned, it's only a matter of time before you will. Someday I'll be a lawyer and maybe I'll find creative ways for you to pay, like child support owed based on your income and net worth. For now, all I have is a warning. Nothing better happen to take me from my grandmother. If anything does, I'll have no reason to protect your lies and greed."

Lance hadn't said anything. His nostrils had flared and his chest had risen and fallen at a rapid pace as he'd considered Jazz's words. He'd rolled his lips, and Jazz was sure he was holding back a litany of insults and denials, but he had been smart enough to keep them to himself. He'd given Jazz one sharp nod. That had been all Jazz had needed, so he'd turned on his heel and walked away.

Jazz hadn't directly been asking for money, but he could see how someone like Lance Dupree, or

Remington Dupree for that matter, might see it that way. Remy was a stuck-up asshole just like his father.

"I have no interest in meeting her," Jazz turned to leave and found Mase regarding him with surprise and confusion.

There was anger there as well, but Mase could take a number on that one. Jazz hadn't asked to be followed. He also wanted to know how the hell Mase had managed it, and he'd find out as soon as they were alone.

"She's leaving you money," Remy said from behind him.

That caused Jazz to pause for a moment, but only out of curiosity. Mase's gaze was aimed over Jazz's shoulder.

"I don't want her money," Jazz said without turning around.

"You don't even know how much she wants to give you," Remy said.

"It doesn't matter. Whether it's twenty dollars or twenty million, I don't want it."

"No way are you worth twenty million," Remy scoffed.

That had Jazz turning around. Only a rich fuck like Remington Dupree would assume Jazz could only afford to turn down less than he was worth.

"No," Jazz confirmed, "I'm not. But I've got enough, and I don't need anything from the Remington family coffers by way of my Dupree blood. I've seen what money does to people. It makes them greedy, and it makes them stay in loveless marriages."

Remy opened his mouth to retort the loveless marriage comment, but Jazz rolled right over him and kept going.

"It makes them do things that are totally and completely reprehensible. It also makes them think they're better than everyone else just because they're rich, and I would never want to be a spoiled, pretentious asshole like you. I can't be bought."

Jazz turned to leave again and threw the last words over his shoulder. "If she's worried about me spilling my lineage and wants to pay me to keep my mouth closed, believe me, I'm more embarrassed about my parentage than she could ever be about her husband having a bastard son."

Remy's words stopped him yet again.

"She's dying. She wants to meet you. She was hoping the money would entice you."

"It doesn't. Just…just tell her you offered it to me, and I turned it down."

"She won't believe me. If you really want her to stop hiring investigators to find you, meet with her yourself and tell her."

With a sigh, Jazz faced Remy once more. There was a family resemblance. He could see that, but the haughty way Remy carried himself made Jazz want to punch him in the face.

"Why won't she just believe you?" Jazz asked.

"Because I was dead set against her offering you any money in the first place."

Jazz felt Mase take a step forward, come a step closer. He didn't need their money. He may not be worth twenty million, but he had a lot of money saved. Their buddy Double-D had grown Jazz's savings into millions, even if it was nowhere near twenty.

He had a nest egg big enough he could retire tomorrow. With Jazz's consulting fees on top of his salary and Double-D's genius with investments, he didn't need anything from his sperm donor or his sperm donor's ex-wife.

Jazz's money was in a family trust, and he had never been more grateful for that than he was after listening to Martin and Charles Coleman.

"I can set up a meeting," Remy offered.

"No. I'm not in town for that long." Jazz had nothing to say to Celia Remington-Dupree.

"Here's her phone number." Remy came around the desk and handed Jazz a slip of paper. "In case you change your mind. If you set up a meeting, I'd like to be there when—"

"Don't get all anxious. I'm not meeting with your mom."

Remy sighed and rubbed his hands over his face. Now that he was standing closer, Jazz could see the dark circles under his eyes, the tension lines at the corners of his mouth.

"I don't think this is a good idea. But if you could have given your mother one last wish..."

Jazz fisted his hands, turned away and strode from the room. Having anyone in Lance's family even mention his mother made Jazz want to rip something apart. If he could have given his mother one last wish?

If he could have given her anything, Jazz would have wished he were enough for her. It would have been selfish on his part, but also might have helped his mom.

He could feel Mase behind him. The skin on the back of his neck prickled, telling him his anxiety was too high. He never liked anyone behind him, but he could usually handle it if it was one of his friends, especially Mase.

Jazz needed to be alone. He was livid, and he was desolate. It had been a day of epic lows in his life and the last person he needed around him was the one person who saw all the cracks in his armor.

Chapter Five

Mase

"Stop following me," Jazz whispered harshly when the elevator doors closed.

"You wanted me to stay and have a chat with your brother, then?"

"He's not my brother," Jazz said through his teeth.

"If you guys have the same father—"

"I don't have a father. If anything, I have a sperm donor."

"Jazz, why didn't you ever tell me you had...a half sibling?"

Jazz shook his head and stomped out of the elevator. Mase followed along, his mind spinning. Jazz had a brother.

Mase followed him out onto the street. When Jazz kept walking without even glancing back, Mase called out to him as he headed back to his rental car.

"I'll meet you at your hotel."

Jazz threw a middle finger over his shoulder and kept walking. Normally Mase would laugh, but today… Today was a day Jazz needed someone to talk to. Mase would get him to talk one way or another. That parting remark had really seemed to send Jazz into a tailspin. Jazz's mother was at the root of this.

Since Mase was already at his car, he rushed back to the hotel and up to the eighth floor where Max had detected Jazz with the GPS tracker. When the elevator opened and Jazz stepped out, he simply huffed out a frustrated breath and walked past Mase.

"Didn't get my room number, then? At least I have a little privacy."

Mase kept his mouth shut.

Jazz stopped and opened the door of room 843 and stepped inside. Mase followed him. The room was so quiet and tense that the slamming of the door sounded like a gunshot. After a beat, Jazz whirled on him.

"What the fuck, Savage? I don't need a babysitter."

Jazz rarely used Mase's call sign and usually only when he was pissed.

"First of all, it's called backup. We give it to each other all the time."

"I haven't had backup since I left the military. I've been on my own—and so have you."

"That's not true. Sam and Ax have been my backup at times, and yours. Besides, this isn't an op. This is a revenge mission, which leads me to believe you do, in fact, need a babysitter."

"I don't need any of the guys knowing about my personal life."

"I'm not 'any of the guys', Jazz," Mase stepped forward as anger boiled inside him.

"I don't want anyone knowing about this part of my life. I didn't even tell *Mémère* I was coming."

"And yet somehow she knew you would."

"She told you about this?" Jazz waved his hand around the room as if that encapsulated the mess Mase had walked into.

"No. She told me she was worried about what you were up to. Ever since the gala—"

"Would everybody stop fucking bringing that up? It's humiliating."

Jazz covered his eyes, only to rub his hand over his face. He looked exhausted. For the first time in years, he looked worried.

"Is it? I'm sorry you feel that way. I found it very insightful."

In his drug-induced haze, Jazz had only said one name...Mase's. He'd talked *about* Coleman, but he hadn't said his name, only Mase's. He'd told Mase he needed him. Mase was grabbing onto that with both hands.

"Sure, because you guys have always had some morbid curiosity about my past."

"No. The guys let the past go. They were only curious because you came in as an officer and you weren't even twenty. I'm the one who wants to know about your past. You know more about my past than any of the guys do."

It was a sore spot. During moments of weakness, Jazz always shut down. There had been a few times Mase had opened up to him and told him about his family, just to draw him out.

"That doesn't mean I want you to know about mine."

"You should have thought about that before you started acting erratic. We were all worried about you. It's not just me, Jazz."

Jazz had accused Mase of being overprotective from day one. There had apparently been a Jazz-sized hole inside Mase that filled up the moment they'd met, when Jazz had applied to Ranger school. He'd been naïve and gorgeous and...lost. Jazz had been lost.

"So it was a joint effort? I don't need any of you backing me up in my personal life," Jazz said.

He'd used a general term, but Mase felt it like a direct hit. Jazz didn't want Mase in his personal life. He never had, and yet Mase couldn't seem to keep himself away. He was like a little piece of metal and Jazz a very powerful magnet.

"You don't want anyone to know you have a half-brother?"

"I don't care one way or the other about Remy Dupree. It's what he represents that I don't want to even think about, let alone have to explain to anyone."

"Then I'll just ask you to do it this once. What does he represent?"

"He's my age, Mase. We're only a few months apart."

Jazz said it like an accusation, but Mase didn't fully get the concept. So his dad was a hound dog. There were millions of stories just like that out there.

"Okay. So your dad was a cheating asshole with a side piece. That's not very original, and it's no reflection on you."

Jazz turned to the window and looked out over the Houston skyline. Mase didn't expect any more out of him, so he was surprised when Jazz spoke.

"My mother was the side piece. She didn't know he was married. Then again, she was a little naïve, considering she was sixteen at the time."

"Fuck," Mase whispered.

Jazz didn't respond. He just took a piece of paper out of his pocket and stared at it. Mase was quiet for a long time. He let Jazz settle down before gently prodding him.

"Why don't you pack it up? Let's head back to Virginia. There's nothing for you here."

"I'm jealous of Remy Dupree," Jazz said.

"Because of your father?"

Jazz laughed, but it sounded more like a disgusted snort. "Hell no. That fucker can rot. I'm jealous because he gets to give his mom one last wish."

"Jazzy."

Mase walked across the room. He sidled up to Jazz's side and put his hand on Jazz's arms, careful not to touch his back. For the first time in so long, Jazz turned toward him instead of away and accepted the comfort. He leaned his cheek against Mase's chest.

This was where Mase always seemed to falter. Jazz felt so right in his arms that his body began to react. Mase pulled his hips back so Jazz wouldn't feel his erection. He moved his hands up and down Jazz's arms.

He didn't do anything more than rub Jazz's arms. He'd deduced enough over the years to know what he called Jazz's no-go zones, and his back was the biggest one.

Mase cupped Jazz's cheek with one hand and continued to rub his arm with the other. He kissed the top of his head. After just a few short moments, Jazz pulled away and looked up at him.

The breath froze in his lungs as he looked into Jazz's eyes. This was always the hardest part, having to pull away before Jazz rejected him.

Jazz's gaze dropped to Mase's mouth. Mase barely held back a groan. He was pretty sure Jazz didn't mean to tease. He'd come to that conclusion over the years. He couldn't seem to help how tempting he was, just like Mase couldn't help being drawn to him.

Jazz kept everything locked up so tight, especially his sex life. Mase was grateful for that, because he wouldn't be able to watch Jazz with someone else, not that he really thought Jazz dated. He also didn't seem to have a problem watching Mase date other people.

That thought more than anything had Mase stepping back and turning away so Jazz wouldn't see the tent in his jeans. Mase cleared his throat and tried to think back to what they'd been talking about.

He knew nothing about the circumstances of Jazz's mother's death. He knew only that she had died very young. That was all Dee had ever told him. She said that a parent should never have to bury a child, and she had buried two.

"Do you want to help Remy grant his mother's last wish?" Mase asked.

This whole scenario was a little too close to home for Mase. He had his own struggle with his parents. The sacrifices Remy was willing to make were foreign to him at this stage in his life.

His father was dying as well, and his last request was to see Mase. It was part of what had driven Bray to come find him in Ukraine. It was the agenda Nick had been pushing since Mase had started accepting emails from him.

Mase's father was the bane of his existence. He and Jazz seemed to have that in common. But Remy's mother wasn't part of that. If anything, she was probably just another victim of the situation.

"If she were still married to Lance, I'd say no." Jazz ran his thumb over the phone number on the piece of paper.

"Why don't you just give her a call? You can decide after you talk to her if you want to see her."

Jazz nodded and pulled out his phone.

Chapter Six

Jazz

She'd sounded elated to hear from him. That was the only reason Jazz was standing outside the door of Celia Remington-Dupree's home. Jazz didn't know if it was because he wished his mother could see him all grown up or if it was a final 'fuck you' to his father, but he was there, waiting for the door to open.

When it did, Jazz jumped. Mase lay a calming hand on his arm and, though he hated that he needed it, Jazz appreciated the gesture.

"May I help you?" a woman asked from the doorway.

"We have an appointment with Mrs. Remington-Dupree," Mase said after Jazz gave no response. "This is Mr. Thibodeaux."

"Of course," the woman took a few steps back and opened the door further. "Please come in."

Mase grabbed Jazz's wrist and pulled him into the house. Suddenly, this was the last place in the world he wanted to be.

"Right this way," the woman said. "She's been expecting you."

Mase moved to follow her, but Jazz pulled him back. He sent Mase a pleading look. He had never needed Mase's protection, but when they first met, he'd reveled in it just as much as he'd fought it.

"We're just here to kindly decline her money," Mase reminded him.

Jazz nodded as he began to trail after Mase. He looked around at the royal opulence of the mini mansion. This was how his father had been living while Jazz and his mother lived in a tiny shack and struggled to buy food. It pissed him off. He and his mother had been a secret, hidden away while Lance paraded his other family around.

Jazz and Mase were shown into a large sitting room. Celia Remington-Dupree was seated in a cushy leather chair with a blanket over her lap. Her smile was warm, but she seemed stymied.

"I'm so happy you decided to come," she finally said.

Her voice was soft and quiet. Jazz imagined her playing games with her children the way his mother had with him. He imagined her singing to them with her quiet southern lilt, so different from his mother's.

"Won't you please sit here with me? I know who you are, Jasper. You look so much like Remy. May I ask your friend's name?"

"This is my boyfriend, Mason." The lie rolled off his tongue as if it belonged there.

Mase stumbled a little as he made his way to the sofa next to Celia's chair. He'd probably expected Jazz to say 'friend' or even 'babysitter'. For some reason, Jazz wanted to shock the woman he still thought of as his father's wife.

"So nice to meet you, Mason. I'm Celia," she said as she reached out.

Mase gently took her hand but didn't shake it, just held it for a moment. She seemed frail. Her cheekbones protruded harshly from what had once been a delicate and lovely face. Her shoulders and elbows were sharp and bony. Even if Remy hadn't said anything, Jazz would have known she was sick.

"I'm sorry to hear you're ill," Jazz said when Mase sat next to him.

Her eyes widened. "Most people avoid that topic like the plague."

"Remy said that speaking to me was a wish of sorts? I'm not sure why? If you're worried that I'll bring up my parentage—"

"It's so far past the point of that, Jasper."

His name sounded so foreign to him.

"Jazz. I go by Jazz."

"Jazz," she corrected. "I..." Celia smiled, but it was forced. Tears sprang to her eyes, but she shook her head as if to deny they existed. "I wanted to set the record straight," she said. "When you're facing death, things that seemed like mountains become molehills."

Mase shifted uncomfortably at Jazz's side—and he had a good idea why.

"I didn't know about you, Jazz. I just wanted you to know that I wasn't some pretentious wife who knew and hid her husband's indiscretions. I thought myself in love with Lance Dupree when I married him. He can be quite charming when he chooses to."

"I've never seen that side of him," Jazz said.

"I imagine not. Probably for the better. Remy wanted to be just like his charming father until... Well, he still bends over backward to please a man who is only pleased with himself."

Jazz sucked in a breath at the harsh words.

"You and Remy were the collateral damage of the workings of a very selfish man, and I'm so sorry about that."

"What do you mean, Remy?" Jazz demanded.

Remy had been raised in luxury. He'd had both parents, even if one had been an asshole. He'd known who he was and where he belonged.

"I was young and idealistic when I married your father."

"He's not my father," Jazz said through gritted teeth.

"No, I suppose not. Your grandfather filled that role—and hopefully with love and affection. My parents' marriage was more like a business merger. I wanted a love match, and I thought I'd found that in Lance. But when he found out I was pregnant, he changed. Our relationship changed. Everything seemed to turn different."

Celia took a breath. Mase pressed his thigh against Jazz's and took his hand. Jazz looked at their fingers twined together. It looked so right that he was tempted to pull his away so he wouldn't get either of their hopes up, but he left it where it was.

"I wish I could say that didn't affect Remy. I didn't resent *him*, but I resented the change to my marriage, and that *did* affect him. Looking back, I can see that it was probably the stress of having two women pregnant at the same time and trying to keep everything straight that caused the rift. But I didn't know about that until much, much later.

"I didn't find out about you until you and Remy were sixteen. It seemed such a small thing. My accountant questioned a monthly expenditure. I didn't know what it was, so he researched it. Even when he found the money ended up with your grandmother, it didn't really raise any alarm bells until I saw your picture."

She smiled at him, but tears gathered along her lower lids. She shook her head.

"Then I needed to know everything. When I found out your mother had died and Lance had done…nothing, I knew that I couldn't stay with him any longer. I can't honestly say I would have welcomed you into our home with open arms when you and Remy looked almost like twins and were only a few months apart, but I know myself well enough to know I would have done *something*. You'd lost your mother, for heaven's sake."

Jazz's throat clogged. She didn't say it as an accusation. She didn't place any blame in that last statement. She didn't act like weakness had killed her, and for that, Jazz was truly grateful.

Guilt pulled Jazz under like a riptide. He'd been taking his anger at his father out on someone who was just another of his victims. Mase squeezed his hand.

"I'm sorry I was rude," Jazz said. "I've always been resentful of his family, even though I never wanted to be a part of it."

"There are so many mixed feelings around that man." Celia shook her head. "I just wanted to meet you, to lay it out on the table. I'm not blameless, but I needed you to know that we didn't know about you. Remy found out when he was sixteen. We didn't tell Mandy until later. She was only ten when I left Lance."

"Mandy?" Mase asked.

"My daughter, Jazz and Remy's sister."

If anyone else on the planet had called Amanda Dupree his sister, Jazz would have corrected them. But to hear it from their mother was like... Jazz couldn't find words for the way it made him feel — soothed, recognized, seen?

Jazz felt something drip onto the hand that was joined with Mase's. When he looked down, more tears fell, and that was when Jazz realized he was crying.

He looked up. Mase's eyes were tortured, beseeching. Mase was a toucher, and he clearly wanted to hug Jazz but held himself back. He knew, and that had shame slamming into Jazz's gut. Mase knew that Jazz couldn't stand to be hugged, especially by men, and the irony of that was not lost on him.

"I didn't mean... I only meant..." Celia said as her hands fluttered about.

"It's fine," Jazz said. "I guess I assumed you wouldn't see me that way."

"I don't know why not. You've made your grandparents proud. I'm sure your mother is proud of the man you've become."

A strange honking noise burst from Jazz's throat before he covered his mouth with his hand. Mase's hand landed on the top of his head as he pressed his forehead to Jazz's temple. It was as close to a hug as they could get.

"I meant for this to be...not..." Celia seemed at a loss for words, and she was getting anxious.

"Cathartic," Jazz said. "This was cathartic."

Celia took a deep breath, then let it out. She coughed a few times but gathered herself.

"That's exactly what I hoped this would be for you. I've added you to the family trust. I should have welcomed you into our family when I found out about you. You were off at college by then and after that in the military. I used that as an excuse to procrastinate this meeting, but I don't have time to put it off anymore. You weren't easy to track down, but somehow Remy managed it."

Jazz wasn't about to tell her that Remy had done no such thing. If Jazz's handler 'Ann' didn't have a soft spot for him, he probably never would have known they'd been looking for him. She'd told him that his half-brother had employed three different private investigators to find him.

"I don't want your money," Jazz said.

"If that's the case, then you're welcome to donate it to a charity. I just... I've thought about you often, and I regret not trying to meet you sooner. I was so afraid you'd hate me, that it had been too long by the time I found out. Mostly I was worried you'd reject us and that would have hurt Mandy and Remy at a time they were learning the full truth about their father. So, it was my fear that delayed our meeting. Please don't hold it against your siblings."

Jazz was tempted to say 'too little too late', but he couldn't bring himself to do it.

"I'll try," he said instead.

"Is he here?" A voice drifted in from the hallway.

"I'm afraid you're in for it now," Celia smiled and for the first time, her eyes sparkled with joy.

Chapter Seven

Mase

"Oh, my God, you look just like Remy," a woman said as she rushed into the room like a whirlwind.

Mase was dizzy with everything he'd just learned about Jazz's childhood. His father was scum, a selfish motherfucker, and Mase wanted to rip his black heart out of his chest. What kind of father could look at Jazz and not instantly fall in love?

"Mandy," Celia chided.

But it was too late. She hurried over and gave her mother a quick, gentle squeeze. Then she did something that had Jazz's eyes widening in shock. She leaned down and hugged him. Mase felt Jazz's body go rigid, and he clamped his hand down so tight that Mase pulled in a breath from the discomfort.

In a way, it was comforting to know that Jazz didn't like physical affection from anyone. Yet it was still heartbreaking, because Jazz needed physical affection from every single person who loved him.

Mandy pulled back and cupped Jazz's cheeks in her hands. She laughed when she saw the shock on Jazz's face, but she sobered as she assessed him.

"So handsome," she said. "More rugged and confident than Remy. I bet the girls go crazy for you." She laughed.

Celia cleared her throat. "Mandy, this is Mason, Jazz's boyfriend."

"Jazz," Mandy said, as if testing it. "I love it. And oh my, do you have good taste in men," she said with a look in Mase's direction. "Nice to meet you, Mason."

Mandy stuck out her hand, and Mase took it. She gave a hardy handshake before pulling back and sitting on the arm of her mother's chair.

"I can't believe Remy did it. He found you. Took him long enough. I've wanted to meet you since I've known about you. According to Remy, it was never 'the right time'. Did you ask him?" Mandy asked her mother.

"We were clearing the air. I haven't gotten that far yet." Celia said.

"I'm engaged."

Mandy's smile exploded with that sentence, and she looked happy, glowing. She had Jazz's eyes but her mother's delicate nose.

"We're moving up the dates so that mom will have more energy to be a part of it."

Celia gave her daughter an indulgent smile. They all knew exactly why she was moving up the date.

"I'm sorry, but I wouldn't feel comfortable —"

"Oh please," Mandy cut in. "I've wanted to know you for so long."

"I'm afraid it's not possible," Mase answered. "Jazz's work doesn't allow him to be at large gatherings where photos and videos will be taken."

It was true, though, that they could probably work around it if not for the fact that Jazz's father would be there. Mandy pouted prettily, but only for a moment.

"I wouldn't want to put you in danger. I'll accept that answer if you promise to give me your phone number and email."

"Amanda," Celia scolded.

"What? We have him here. You can't think I'd let him leave without finding a way to badger him into coming to Thanksgiving or Christmas or Easter or Halloween — hell, even President's Day."

Jazz smiled.

Mandy was going to be a hard one to resist. She had a natural exuberance and joy about her. She'd definitely had a different childhood than Remy had.

"I'll give you my information, but don't be surprised if it takes me a while to respond or if I go dark for a few months at a time."

"Go dark? Is that military speak?" she asked as she handed him her phone.

Jazz chuckled as he typed his information into Mandy's cell phone. When she took it back, she handed it to Mase. She wanted his information?

"If you're Jazz's boyfriend, you're in this, too. I mean, for all we know, you're the one who convinced him to finally come see us. You and I can conspire to get him to come back."

Mase took her phone and entered in his information as well. If he were really Jazz's boyfriend, that would be his role. He probably wouldn't be good at it, though, considering he'd gone more than half his life without seeing his own family.

"I really wish you could come to the wedding," she sighed. "It would be nice to have more family on my side. Ryan's family is huge, and they're all descending on Houston for the ceremony. They're flying in from all over the world."

"Ryan?" Jazz asked.

Was that a protective tone to his voice? Mase smirked a little. Jazz was getting roped in, not that Mase could blame him.

"My fiancé. Ryan Gold. I met him in college at Rice but then he went to graduate school at Stanford, so I moved out there with him. We may end up in California eventually, but for now, we're back here," Mandy smoothed a hand down her mother's arm.

"Don't worry," Celia said when she saw Jazz's frown. "Ryan has been fully vetted by Remy and me. He's been around long enough that we really know him. They've been together for five years."

"And I didn't think he'd make it through the first six months with my family." Mandy rolled her eyes. "But he stuck it out—well, mostly. I mean, he and Dad don't exactly get along."

Celia snorted, and it wasn't delicate.

"Fine," Mandy admitted. "They can't stand each other."

"I like this guy already," Mase muttered.

Jazz cast a sideways glance. When their eyes met, he knew Jazz was in complete agreement. Mandy continued to talk almost nonstop for another fifteen minutes before she wore Celia out. They were just standing to leave so she could nap when Remy strode into the room.

"I thought we agreed I'd be here for this meeting," he said.

"No, you made a demand I chose not to comply with," Celia said. "There were some private things that needed to be said between Jazz and myself. I believe we've cleared the air. And I don't appreciate you texting your brother," she directed the last statement at Mandy.

"What? He should get a chance to meet his brother, too."

"He's not my brother, but we've already met. Earlier today, in fact."

"Oh. Well, if you're going to be like that, I'm sorry I texted you."

Mandy turned away from her brother in what could only be described as a flounce before slipping her arm through Jazz's and leading him out. Mase followed, after saying a quick goodbye to Celia.

"That was rude, Remy. Better to say nothing at all than throw out a barb. You know that better than anyone," Celia said.

"I'm sorry, mother," Remy replied. "You look like you need some rest."

When he heard that last exchange as he stepped out of the door, Mase was worried that Remy thought he was better than Jazz. It was a crazy notion. No one was better than Jazz.

"Don't mind, Remy," Mandy was saying to Jazz. "He barely thinks of himself as my brother, either. Sometimes I swear he thinks he's my father."

Jazz's back straightened at the word 'father'. Poor Mandy was oblivious, but she was just what Jazz would need to pull him reluctantly into this strange family.

When they reached the front door, Mandy threw her arms around Jazz and hugged him with gusto. Jazz gave Mase a panicked look as he gave her back a stiff pat. What she said next had Mase thinking she wasn't as much oblivious as she was optimistic.

"I know it's new for you, and I know I can be a bit much, but Mom really needs something to focus on. I'll send you her email. If you could just keep the lines of communication open, it would really make her happy. I know" — she held up a hand and cut Jazz off before he could even say anything — "it's not your responsibility to make her happy, but she's a kind woman. She really is."

"I'll think about it," Jazz said.

"Thank you. She's got a lot of guilt, and Remy has a lot of resentment. I guess I just try too hard to make up for it, but I'm a pretty happy person in general. Ryan says I overwhelm people sometimes. He claims it's cute. I don't mean to overwhelm you. I just want a relationship."

"I'll think about it," Jazz said again.

Mandy gave him a twisted sideways grin that was full of sass and reached out to pat his cheek. Jazz reached up and touched her hand. Mase waited for Jazz to pull her hand away, but he just patted it a couple of times before she pulled back with a smile.

"I'll be in touch," Mandy said as they left.

Jazz was quiet on the drive back to the hotel. He'd had a busy day. Mase wanted to ask him about Martin Coleman, but it just wasn't the right time.

Chapter Eight

Jazz

As soon as they got back to the hotel, Jazz started packing his things — not that he'd unpacked much. The last twelve hours had been a rollercoaster ride.

Celia and Mandy had been a huge surprise. Remy was exactly what he'd expected. He wondered how long they'd been looking for him and how long Celia had been sick.

His handler had told him they'd been looking for at least a year. Sometimes it was handy to be using an alias. Not that he couldn't have used his own name if he wanted to, but he was paranoid. His paranoia had paid off many times in his line of work, just as it had earlier that day.

The very thought of Marty's voice had a shiver slithering down his spine. He was relieved Marty hadn't been the one to drug his drink at the gala, but that meant Jazz didn't know the motive behind what had happened.

"What are you thinking about?" Mase asked.

"Nothing important."

"Good. Then maybe we can finally discuss the night of the gala now that I have you pinned down."

"Speaking of pinned down, how exactly did you find me?"

"You open up about the gala, and I'll tell you how we trailed you," Mase said.

Jazz wanted to punch the smug look right off his face. The last thing he wanted to talk about was whatever had fallen from his mouth while he'd been virtually unconscious.

"You do realize that being able to track me could be a danger to me and anyone I'm trying to help?"

"I trust Max. He's the only one who can track you."

Jazz trusted Max, too. The kid had integrity and brains.

"What exactly are you looking for?" Jazz asked.

"Well, I wanted confirmation that Martin Coleman was the man who had you scared, but that was confirmed when you trespassed onto his property this morning, I assume, to plant listening devices."

"If you have confirmation, why do you need me to say it?"

"I don't want confirmation, Jazzy. I want intel. What did he do to you?"

Jazz turned away. Mase was the only one who called him that. He both loved it and hated it. He hated it mostly because it brought back the shame of the past. He remembered vividly the first time Mase had used the moniker. It had been the first time they'd kissed.

"Jazz." Mase's voice was low and directly to his right.

Jazz scoffed even as he stiffened. He knew better than to approach Jazz from behind. He closed his eyes and took a breath. Still, fear blossomed inside him, so he sat in the office chair to have something at his back.

"You're not fucked up, Jazzy."

"I am," Jazz yelled. "You know better than anyone that I am. I actually wanted you to… Fuck. I can't do this, Mase. If you need to trail me, then so be it, but I can't talk about this with you."

Mase jerked his head back as if he'd been slapped. Jazz didn't mean it like that. If there were anyone he'd want to tell, it would be Mase. And yet…he couldn't. The shame would eat him up inside.

"If not me, then someone. For the love of God, Jazzy, talk to someone, maybe a therapist."

He hadn't told a soul. Not even *Mémère* knew. Who would he tell? Mase was the closest thing he'd ever had to a boyfriend. Ghost was the closest thing he had to a best friend but mostly because their paranoias complimented each other. He couldn't tell anyone who might tell Mase or *Mémère*. That left exactly no one.

Jazz didn't realize he was shaking his head until Mase knelt before him and stopped the movement with a hand on each cheek.

"You've passed plenty of psych evals. You've never talked about it? Not to anyone?"

Jazz looked into Mase's eyes. He couldn't shake his head because Mase was holding him still, but he didn't need to. He saw the exact moment Mase realized it was true.

He didn't mean to hurt Mase. What he felt for Mase was like nothing he'd ever felt for anyone else in his life, but he couldn't do anything about it. It was absolute torture. So he tried his best to stay out of the way, to let

Mase move on, to let Mase have friends and a support system.

Mase leaned in and pressed their mouths together. Jazz groaned and immediately went hard as a rock. There was no tongue. It was just a chaste touch of lips.

Jazz grabbed the back of Mase's head and pressed his tongue against the seam of Mase's lips. Mase growled and opened for him but kept his hands gently on Jazz's cheeks.

The joy and fear these moments caused always sent Jazz into a tailspin. He wanted Mase's touch more than anything, yet that very touch made him break out into a cold sweat and had nausea rising in his gut.

Just before he was about to break away and push Mase off him, Mase slowly pulled back. He'd learned how to read Jazz. The shame that there was a need for that swallowed Jazz whole.

He had been the one to instigate it, yet he had no right, because he'd always be the one to put an end to it as well. Mase deserved better than that.

"You're not fucked up," Mase said as he touched his forehead to Jazz's.

Jazz pushed hard against Mase's chest and stood. With jerky movements, he threw his toiletry bag into his carryon and zipped it up.

"I am. Don't tell me this isn't all fucked up. I can't even…"

He couldn't even say 'sex' or 'fuck' or 'make love', let alone do any of those things. He'd never been able to, not even when he'd wanted to — with Mase. Only with Mase.

"Maybe that's not what I'm looking for," Mase said.

Jazz snorted.

"I'm not saying I don't like sex. I do. But maybe I like you more."

Jazz whirled around to look at Mase. He needed to see his face to know if he was telling the truth. He was.

"What does that mean?"

"It can mean whatever we want it to mean. I just want to be with you. I've always wanted to be with you. We have this time, Jazz. We have to be together for the next few weeks, at least until we get new orders. Can't we just try?"

"Try what? You know I can't cuddle or sleep in a bed with you." Jazz swallowed before he could get the next word out. "Sex is off the table, too. What's left?"

"I'm just asking you to try to test your limits. I won't force anything. You can control it all. Just try to see what you can feel comfortable with."

Jazz shook his head. "I can't think of anything I'm comfortable with."

Mase's chest rose and fell twice, then he walked over to the bed. Jazz had to work to get air into his lungs. Every time they'd tried anything sexual, Jazz panicked and ruined everything.

Then the humiliation would take hold, and he wouldn't be able to look Mase in the eye, so he'd avoid him for days or weeks or even months. He'd back away from all their friends so that Mase would have someone to be with, someone to talk to.

Jazz wouldn't have talked about it, even if he had been around friends, so he let Mase have what he needed to recover. And the next time, Jazz would try not to be selfish, not to try to take something that wasn't meant for him. But he couldn't resist the allure of Mason Hart.

Mase took off his shoes and crawled onto the bed. Jazz was confused. He was fully clothed. He turned away from Jazz and curled up on his side then... nothing.

"What's going on?"

Was he expecting Jazz to get undressed because he wasn't looking? Was he expecting Jazz to take the lead? Because that was not going to happen. It was hard to guide a ship if you didn't know how to sail, or even float.

"I have a feeling you might actually like cuddling. Call it intuition," Mase said.

Jazz licked his lips. He didn't really know how to cuddle. He might have cuddled with his mom at one point, but by the time his grandparents got custody, he was probably past that point.

"You be big spoon." Mase reached back and patted the space behind him on the bed.

Big spoon. Jazz nodded. Maybe he could do that. No one would be at his back. He'd be in control and could back away if he needed to.

Crawling onto the bed, Jazz knee-walked to the center where Mase was and gently lay down behind him. He stilled for a moment to see if any anxiety hit him. He felt calm, even a little excited that he'd be able to touch Mase.

Jazz scooted forward until he was directly behind him. He slid one arm around Mase but wiggled around trying to get the other arm comfortable.

"What do I do with this arm?" he asked.

Mase let out a choked laugh. "Ah, the curse of being the big spoon."

Jazz smiled as he curled his arm up and used it to cushion his head. The stress of the day seemed to melt away with Mase in his arms.

Leaning forward, he nuzzled the back of Mase's neck and sucked in a deep breath. Mase smelled clean and citrus-y. There was a musk underneath it all that had Jazz once again, hard as a rock.

He pulled his hips back a little but pressed his chest forward so there was no space between Mase's spine and his torso.

He was so turned on that his cock was throbbing. He was so relaxed he could have fallen asleep. He didn't know what to call the mixed feeling, so he guessed that was the curse of cuddling?

Chapter Nine

Mase

His eyes stung, his throat was on fire, his cock could pound nails, yet Mase lay as still as a statue while Jazz experimented. Finally, he felt Jazz all along his back. Mase closed his eyes and reveled in the sensation.

Then Jazz leaned in and nuzzled him. His dick pulsed against his zipper, begging for some extra space, but he was just going to have to wait. In all the years he'd known Jazz, this was the closest he'd come to instigating any intimacy.

Jazz sighed and his body seemingly dissolved into the bed. He ran his hand up and down over Mase's chest and abs. Mase did his best to relax, but his muscles twitched and danced under Jazz's touch.

It was the perfect way to round out a perfectly fucked-up day, wrapped in Jazz's arms. Mase stayed quiet and fantasized about a world where he could end every day just like this.

It would be a world where Jazz finally slowed down a little and where he actually had a family who loved him. His family wouldn't be just Dee anymore. It could include his sister and maybe his brother, too.

Mase was enjoying having his brothers around...and his mom. He'd been unfair to her. He needed to hear her out. Someday they'd probably all meet each other. Mase pictured what a family get-together would be like. He laughed at the chaos he knew would manifest.

"What's so funny?" Jazz asked.

"I was just thinking about Mandy. She's a spitfire."

"She is."

"I can't wait to see what happens when she and Dee get together." Mase laughed harder.

"What? Fuck. I didn't even think about that. That can't happen. No way."

"It's inevitable. They're both inevitable. Why fight it?"

"Mase, you have to promise not to tell her about Mandy."

Jazz put his hand on Mase's arm to punctuate the demand. Mase would do everything he could to make sure the two met, because it would create a family for Jazz.

"No can do, Jazzy," Mase said. "No one can keep a secret from Dee. I have a feeling Mandy's the same."

"They're two peas in a pod," Jazz groaned. "I'll lose control of my own life, what little is left to me while I'm not working."

That's just what you need, Jazzy, Mase thought.

"Seriously. Don't tell *Mémère*."

"Chances are she'll get it out of you first, anyway, but you know I won't risk her wrath by hiding something from her. The woman's like a second mother to me."

"Second mother?"

The question had guilt pushing at Mase's chest. That wasn't how he used to describe Dee.

"I've been emailing my mom. I assumed a lot of things when I left home, like her being on the same page as my dad. I'm not sure that's true anymore."

"She wasn't?"

Mase shook his head. "Bray said they got divorced over it."

"Oh."

"Yeah. Guess I should have responded to one of those emails she sent over the years."

"Why didn't you?" Jazz asked.

"Assumptions, I guess. I assumed she was trying to get me to apologize to Dad," Mase shook his head. He hadn't done anything wrong. "Well, anyway, I assumed she was trying to get me to reach out to him, that she was going behind his back or else he would have emailed himself."

"And your brothers?"

"Mostly Bray. Nick didn't reach out until recently. Bray tried to get in touch just before he turned eighteen. I assumed that was morbid curiosity. He tried again when I was in the middle of the whole trial. I definitely didn't want to talk to him during that. Then he landed in the middle of the Kyiv op and took a bullet for me."

"Yeah, that's not curiosity."

"No," Mase agreed.

It was love, and he felt it coming from Bray like warmth from the sun. Their mom was the same way — or at least she had been.

Nick was a little different.

"I feel like Nick is a covert operator reporting to my father," Mase admitted.

"Really? I figured he joined HC to follow Bray. Y'know, the twin thing."

"Maybe that's part of it, but I can't recall one conversation I've had with Nick, whether by email, phone or in person, where he didn't bring up our father, even after I asked him to let it rest."

"Was he that bad?" Jazz asked. "Your dad?"

"Was yours?"

Mase was met with silence.

"Why didn't you tell me?" Mase asked.

"We don't really talk about our pasts. Isn't that the deal?"

"I don't mean picking over all the details. Why didn't you tell me you know who your father is? I assumed either your mom didn't tell you who he was before she died or he died before she did."

"No. He's still alive. He just abandoned her so he could move on to someone else, I assume."

"But he didn't abandon you?"

"What?"

"You said he abandoned her."

The silence drew out for a few minutes. Mase was sure he wouldn't get an answer until he heard Jazz speak so softly that he would have missed it if they hadn't been pressed together in the quiet hotel room.

"There was nothing to abandon. I had no relationship with my father."

Oh, Jazzy, Mase groaned in his head. Life had just given him a shit hand then kept adding to it.

It was such a rare and honest admission that Mase couldn't even form a response. He was learning so much about why Jazz was who he was. Maybe by learning about Jazz's past, he could forge a future for them.

By the time Mase thought of something to say, he realized Jazz had fallen asleep. His hand had stopped moving and his breath was deep and even. Mase smiled. Maybe someday—with a little work—Jazz might feel secure enough to fall asleep in his arms instead of the reverse—not that he minded being held, on the contrary. He snuggled in and let his body relax.

Chapter Ten

Jazz

It was one of those torturous dreams — the ones that fill your heart with hope, only to rip it to shreds once your eyes open.

The actual dream was the best he'd ever had, but the aftereffects upon waking were just as bad as the worst of his nightmares.

He could feel the solid length of Mase on top of him. He wasn't scared. He vibrated with need. His whole body throbbed with the desire to do what that very body stopped him from doing.

Mase kissed down his neck. Even that had his cock pulsing. His nipples itched for Mase's touch, but Mase worked his way back up and pressed their lips together.

Jazz groaned. He wanted. He needed. But he didn't know what he needed. Sex wasn't an option. It would never be something he'd enjoy. Then again, he never thought he'd want it at all until he met Mase.

Mase rubbed their erections together through their clothes. Jazz moaned and thrust his hips forward. He knew how that felt. He'd allowed it once when he'd been tipsy enough to come on to Mase – before he'd panicked and ended up puking all over him.

That one small experience was the basis of his entire spank bank, not that Jazz jacked off that often. At least he hadn't over the past few years.

Recently, his sex drive had roared back to life with a vengeance. It coincided with seeing Mase again, which wasn't too much of a surprise. Almost every jack-off session he'd had since joining the military had been instigated by sexual frustration over not being able to touch Mase.

It was why part of him was happy to stay away from the guy. The dichotomy inside him eased when they weren't together. He could be satisfied with the label he'd given himself—asexual. It felt like a lie whenever Mase was anywhere close by.

Jazz took control of the dream, as he was sometimes able to do. He rolled them so he was on top and thrust his hips against Mase's. He used his hands to feel the steely strength of the man he wanted more than he wanted his next breath of air.

It had always been that way between them, right from the start. He was sure Mase would end up hating him at some point. He'd called him a tease once. It probably appeared that way on the outside.

On the inside, two monsters fought for dominance. His desire for Mase would always be the second most powerful emotion. Fear always won that fight.

But here in his dreams, Jazz was in control. He imagined that experiencing an orgasm with someone else was probably better than the ones he was able to give himself. With no experience in that area, he'd let the dream take hold.

He gripped Mase, but Mase was facing the other way. When had he rolled over? Jazz dug his fingers into Mase's hips and the heel of his hands into the sides of his ass.

When he pressed his hips forward, it was into the firm cushion of Mase's butt cheek. It was something he'd never experienced in real life, something that would usually feel muted or even numb in his dreams. But it still felt real and just as good as the time they'd rubbed cocks.

Mase moaned. Jazz smiled. He loved making Mase feel good. He'd do anything to make Mase feel good — anything that wouldn't cause his heart to seize with fear.

Unfortunately, that meant keeping Mase safe and happy from afar. When they were together, it ended in disaster.

As punishment for the shit that spilled from his mouth when he panicked, Jazz would then have to watch Mase try to move on with someone else. That was their pattern.

Mase moaned his name. "Jazz."

Jazz could count on one hand the times Mase had said his name in that tone of voice. It was that raspy tone that both titillated and frightened him.

He pressed his dick harder against Mase's ass and tightened the grip on his hips. Mase gasped. Jazz smiled wider. They'd never continued for so long, especially not as Jazz's balls drew up and his pulse began to race with both uncertainty and exhilaration.

His pulse beat in his ears. His cock throbbed. His hands gripped tighter. His muscles coiled. His palms slid up a fraction of an inch, and he felt the warm satin of Mase's skin. Muscles twitched and bunched under Jazz's fingers.

The unfamiliarity of the feeling caused Jazz to shoot inside his pants, even as his eyes popped open. He scurried backward before his brain fully clicked on.

He was at the edge of the mattress where he had been pressed against a very real body. Mase flipped around, his pupils dilated, his breathing harsh, his pants unzipped. The very detailed outline of his erection encased only by the gray cotton of his underwear had Jazz in a frenzy to get farther away.

With no room left on the bed, he fell onto the floor but immediately popped up onto the balls of his feet.

It's Mase. It's Mase. It's Mase.

Jazz tried to repeat it over and over in his head, but he couldn't lift his eyes from the large, hard dick long enough to verify the face belonged to the man he'd been crazy for since he was a twenty-two-year-old Ranger candidate.

When he was finally able to tear his gaze away, it was only to dart all over the room, looking for safety. They were in a hotel room. There had to be a bathroom.

There was light spilling from an opening down the hall. Jazz hurried toward it. He slammed and locked the door as he took in huge gulping breaths and tried to calm his racing heart.

He slid down until his butt hit the tile. Pulling his knees to his chest, Jazz let the tears of relief fall. Taking slow, even draws of air, he tried to calm the chaos in his mind.

Where was he? What had happened?

After a few breaths, reality pierced the haze of the past and flashes of memory came through, grounding him in reality.

The day flooded back. He was in Texas, and he'd done what he came to do. Jazz nodded to himself. He'd done what he came to do.

He pulled more air into his lungs at the memory that popped up next. The memory of him crawling into bed behind Mase, of wrapping his arms around the man he wanted more than anything and...relaxing.

Jazz rubbed his hands over his face. He'd gone and fucked up again. Mase was probably hurt…again.

And this time Jazz wouldn't be able to back away and disappear as Mase tried to move on and started dating some other man or woman. His stomach rioted at the thought.

These were the choices his past had given him — force himself to do something he loathed or lose the man he loved.

Chapter Eleven

Mase

Mase paced the hall outside the bathroom. He listened to Jazz's pants and incoherent mumbles echo around the room.

Jazz had calmed down quickly, which was a relief. He didn't want to have to tear the door from its hinges to make sure he was okay.

After a few moments, when the bathroom was silent but for some deep breathing, Mase slid his butt to the carpet and slumped against the wall.

This was the way of it.

Every. Fucking. Time.

Each time, he thought he had a grasp on Jazz and what he needed. Then there was the inevitable panic attack. This time it had been his dick, though that was probably the root of all Jazz's panic attacks.

The first time Jazz had backpedaled like Mase was a leper, he'd been so pissed. He'd been determined to stay away.

Like a siren, Jazz drew Mase to his demise. It didn't matter how many times he crashed into those fucking rocks, he just kept coming back for more.

Over the years, Mase had watched him. He'd memorized Jazz's every expression. Even knowing Jazz didn't do this on purpose didn't stop the pain it caused.

So many times he'd backed away, tried to move on, tried to find someone else he might want half as much as he wanted Jazz. He'd just ended up filling the time until he and Jazz would bang together, only to swing apart again like the metal balls on one of those Newton's cradles of perpetual motion.

At first, he'd thought Jazz was a tease. Then he'd thought him a scared virgin. It wasn't until he'd picked up on more of Jazz's fears that he'd known it was something more insidious. Jazz never wanted anyone at his back…ever.

Mase had known from the beginning that group showers had been painful for him, but he hadn't tried to reason out why. He'd discounted it as shyness. Jazz was a very private person. Mase hadn't thought it connected to the sexual fears until much, much later.

This time, though, he wasn't giving up. This was the perfect time to dig his heels in. Jazz couldn't run from him, at least not far. They were supposed to be like Tweedledum and Tweedledee.

The water gushed on in the bathroom. He wondered idly if Jazz would spend the next hour in there, avoiding him. When the bathroom door clicked open, Mase scrambled to his feet and turned to face a glassy-eyed Jazz.

This was the hard part. Jazz didn't want to be coddled, but he wouldn't apologize, either. They stood there for a moment in silence. In the past, this was the point where Jazz would run.

"Do you need the bathroom?" Jazz asked as he stepped aside and pressed his back to the closet door, making room for Mase to pass him.

Mase shook his head. He watched Jazz's expression closely.

"Don't you need to…?" Jazz's gaze flicked down to Mase's zipped pants.

"No, your face did that for me."

"My face? What does that mean?"

"The fear in your eyes had my dick wilting before you even shut the door to the bathroom."

Jazz leveled him with an intense stare. Was he going to deny being afraid? Every time he tried to discuss these episodes, it ended in a fight with each of them laying blame. This time, Mase had changed. He didn't know if it would end up better or worse, but it would damn well be different.

They stared at each other for a long, tense moment. When Jazz was the first to look away, Mase let out the breath he'd been holding. His lack of denial was as good as an admission.

"I need to shower and change then we can head to the airport." Jazz moved past Mase to pull some clothes from his suitcase, then shut himself back in the bathroom.

"I'll buy the tickets," Mase said as the door shut and the lock clicked back into place.

It both pissed Mase off and ripped him to shreds that Jazz felt the need to practically barricade himself in a room before he could get naked.

When the shower sputtered on, Mase took a breath. He felt like he'd won a battle. It wasn't a big battle, but it still felt like he'd finally done the right thing where Jazz was concerned.

Mase pulled out his phone and dialed HC. Wade answered immediately and they went through the safety protocol as he listened for the water to cut off.

"We're heading to the airport now," Mase said.

"That was quick. I thought it would take a few days of convincing."

"He's efficient. He already did what he came to do. He'd probably be heading back today, with or without me."

Wade snorted.

"All right, so he'd be back by Tuesday even if I hadn't corralled him."

"Should we be expecting a shit-storm of any kind?" Wade asked.

"Always expect a shit-storm. I just don't think the next one will come from this direction."

"Your tickets will be ready when you get to the airport. Debrief at twenty-three-hundred hours."

Wade disconnected the call before Mase could answer. They were going to have to tie Jazz to a chair if they thought they were going to get a debrief from this 'mission'.

They drove to the airport separately in their rental cars. Mase liked knowing that if Jazz deviated, he'd be able to find him, not that Jazz would miss their meeting on Wednesday. No matter what, he wouldn't risk his job. That's what Mase was counting on.

As soon as they boarded the plane, Jazz popped in his ear buds and closed his eyes. Mase smiled. He wouldn't be able to ignore him forever.

As he relaxed back in his seat, Mase remembered the noises Jazz had made in his sleep. There hadn't been any groans of pain as he'd humped Mase's ass. It was the first time he'd ever seen Jazz come, and it was a sight he'd never forget.

The sound of his name on Jazz's lips, the feel of strong fingers digging into his skin, that little gasp of surprised pleasure, the pulsing throb against the cheek of his ass where Jazz's cock had been pressed tight... Mase had spun himself into a pretzel so he could turn and see the agonized pleasure of Jazz's scrunched face as he shot his load.

Mase adjusted himself in his seat. He'd almost come in his pants just knowing he'd finally made Jazz come in his.

His only mistake had been to pull down the tab on his zipper so his pants didn't strangle his cock. The look of fear and pain in Jazz's eyes as he'd stared at Mase's erection had made his stomach cramp and his dick wilt. He was going to have to figure out a way to separate those two memories, because there was no way he was going to forget either one.

Chapter Twelve

Jazz

"You have to give us something. What the hell were you doing in Martin Coleman's house when we damn well know you weren't invited?" Wade paced the war room, running his hands through his hair.

He had to be frustrated or pissed — or worse. Wade was a big guy, but he was one of the kindest people Jazz had ever known. Jazz had never seen him lose his temper.

"We know he's the one," Sam said quietly.

Jazz closed his eyes. He was so glad Mase wasn't in the room. This was Jazz's debrief. Mase's was scheduled directly after. It was standard protocol that operators couldn't be present during another's debrief if they'd been on a mission together. He was sure Mase knew every fucking detail Wade and Max had uncovered, but Jazz couldn't bear for it to be discussed in front of him.

"You need to keep us in the loop so we can have your back," Sam continued. "We will always have your back, Jasper."

No one called Jazz by his real name. Most of the guys called him by his call sign, Woody, since they thought it was funny — or people called him Jazz. He was more used to his alias than he was his full name. Not even his grandmother called him that — unless he was in big trouble — so the name made him cringe.

But Jazz wasn't going to tell them what he'd been doing in Marty's house. He didn't really have a full-formed plan. He also wanted everyone he cared about to have absolute deniability if any of this ever came back around to bite him in the ass.

"Jazz" — Sam shook his head — "you're not an island or a one-man army. You can't do everything alone."

"I don't plan to do everything alone," Jazz said, *but I'll handle Marty on my own.*

"Okay then. Max saw you placing listening devices in Coleman's home. I'm guessing no one at the Company sent you to do that, especially since you used Max's devices."

Jazz's mouth tightened. He had been all gung-ho to hire Max, but he'd misjudged how good the kid was. They'd been able to tail him. Jazz's stomach roiled at the implications.

But Wade was right. He had to give them something, even if it was only a small portion of the real truth.

"If you need me to confirm what you already know, so be it. Martin Coleman and I have a history, a bad one. I haven't seen him in years, but I still don't trust him. I need to know what he's up to."

"Okay, but keep us in the loop," Wade said.

Jazz sat back in his chair and assessed his friends. It wasn't that he didn't trust them. He did, explicitly. But the protective instinct was strong in his friends — especially Mase.

If they happened to overhear any of his past, would they jump in and put themselves in danger? Would they think less of him? Did it matter? If they kept digging, he didn't know what they'd uncover or how it might blow up in their faces.

"Fine."

Sam let out a breath. Jazz wondered if his friend thought he'd fight it. He probably would have if he thought he could get away with it.

Max could no doubt hack into his own devices and likely already had. He'd just have to figure out which ones Jazz had taken. In the end, Jazz didn't change the outcome. They would know what was happening.

"Good," Wade said.

Jazz nodded, though the thought of any evidence being discussed made the little he'd eaten want to revolt.

"Let's discuss the meeting on Wednesday with William Campbell." Sam slid a folder closer to Jazz.

He opened it, but there was nothing in it he didn't already know. He'd combed over Campbell's file. He'd gone so far as to do his own separate research.

Two weeks ago, Campbell had called upon one of Lucien Bernard's associates — Ax — to take care of a problem for him. And since Jazz was Lucien Bernard, he needed insight into the situation.

The problem had been one Peter Thornton. Peter, Campbell's personal assistant, found out that Campbell, a lawyer and advocate for women's rights, was secretly running his own human trafficking ring.

Campbell had tasked Ax with getting rid of Peter but making sure his body was discovered. They were currently working around that requirement, which is where Jazz had needed to get involved.

"How's Peter doing?"

Wade sighed and sat down. "He's grateful. He knows exactly what would have happened if Ax hadn't gotten him out of there, but he's having a hard time accepting that he can't contact his sister or his aunt and uncle."

"And you think his sister's safe?" Jazz asked.

"I think she's probably one of the safest women in San Francisco at the moment," Sam said. "Since Campbell won her sexual harassment case against her former employer, she's got a connection to him as well. He's smart enough to know that if two people who are related and so closely attached to him disappear, that he'd be looked at through a microscope."

"And he doesn't want anyone looking too closely," Jazz agreed.

"We're keeping tabs on her," Wade said.

"Is there anything else you need from me?" Jazz stood.

Wade looked at him for a long time before answering. "We need your full cooperation in this, but I don't think we quite have it yet."

Jazz held his gaze. He was used to lying. It was his job after all. Yet he couldn't bring himself to do it to his friend. "I'm giving you all I can."

Wade nodded.

Jazz took a deep breath as he left the room.

* * * *

It was three in the morning before he got back to his penthouse apartment. He hated the place. It was too big, and there were too many empty rooms. When he'd lived with his mom in that tiny little house, he'd always wanted more space, and now he wanted less.

When he'd listened to his mom fight and make up with his sperm donor, he'd been sure there was no such thing as too much room.

"You're home late." Mase's voice came from somewhere in front of him.

Jazz didn't jump. The truth was that he wasn't surprised Mase had broken in. Jazz, or rather Lucien Bernard, had placed Mase in a condo just two floors down from his. Lucien was his host, after all, and made sure he had appropriate accommodations.

A light flicked on and shined down on Mase as he sat forward from the corner of the sofa.

"You're just pissed because you couldn't tail me without Max's gadgets."

Jazz had gone out of his way to make sure he couldn't be tracked. He'd bought new clothes to wear. Everything from his underwear to his socks and shoes was new.

Mase shook his head. "I don't need gadgets."

Jazz's blood ran cold. Did Mase know where he'd been? He looked at his friend and tried to gauge his reaction.

"I stayed to make sure you wouldn't need backup, but there was no need to confront you." Mase rubbed his temples. "I hope you're not getting in over your head here."

Jazz's heart began to race. Maybe he was losing it. He hadn't spotted Mase. He hadn't even felt himself being followed.

"Is this really worth it, Jazzy? Is this what you need? Because I could find a million ways to get rid of him that aren't so fucking complicated."

Jazz hung his head. Mase had pieced it all together. He'd known this would be his last assignment for the Company, but he thought it was because he was making the choice, not because he was losing his touch. Sam wanted him to join HC. He likely would, but he hesitated to tie himself so closely to Mase.

He wasn't sure he needed Marty dead. Part of him wanted that, sure, but was it the right thing to do? His morality was skewed and stretched from years of pretending to be someone with no morals.

At this point in time, he just wanted to keep eyes and ears on Marty and his father. And if Marty did need to die, Jazz would be the one to pull the trigger.

"I don't know what I need," Jazz said.

"How about you try needing me for a little while?" Mase asked as he stood from the sofa and took a few steps closer.

"Mase, it didn't work at the hotel. It—"

"Don't interrupt. I only want a kiss."

"Just a kiss?"

Jazz looked at Mase's mouth. In truth, he was obsessed with Mase's mouth. He had a beard now, and his dark blond hair was a little too long but looked silky. Jazz shaved off his own facial hair for his trip to Houston, and he wondered how Mase's beard would feel against his bare skin.

"All right."

Mase didn't move except to lick his lips. He was going to let Jazz decide...so he did. Jazz stepped forward, leaned in and pressed their lips together.

When Jazz didn't open his mouth right away, Mase started pulling back.

He was so sick of pushing Mase away, of Mase having to push himself away before Jazz did it for him. Mase deserved so much better. He deserved everything. And in that moment, Jazz was determined to prove it to him.

He reached up and grabbed fistfuls of Mase's hair to keep him from retreating. He felt cool air hit his lips as Mase gasped. Jazz took the opportunity to press his tongue inside Mase's mouth.

Mase lifted his hand and gently cupped Jazz's cheek.

Jazz tightened his grip in Mase's hair.

Mase groaned.

The sound was too raw, too desperate. Jazz immediately pulled back. Mase dropped his hands to his sides. Jazz still had his hands tangled in Mase's hair as they both panted, their foreheads pressed together.

The feel of Mase's breath on his lips had his cock leaking inside his underwear. He tilted his head as he prepared to try another kiss at a better angle. As he leaned in, Mase reached up and loosened Jazz's grip as he stepped back.

"I think that was a good first step." Mase smiled. "Night, Jazzy."

Jazz stood there, bewildered and bereft, as his front door clicked shut behind Mase.

Chapter Thirteen

Mase

Mase sighed when he looked up and saw Wade waving him over. He'd started HC out of necessity and he loved that he'd made a place for all the guys to belong, to make a difference and still be able to be open about who they were. That was great.

He just didn't like the day-to-day operations. That had never been his desire or his strong suit. So when he saw Double-D stride through the office, he let out a quiet groan, but stood and headed for the war room.

"Savage." Double-D smiled and gave him a half hug. "Holy shit. You look different. Hot, but different."

Mase huffed out a laugh and shook his head. Double-D had always been a flirt. The asshole knew exactly how gorgeous he was, and he didn't hesitate to use it to his advantage. Fortunately, he was also fun to be around and a financial wizard.

"Well, gentlemen," Double-D said when they sat around the conference table. "As always, I bring you good news. We're all a little richer, thanks to me."

Wade chuckled and shook his head. "I hope we can go into a little more detail since this is the first time in three years that Mase has been able to sit in on this meeting. Also, we want to talk about the reserves."

"It's all here," Double-D said as he tossed a folder into the middle of the table. "I printed it out, but you might want to make copies. I've lost another assistant."

"Sexual harassment?" Sam asked.

"Yeah, only *he* was harassing *me*."

Mase snorted.

"Seriously, Savage," Double-D said. "I don't dip my pen in the company ink. This guy was really pushing it, so I finally had to tell him it was never going to happen. I was paying him enough that I thought it would make up for me being so frank. Apparently, not."

"You've changed, D," Mase said. "I don't remember you wanting to turn down any offer."

"I didn't say I *wanted* to turn it down, but the last thing I need is a sexual harassment lawsuit."

"Speaking of lawyers and sexual harassment," Wade said, "we need to figure out what we're going to do with Thornton, so let's talk about the reserves. It won't be cheap to try to give him a new identity."

"I'm not sure he's ready, anyway. He might be grateful, but he's devastated his law degree's going to be useless," Sam said. "I'm worried he'll do something stupid."

"You have someone with a law degree?" Double-D asked.

"You need a lawyer?" Mase joked.

"Was he licensed to practice in Virginia?"

"He was just finishing his degree," Sam said. "He wasn't licensed anywhere, but he was a paralegal in California. I do have to warn you that his family history is pretty colorful. He flat out told Nick that he came from a long line of con artists."

Something flashed in Double-D's eyes, and his lips curved up. "I do need a new assistant, and someone with legal knowledge would be even more valuable. I'm trying to expand a few things."

Sam and Wade shared a look. Sam stood from the table. "Gentlemen, would you mind taking this meeting to the first floor? I'll make copies of the statements and bring Mr. Thornton. You can meet him, D, and see what you think."

As Sam left the room, Wade and Mase stood.

"Why can't he just bring the guy here?" Double-D asked.

"Thornton has no security clearance."

Double-D snorted. "Mine's not exactly up to date."

"But you were cleared," Wade says. "Besides, you have access to some of our most valuable records — our financials."

* * * *

By the time they were settled into a conference room on the first floor, Sam led Peter into the room. Double-D, who was sitting next to Mase, leaned forward in his seat, a half-smirk pulled at one side of his mouth.

Sam handed a stack of papers to everyone around the table. Peter shot each of them a wary gaze before he sat in the chair farthest from everyone else.

It seemed he trusted the guys at HC only so much. Mase had heard that Nick was the one he felt most comfortable with. He closed his eyes and took a deep breath. The last thing he needed to think about was family bullshit.

"Peter, this is Dominic De Luca. He manages our finances."

Peter frowned. "What does that have to do with me?"

"We need to talk about your future."

"I thought I didn't have a future," he sniped.

Wade sighed. "You can't use your law degree. That doesn't mean you don't have a future."

"Does that mean that eventually you're going to let me go?"

"Peter," Sam said, "we know this is hard, but you do realize what will happen if you try to pass the bar in any state in the union?"

Peter huffed out a breath. His gaze dropped to the floor, and he nodded. "It's not that I'm not grateful for what you guys did."

"We know, kid," Sam said. "But at this point in the game, it's not just your life at stake. Ax and Nick were supposed to take care of you, and by that I don't mean put you into a cushy apartment on the fourth floor of our building."

"I know what Campbell wanted them to do."

"You staying invisible keeps them alive as well," Wade said. "Nick, Ax, Jett, Brody...all four who got you out of there alive, not to mention Sam, Mase and Jazz? Their lives are at stake, too."

"I get it. I just... I can't remember the last time I've gone more than twenty-four hours without talking to my sister. Now she thinks I'm dead. *Dead.*"

"But if she knows you're alive, her life would be at risk," Wade says.

Peter widened his eyes, then darted them frantically around the room as he clearly thought that through.

"If Campbell knows you're alive but can't find you, he knows your weak spot. He knows exactly what leverage to use to get you to give yourself up. And don't think he'd let your sister go because he found you. No matter what he promised, once he found you, you'd both—"

"Okay," Double-D said, "look at the poor kid. You're scaring the shit out of him."

Wade leaned back in his chair, content to let Double-D play good cop.

"Hey, Pete, I'm Dom. My friends call me Double-D."

D's call sign seemed to distract Peter as he gave D a long look. Then he snorted.

"Why do I get the feeling your nickname has nothing to do with your first and last name?" Peter asks.

"Maybe you're smart." D shrugged. "Either way, I have a proposition for you."

Peter raised his brows in surprise. He looked a little too interested. "What kind of proposition?"

"I'm a wealth and asset manager—mostly for myself, at this point—but I'm in need of an associate who could help me, and I think you have just the skill set I need."

Peter narrowed his eyes. "You want a lawyer who can't practice law?"

"I need someone who can read legalese and someone who can read people."

"I don't take advantage of people," Peter said.

"And I won't ask you to. I just want your insight."

Peter stared at D for a long moment. "I might be willing to help you."

Mase noticed that everyone's shoulders relaxed in unison, even his. No one mentioned that Peter would still be kept under lock and key most of the time. He'd learn that soon enough.

Chapter Fourteen

Jazz

"Do we know why he wants to meet at a hotel?" Jazz asked.

"He's paranoid," Sam said. "And rightfully so. No one's been in the townhouse where he was holding Peter since that day. He had professional cleaners do a deep clean, and it seems he's thinking about selling it."

Jazz nodded, only slightly concerned that Campbell changed the meeting location at the last minute. Max had an eye on everything, regardless. Ax pulled the car into the underground parking at the hotel. As the lowest man on the totem, he reverted back to lackey. It hadn't surprised Ax, and he didn't seem to mind.

What had been a surprise was that Sam decided to sit up front with Ax, leaving Mase and Jazz in the back. Wade and Jett followed in a separate car. Technically, that made sense, too, since Mase was supposed to be their guest. But having his thigh press against Jazz's as they drove to a meeting like this was infuriatingly distracting.

Jazz cleared his throat and pulled his legs closer together. When he looked up at Mase, it was to find his lips rippling to hide a smirk. The man knew his effect. As soon as the car stopped, Jazz unbuckled his seatbelt with one hand while he opened the door with the other. He slipped out, shutting the door to cut off the sound of Mase's laughter.

As they headed for the elevator, Sam gave Jazz a look. They were all watching him a little too closely. Sam was the worst of them all, because he and Sam were more than army buddies. They both knew the isolation of working for the Company and maybe they'd both used it to distance themselves from everyone.

"What's with the mood?" Ax asked as he pressed the button for the lobby. "This guy has such a hard-on to meet you. He might have an orgasm from the sight of you."

Jett snorted.

Sam rolled his eyes and shoulder-checked Ax, who shrugged.

Jazz had learned long ago not to trust people who were so happy to meet him. Most of them wanted to take his place.

In the lobby, two bruisers in suits were waiting stiffly near the elevator from the parking garage when they got out.

"Oh, here we go," Ax grumbled under his breath.

One of the men narrowed his eyes at Ax until the other man elbowed him. Ax ambled over to them and gave them a nod.

"You gentlemen here to escort us up?"

One man nodded. "No weapons," he said quietly.

Ax laughed. "You guys don't know how this works. Let me clue you in. You want this on your turf, we bring whatever the fuck we want. If Campbell wants to meet somewhere neutral, then we'll talk."

The men gave each other a look. The one who'd given Ax the stink eye turned and stepped away to make a call.

Jazz stood by and looked impatient. This was a power play. Even if they took his weapon, he'd just take theirs. And every man on his team was capable of the same.

Ax and Sam chuckled as the guy ended up whisper fighting with whoever was on the other end of the line. Seemed he really didn't want to let Ax get his way. But before long he hung up, gave them a dejected nod and pressed the call button for the elevator.

With six in Jazz's crew plus the two bodyguards, they had to split up into two elevators. Even with Jett, Wade and one of the guards in the second elevator, the small space was cramped. And of course Mase was right next to Jazz, who made sure to put himself in the back corner. He felt safe cradled by two walls, especially with a man he didn't know or trust in the elevator with him.

When the doors slid open, they were in the foyer of the largest suite in the hotel, and yet another guard stood at the edge of the living room. As they entered, he turned and left.

"Sit there," said the man who had narrowed his eyes at Ax.

"Thanks. What was your name? Jason?" Ax said as they moved slowly toward a long dining table.

"No," he gritted out through his teeth. "Jason's the one you shot. He's still recovering."

"Wow, you guys have health benefits? You hear that, Bernard?" Ax turned and gave Jazz a sly wink that the other man couldn't see.

According to the debrief, it had actually been Jett who'd shot Jason, but they didn't argue the point. Instead, Jazz gave Ax a flat look.

"I pay you enough that you can afford your own health insurance," Jazz said, his French accent thick.

Ax shrugged. "I'm healthy as an ox — and I got my insurance right here." Ax patted the side where he kept his firearm as he smiled at the guard who wasn't Jason.

The elevator pinged again. The doors slid open and out stepped Wade, Jett and Campbell's other guard. As they walked toward the table, someone called Jazz's alias.

"Mr. Bernard?"

Jazz turned to find an older, distinguished-looking man approaching. He was well dressed, maybe an inch or so shorter than Jazz's five-foot-ten frame. But where Jazz was fit and slender, the other man was thickening around the middle.

"Mr. Campbell," Jazz said with a nod.

"It's a pleasure to meet you, Mr. Bernard. Shall we sit?"

Campbell sat at the head of the table. Jazz sat next to him, his back to the wall. Sam and Wade sat across from Jazz, and Mase sat beside him. Jett and Ax stood at the wall behind Sam. After introductions were made, Campbell tried to take control of the meeting.

"Thank you for meeting with me," Campbell said. "I think we have a lot in common."

"I'm going to be frank and tell you that, though I'm intrigued by your offer, I'm not pleased that you used my men to clean up your mess."

Campbell paused, swallowed, nodded. "I understand. I'm very careful about keeping my business private. I have everything under control again."

"I imagine your friends at this club would prefer you keep things that way."

"Yes, of course. I did make them aware of my slight security breach. I also was sure to tell them that you and Ax were the ones who helped me. That definitely improved your chances, especially since it was on the news that a certain Peter Thornton was found dead in a motel room outside San Francisco this morning."

Jazz nodded.

"I'd like to speak to you about working together and shall we say…sharing inventory?"

Jazz lifted his brows in surprise and looked at Ax, then back at Campbell. "I thought we were here to discuss connections, Mr. Campbell."

"Yes. I have connections that I'm happy to share with you, but I also have a thriving business of my own that's growing. My clients have very specific tastes. They're also impatient. They are powerful men. You have a lot more…inventory. I was simply hoping that I could give you a list of what I'm looking for. I'm happy to split the profits with you if you're able to fulfill any of my needs."

"For today, let's discuss this membership you promised. I'll need to know more about your organization before I consider working with you, Mr. Campbell. The fact that you're an attorney who specializes in women's rights is intriguing. It's an excellent cover..." Campbell puffed up his chest and smiled just as Jazz took a breath to burst his bubble. "But it also seems to have drawbacks, obviously. The people you work with are much more likely to blow the whistle if they catch something amiss."

Campbell nodded sadly, then cleared his throat.

"Tell me more about this club. I've heard whisperings, but as I'm mostly in Europe, I haven't attempted to see if they're true."

"They're true. I can assure you. The club has no name. There is, of course, an LLC behind it to which you would pay your dues. They also request a payment to set up a membership meeting."

Jazz raised his brows as if surprised, but he was practically drooling to get the bank account details that would surely lead to a maze of shell companies. But maybe, just maybe, they'd get a name or two from following that maze.

"What's the fee for a membership meeting?"

"Fifty-thousand per person. I've received approval to give you two applicant spots. There's also a possibility of a third, but that's still up for debate. For now, there's one for you and one additional, maybe as a reward for your men?"

Jazz shook his head slightly. "It depends on what's required to join."

"It starts with a meeting. There are a lot of questions that will be asked and a little proof of your commitment, so we all have a reason to be loyal to the club."

"It won't be possible for me to have sex while being observed," Jazz said.

"They're more than happy to cater to your tastes."

"That wouldn't be possible." Jazz shook his head.

"I don't understand," Campbell said.

"I'm asexual, Mr. Campbell."

Jazz heard the creak of Mase's chair as he shifted beside him. This wasn't a conversation he would have chosen to have in front of Mase, but it seemed it couldn't be avoided.

Chapter Fifteen

Mase

Asexual. The shock of Jazz using that word to describe himself reverberated inside Mase's head. The first thing that popped into his mind was the look of raw desire he'd seen in Jazz's eyes countless times. The second image — one that had him blinking to try to forget — was the tortured fear in those same eyes as Jazz scrambled off the bed and away from Mase as fast as his feet could carry him.

Jazz wanted him — at least Mase thought he did. For over a decade, Mase had been trying to get Jazz past all the hurdles in his head. But hearing Jazz label himself that way, with such a definitive tone, Mase felt blindsided. Why hadn't Jazz ever told him he thought of himself that way? Did he really think of himself that way or was that part of his cover?

When he looked up, Sam held his gaze for one heartbeat, then two. There was a mix of warning and comfort in his friend's eyes. He'd been there from the beginning. Sam, Mase and Kota had met in basic. They'd been there, watching Mase trip over himself when Jazz joined the Rangers.

They'd helped Mase protect Jazz from a couple of assholes. It was right at the end of the 'don't ask, don't tell' bullshit. A few guys had tried to out Jazz. And though Mase had hoped they were right about Jazz's sexuality, Jazz deserved to come out on his own terms.

The problem was that even after that had been resolved, Mase hadn't been able to let go. He had still felt the need to protect Jazz. He still felt it to this day.

Asexual?

In Mase's mind, asexuality was no different than being gay or bi or demi or pan. It was in the DNA, something you were born with, something you couldn't fundamentally change, even though sexuality could evolve. He'd thought that Jazz suffered from sexual aversion due to past trauma, not asexuality since birth. Was he really ace or had that aversion grown into part of his sexuality?

Mase had researched this long before working with people who were forced into prostitution. He'd started researching it before he left the army, when he realized that was why Jazz would pull him close, only to toss him aside with such a broken look in his eyes.

"This is a business to me, strictly a business," Jazz said. "It wouldn't pay to get emotionally attached to my inventory, as you say."

"That makes a lot of sense. You don't have to worry about being manipulated by the fairer sex. And if you find someone untouched, you're not tempted to sample the merchandise."

Mase had a strong stomach, but he would never get used to these monsters talking about people as if they were furniture.

"Exactly," Jazz agreed.

"Then who would you like me to sponsor?"

Jazz pretended to think about it, though they'd already discussed it thoroughly. Wade rarely went undercover, but he was perfect for this role.

He was a big, imposing guy who clocked in at close to six-four. He couldn't blend into a crowd while under cover when he was head and shoulders above everyone, but no one would fuck with him, either. As a former Navy SEAL, the man could take care of himself.

And, though some might assume he was all brawn, Wade was incredibly intelligent. He might not think that about himself because he was the lowest performing member in his family academically, but he was a genius when it came to logistics.

Wade was also single and pansexual, so if he had to play sexually with someone, he was a good choice. Then again, so was Mase.

Mase was bisexual and also single, but Jazz had shot that idea down because Mase wasn't part of Lucien Bernard's organization. Jazz had been right, but it had still made Mase feel good that he'd responded so quickly, as if maybe there were other reasons Jazz didn't want Mase involved.

"Wade Laslow," Jazz said as he nodded in Wade's direction. "He's here in the area more than the rest of us. I would like to join myself if there's a way to do it without fucking anyone. If not, I'll choose someone else."

Mase didn't like the thought of Jazz going into a place like that alone. Then again, Wade would likely be there. Jazz had been in worse places over the years and probably all by himself. But fuck if Mase didn't want to have his back.

He was so distracted that he'd lost half the meeting. When he looked up, Sam's eyes flashed with reprimand. Mase gave a slight nod. He needed to keep his head in the game.

Campbell handed Jazz a slip of paper with a long string of numbers as they all stood from the table. *Bingo.* That was exactly what they'd come for, a place to start digging.

* * * *

When they left Campbell's hotel suite, Sam held Mase back, pulling him aside long enough to make him wait for the second elevator. Mase didn't fight him. If he were in the elevator with Jazz at this moment, he might explode from trying to hold in all the shit he needed to say.

As it was, he tapped his foot on the elevator floor the whole ride down. Sam ignored him, but Campbell's guard kept looking over. He'd never been so close to breaking his cover. He'd watched Kozak's men do unspeakable things to women. He'd had to laugh when he wanted to puke, yet he'd kept his mouth shut. Why couldn't he keep quiet now?

When he and Sam reached the car, Mase was surprised to see the other SUV already gone. He looked at his friend with suspicion.

"What's going on?"

"I wanted to talk to you alone and not here. Get in the car, Mase."

Mase smoothed his tongue over his top teeth before moving toward the SUV. As soon as he heard the click of the lock disengaging, he pulled open the passenger door and climbed in.

"You need to give him space," Sam said as he backed out of the parking spot.

"You heard what he said. Has he labeled himself asexual before?"

Sam shrugged. "Jazz can label himself whatever the hell he wants."

"I can't help worrying that he's denying himself — or at least a part of himself."

"Would it be the end of the world if he was ace?" Sam asked. "Does him being ace make you love him less?"

"No." But it did make him feel lost, directionless. He'd been honest when he'd told Jazz that he wanted him more than sex, but even nonsexual touching was off the table. "Do you think he's happy?"

Sam gave Mase a startled look. "What do you mean?"

"Do you think he's happy with the way things are. Do you think he's happy without having a relationship of any kind?"

"I..." Sam sighed. "I wouldn't call Jazz happy. When he's not around you, work is his sole focus."

"Do you think that makes him content?" Was he more settled — happier — when Mase wasn't around?

"I don't think content is the right word. I'd say Jazz is resigned. He has reconciled himself to his fate, until you're there, determined to prove he's not as untouchable as he wants to be. Then again, I wouldn't call you happy, either. When you're together, I think tortured is the best way to describe you both."

"I want Jazz to be happy. I always hoped he'd to do what it took to move beyond his past. What if I'm just making it worse? What if instead of helping him, I'm hurting him?"

"Mase..." Sam blew out a breath. "Do I think Jazz would be happier if he could really be with you, with no fear? Yes. But it'll take a hell of a lot of work to get there, and maybe he's not ready. Maybe he never will be. What if he's never ready for that kind of intimacy?"

"If I could hold him, kiss him, sex wouldn't be as much of an issue. I can't do any of that. But maybe the real question is, is that even what Jazz wants?"

Sam snorted. "Jazz wants you. There's no question in my mind about that."

Mase closed his eyes. "I need to be able to touch him. Now that I know what it's like to have him in bed with me..." Mase shook his head then looked at Sam. How was he supposed to describe what happened?

"Seems like a lot went down in Houston," Sam said with eyebrows raised.

"He fell asleep on the bed with me, his arms wrapped around me. That should mean something. It meant something to me."

"You know as well as I do that ace doesn't mean aromantic. We all know Jazz has romantic feelings toward you. I think it means he trusts you more than anyone."

"He touched me in Houston," Mase said quietly. "More than touched me."

Sam looked over at him so fast that the car swerved a little. "By touch, you mean... No, don't tell me. I don't need details."

"Sexually. And he was into it. He got off."

"Fuck," Sam whispered. "I so did *not* need to hear that." Sam sighed.

"When we're alone, it seems like he wants to have sex but is scared. I always figured that if he was ace, it would lean more toward disinterest rather than fear."

"The bottom line is that only he can decide what he is or what he's ready for."

Mase sighed because he couldn't refute that. In all honesty, he didn't want to argue the point. He didn't want Jazz to turn himself into something he wasn't, but Mase also wanted to touch the man he loved.

"Maybe this makes me selfish, but if he's ace, where does that leave me?"

"In the same place you were before you heard him say that word, in love with Jazz."

He was in the same place, on the outside looking in. Mase shook his head. He would never force someone to change who they were for him. That had been what his father had done to him, and his father was the last person he wanted to emulate.

When Mase had come out to his father, Russell Hart had made him choose his family or living his truth. Mase had walked away, and that had been when his father had twisted the knife.

He shook his head. Years had gone by without him thinking about his father for more than a second here or there. Now that his family was surrounding him, that rage bubbled up inside him all over again.

"What if I'm making things worse? What if the best thing for Jazz is for me to just walk away?"

"We've all watched you do this tango, and we all know that it takes two. If he didn't want you, didn't long for you, we know you'd have backed off years ago.

Jazz does want you. He just doesn't know what to do about it."

"Yeah, well, him and me both. I mentioned talking to a therapist, but I think he sees himself as a lost cause."

Sam gave him a sidelong glance.

"What?"

Sam shrugged.

"*What?*"

A huff left Sam's lips that was half exasperation, half giving in. "I have my own set of...aversions."

Mase pulled his brows together. They'd talked about sex in general but not specifics. And now that Sam was dating his brother, he said, "Dude, I do not want to know what you get up to with Bray."

With a shake of his head, Sam chuckled. "And I'm not going to tell you anything about Bray. I'm telling you that part of the reason I'm so protective of Jazz is because I have my own issues. I thought I wouldn't be able to have the full...intimacy of a real relationship."

Mase groaned and covered his face with his hands.

"Fine. I won't try to tiptoe around it. Tie your hands behind your back."

"What?" That was not what he'd expected Sam to say.

"He's afraid of being overpowered. We all know that. Make it so that overpowering him is physically impossible."

The idea had merit, to put the choice in Jazz's hands like he'd done in Texas. It was so simple that he was shocked it hadn't occurred to him before. And there were plenty of sexy ways to do that. But then Mase realized that Bray had probably needed to do something similar for Sam, and his stomach turned.

"I don't know whether to thank you or beat the shit out of you."

"I think it says more about Bray than it does about me. I never asked him." Sam blew out a breath and shook his head. "What I mean is, he figured that all out on his own. He's intuitive and so fucking selfless."

Mase nodded.

"Speaking of Bray…"

"We're not. In fact, I'm not sure I ever want to talk to you about my brother again."

"Look… I know Nick's pressuring you, and—"

"No." Mase shook his head. "No. You're my brother, too. Don't make it so that I have no safe space from all that bullshit."

"Okay. You won't hear another word from me. You might want to steer clear of Ax, though."

"Fuck." Mase pulled at his hair. "Why did you guys have to hook up with my brothers?"

"I don't know if you noticed, but it's not hooking up. I'm not letting Bray go…ever."

"Thank fuck I don't have any more brothers. And if Bray had to be with anyone, I'm glad it's you."

"I'll believe that after you apologize for that gut punch in Kyiv."

Mase snorted, but he didn't apologize. "You deserved it."

Sam shrugged. "Probably."

Chapter Sixteen

Jazz

When Sam pulled Mase back, the elevator doors closed between him and Mase's pissed face. Jazz knew that the reprieve was only temporary. Mase would want to talk about what had been said during the meeting with Campbell.

The car ride back to HC was quiet without Mase in the car. As he looked out of the window, Jazz ran a hand over the beard that wasn't quite as long as it should be for his cover. He'd only had four days to grow it back since shaving it off. Not that he ever let it get very long, and it was always well groomed.

He snorted at his train of thought. Even his mind was determined not to think about Mase...and yet there it was again. He wanted to know what Mase thought, but the roiling in his gut told him that he already knew. Mase would fight him on this.

Mase would find a reason to say that Jazz wasn't ace. Not that Jazz himself was one-hundred percent sure, but it worked for his cover. It was part of the reason he had been picked for this particular assignment.

It was easy to say you were asexual, but Jazz could back it up. The visual stimuli didn't matter. The agency had tested him. Strippers, porn, even someone touching him — especially someone touching him — couldn't make his dick twitch.

There was only one person who had turned him on since his encounters with Marty had fucked him up — Mason Hart.

He remembered the first time he'd spoken to Mase. He'd been in phase one of Ranger Assessment and Selection Program — RASP. Mase, Sam and Kota were already Rangers. Because Jazz didn't talk about tits and ass with the other recruits in RASP, a few of the guys started getting on his case about it.

The problem was, they were right. Jazz had known he was gay since he'd been about thirteen. He hadn't had the time or energy to do much about it, but he knew it was there. He'd never been a really horny kid. His attraction to other guys or movie stars was a sort of laid-back buzz in his brain, not a pressure to hump and get off.

Then in college, Kevin had come on to him. Jazz could tell right away that his best friend Marty had been a little jealous. Jazz had turned him down because he hadn't been attracted to Kevin. He hadn't found anyone he wanted enough to have sex with. Then again, he'd only been sixteen at that point.

He shook off all thoughts of Marty. That man had taken up more headspace than he'd ever deserved in the first place. But if he wasn't thinking of Marty, he went right back to Mase. By the time he'd reached RASP, Jazz had known he was fucked up.

The guys giving him a tough time didn't let up. Finally, Jazz had told them they'd be more likely to pop a boner watching gay porn than he would. He'd known it was one-hundred percent true. Watching porn was more likely to make him puke. But those homophobes had taken offense and were about to gang up on him.

That was when Mase, Sam and Kota had stepped in. They must have heard the guys calling Jazz a faggot as they'd followed him out of the mess hall.

Mase's deep voice had boomed. "What's going on here?"

That was all it had taken. Jazz had been surprised to find that the sound had moved down his spine to zap him in the balls. He hadn't gotten hard — thank God — but he'd felt a twitch, something that hadn't happened since before Marty had held him down and told Kevin to take what he wanted.

"Jazz."

He turned at the sound of *Mémère's* voice. He didn't even remember getting out of the car and walking into HC. Jazz gave *Mémère* a smile, even though he cringed inside. There would be no escaping Mase now. The other car was probably moments behind them, and there was no hurrying away from *Mémère*, especially since she'd been watching him closely, too.

"Come have some tea, *mon petit*," she said.

Jazz took a deep breath and nodded. He followed her into her apartment on the first floor of the HC building, the only living quarters below the fourth floor. *Mémère* was superstitious. She didn't like elevators, and she didn't like stairs.

So when Mase had recruited her to work for HC, he'd built her apartment on the first floor. Mase loved *Mémère* almost as much as Jazz did. It was why Jazz knew that he would never truly escape Mase and the feelings he had for him. *Mémère* had had enough loved ones taken from her. Jazz would never be responsible for taking away someone else she loved.

"Did you two quarrel again?" she asked as she put the kettle on.

Jazz huffed out a breath as he sat at her kitchen table. *Mémère* called them lovers' quarrels. It was more than that.

Mase didn't get a say in Jazz's sexuality. That didn't fully ring true when Mase was the entirety of Jazz's sexuality. And it wasn't just Jazz's dick that was drawn to Mase. As hard as he tried to protect his heart, that belonged to Mase as well.

Every time Mase moved on, every time he had a relationship with someone else, a piece of Jazz died inside. That was why he left. He couldn't stand by and watch Mase be happy with someone else.

He also couldn't divide everyone's loyalties. Sam was always reassuring him that Mase still wanted him, still cared for him. Jazz was the fucked-up one, the one to run from Mase, so he was the one to bow out of making their friends feel divided as well. The least he could do was allow Mase to have the support of his friends.

And even though all Mase's relationships so far had ended, Jazz had to watch him find bits of happiness with other people. Someday it would stick, and Jazz would be left alone…again.

Chapter Seventeen

Mase

As soon as they were at HC, Mase sought him out like a heat-seeking missile. He knew exactly where Jazz was. He was either with Dee or he'd already left. If Jazz thought he wouldn't beat down his grandmother's door—or the door to his condo—he had another think coming. When Mase knocked, he heard a groan.

Bingo.

"Mase," Dee said when she opened the door. "You're just in time for tea, *cher.*"

He stepped inside as Dee flittered around, happy to have Jazz and Mase in the same room when Jazz had been cagey as fuck since the incident at the gala. When Mase offered to help, she made him sit across from Jazz.

"Are you two going to tell me what I missed? You usually at least pretend to get along for my sake."

"It's fine, *Mémère.* Mase is just pissed because I said something he didn't like."

"It's more than just saying something I don't like, if it's true. Is that part of your cover or do you really consider yourself…" Mase looked at Dee.

"I'll give you five minutes to work this out. Then we're having a nice *veiller*."

With that, she slipped out of her front door and closed it with a click. The electronic lock engaged with a quiet, mechanical *whoosh*. Jazz, who had been avoiding Mase's gaze, finally looked him in the eye.

"You don't get to choose my sexuality. You don't get to change it because you don't like it, either."

"That's not what I'm trying to do, and you didn't answer the question."

"I'm not affected by sexual stimuli, Mase. Even the CIA has classified me as asexual because I passed their tests."

"They have sexual classifications?"

"What do you think? They have to know which way you bend or you could end up blowing your cover. It's hard to pretend to be gay or straight or anything but asexual."

Mase leaned over the table toward Jazz. "The CIA doesn't know what's between you and me. They didn't put us in a room together. They didn't hover your lips over mine or lie us next to each other in a bed. They didn't press my back to your front so you could feel my ass against your hard cock."

Jazz's throat clicked as he swallowed. "What happened in Houston doesn't change anything. In fact, it proves I was right."

"It proves you're scared, just as scared as you were three years ago, five years ago, ten years ago." Mase growled in frustration. This was not how he wanted the conversation to go. He didn't want Jazz to think he was fighting him on this. He just wanted to know the truth, but when Jazz got defensive, so did he.

"Exactly. It doesn't change. It's not something I can shake off," Jazz pushed back from the table, then stood and paced. "This is not going away. This is my sexuality."

"Sexuality is in your genetic makeup. I was always bi. My brothers were always gay. But there are things that can change your sexuality, Jazz. I don't give a fuck how the CIA classified you. What I need to know is, were you always ace, Jazzy? Or did something happen to make you sex averse? Perhaps something with Martin Coleman?"

Jazz swung around, anger and shame blazing from his narrowed eyes. "You don't know what the fuck you're talking about."

"I think I do. I may not know the specifics, but I know that douche is the reason you can't stand to be touched. I want to kill him, Jazzy. I want to rip his guts out for doing that to you. Maybe that's exactly what I'll do. What if I get to him before you do?"

"Don't," Jazz said through gritted teeth.

"You want to ruin him politically. I think that would be easy enough. But I want to tear him limb from limb."

"It won't change anything. I'll still be broken. I'll always be broken, Mase. Why do you keep coming back for more? Every time you break up with someone, you swing by to see if anything's changed. Nothing's going to change."

"Swing by? What a crock of shit. You think you're an afterthought? Jazz, you're the *only* thought. But none of that matters if you don't want me. That's the bottom line here, Jazz. Do you even want me? You know I want you. I'd twist myself into a pretzel for you, literally tie myself up in knots to put you at ease."

"What I want and what I can have are two different things."

"No. If you want me, you can have me. We could figure out a way. But you won't even try."

"I've tried," Jazz screamed. He cleared his throat and repeated it in a calmer tone. "I've tried."

"I'm conceited enough that I assumed I could be what's best for you. Maybe I'm not. Maybe I'm the worst thing for you."

The words hurt as they moved over his burning throat like shards of glass, ripping him from the inside. Mase had laid himself bare for Jazz so many times. Why wouldn't he even try? He stood from the table and slammed out of Dee's apartment before he said something he'd regret.

Chapter Eighteen

Jazz

How the fuck could Mase think he wasn't trying? Every time they were together, he tried. Every time it didn't work and he freaked out, another piece of him shattered. Then he'd do something stupid like tell Mase to move on, to find someone else — and Mase would try.

At first, Jazz made himself watch. He'd watch Mase date men and women. He'd smell the sex on him when he came back to base. He had hoped then that the jealousy would help him get his head out of his ass.

Those first few years had been a torture of push and pull. Every time Mase was single, they'd try again, because Jazz had been determined not to see the man he wanted with anyone else. But then he'd shut down. He'd feel so completely inadequate. He'd tell Mase it wasn't working.

Then came the time that Mase didn't even want to try when he was single. That was when Jazz finally accepted the offer from the CIA. He'd needed to get out of the military and away from Mase.

Before all those memories even processed in his brain, Jazz went after Mase. He wasn't sure what had him panicking. Mase had left in a huff many times before, but those last words had been garbled with emotion.

Jazz caught the door before it closed, but before he could say anything to Mase, Wade came around the corner.

"Mase, Jazz, just who I was looking for. Max found more information about Kota. You both need to see this."

Mase stood still for a moment, his hands fisting and un-fisting. Without turning back to look at Jazz, he nodded and followed Wade into the elevator. They both turned once they were inside. Wade held the door and looked at Jazz. Mase looked everywhere except at Jazz.

If the meeting hadn't been about Kota, Jazz would have bowed out, but Kota was family. If he could help get their brother back into the fold, he'd do it. He hurried toward them and quickly pushed between them to put his back to the wall.

It didn't matter if he was at HC, and it didn't matter that he trusted every single man in the building. He couldn't relax when someone could come at him from behind.

He watched the back of Mase's head as the elevator ascended. He knew all Mase's moods. He knew his every tick and facial expression.

In *Mémère's* apartment, he'd been both hurt and angry. Jazz rubbed his hands over his face. The anger he could deal with. It was the hurt that twisted his guts.

He was sick to death of hurting Mase. And it wasn't often at this point in his life that he had no clue what to do…only around Mase.

Mase had thrown him for a loop from that first day they'd met. Jazz had seen the three Rangers around the base. His eyes had lingered on Mase, but he hadn't really known why. Jazz had liked the way he joked with his friends.

Then he'd heard Mase's voice, felt it against his skin. Mase had leaned down the few inches that separated their height and spoken low into his ear.

"You okay?" he'd asked.

That was all it had taken for Jazz's body to come back from the dead like a phoenix rising from the ashes. His dick hadn't twitched from any external stimuli in years, yet Mase had made him hard with two raspy words. Luckily, Mase had touched his lower back. That had deflated his boner so fast that he could almost convince himself it had never happened — until it happened again.

The elevator pinged, and the doors slid open. Jazz had been so wrapped up in his own thoughts that he hadn't realized that Wade had pushed the button for the third floor.

The whole building of HC was secure. No one got in unless they were granted permission. The first floor was the lowest level security, not requiring much security clearance, just a thorough background check. To visit floors two, three or four required higher security clearance, because most of HC's clients were currently government agencies who required it.

The second floor was where everyone worked, the fourth floor was only living quarters. The third floor had been mostly unused until Max joined the team a few months ago. And when Jazz stepped off the elevator, he was surprised at how much had changed.

The floor plan was laid out like the second floor. The large space that made up the bullpen on the second floor was mostly bare on the third floor. Then Wade stepped into a huge office of sorts. It was as big as the war room one floor below it, but it was now full.

Monitors covered one entire wall. A train of tables circled the room, each one supporting a computer. Some of them were powered on and had their own monitor. Others were pulled open with the wired guts spilling out onto the table.

On one side of the room, Max sat at a desk that looked like a donut with a slice taken out. Sam stood behind him, hovering as Max tapped away at his keyboard.

"What did you find?" Wade asked.

Max looked up. After making sure everyone was there, he nodded toward the wall of monitors.

"We know what Kota was convicted of. I just found proof he's innocent."

That got everyone's attention. They all turned in unison to watch as a grainy video played with no sound.

A man approached a car, then a woman stopped him. Her body was curved inward as she tried to pull him away from the car. The man backhanded the woman, and she stumbled back a step or two, but she kept pleading.

The man grabbed her and slammed her against the car. He wrapped his hands around her neck. She struggled against his hold but obviously had no idea how to break free.

That's when Kota strode into view. He quickly pulled the man away and pushed him back so hard that the man stumbled and fell. Kota spoke to the woman, but the man wasn't done. He marched forward and swung at Kota, who dodged the punch and threw the man onto the ground again.

As the man rolled around and struggled to get back up, Kota talked to the woman. She nodded, then shook her head. Kota fisted his hands and said something else. The woman shook her head again.

With one final nod, Kota walked away. The man on the ground said something to the woman that made her entire body still.

A chill skittered down Jazz's spine. He felt the fear right along with her. It was a threat. He couldn't hear the words, but he knew what that woman was feeling. He'd felt it too—powerlessness, terror, hopelessness.

Before the man could get back up, the woman hurried offscreen. Max typed wildly on his keyboard that looked to be broken into two pieces. Another perspective popped up. Kota was getting into his car and the woman must have called out to him, because he turned.

They were about ten feet apart when she came on screen. They spoke for only a few seconds before Kota nodded. The woman moved to his passenger side and got in of her own free will—not kidnapped, just as they'd known.

"Get this to the DA," Mase said. "*Now.*"

"The DA had access to these tapes," Max said quietly. "I got them off his servers."

Mase banged his fist down on the table closest to him. The loud thud reverberated through the room.

"Who's going to Missouri?" Mase gritted out through his teeth.

"I'm logistics. I'll figure it out within the next forty-eight hours," Wade said. "Max, we need background on the DA and the defense attorney who represented Kota."

"On it."

With one final nod, Mase left the room. He needed to cool down. Jazz knew he needed to cool down. Normally, Jazz would try to help with that by talking him down, but today he was part of the reason.

Chapter Nineteen

Mase

He needed to blow off some steam. What he wanted to do was find that DA in Missouri and beat the ever-loving shit out of him, but the heavy bag would have to do. He took the stairs to the first floor and kept his head down as he made his way to the gym. Luckily, the hall was empty and so was the locker room.

He stripped down to his underwear and pulled on some athletic shorts before heading into the gym, keeping his gaze on the floor in front of him.

He hadn't been this full of rage since he'd first joined the army. His dad pushing him out of the family had ripped something open inside him. He'd gone from a kid who skirted the line to a complete troublemaker.

He'd lost count of how many fights he'd started in basic — and he'd won every one of them. It was how he got his call sign, Savage. That was how he fought. Most of the guys in his unit learned to steer clear of him.

Kota had been in his unit. He steered clear of Mase, too. But then a few of the guys had started using slurs about Native Americans. That was a fight Mase didn't regret starting, even if he did get in trouble.

He could still hear the confusion in Kota's voice when he asked Mase, "Why did you stand up for me?"

"I know what it's like," Mase had told him. "I know what it's like for people to think they know something about you when they don't know *shit*."

Sam had been the one to teach Mase not to be a hothead. He'd come in at the same time, but he was a few years older than Kota and Mase. He'd come in as an officer because he'd used an ROTC scholarship to get through college.

That's how it had started with the three of them. They'd all come to the army for the steady income and the possibility of a future. They'd all had a hard time with the hetero-normative expectations. They'd bonded.

Eventually, they figured out that they were drawn to each other because they were all queer. They watched each other's six, both in battle and in life. And now Kota was in jail — and the fucking DA knew he was innocent.

Mase had just finished taping up his knuckles when he saw Nick step into the gym in workout clothes. He groaned, then turned away, hoping that if Nick saw him, he'd walk right by.

"Hey, Mase," Nick said from behind him.

"Now's not a good time."

"It's never a good time."

Mase pulled in a deep breath as he tried to steady himself. "It's never a good time to talk about Russell Hart."

"Dad. His name is Dad."

Mase turned to face his brother. "Not to me, it's not."

"Look, Mase. I know he said some things that hurt you—"

"If you know that, then why are you here asking me to see him?"

"He's sorry. He's miserable. He's going to die, and his one last request is to apologize to you in person."

"His last wish isn't my concern." Mase turned back to the heavy bag.

"Why? You're the only one who can give it to him."

He swung around again and got in Nick's face. "Because he doesn't deserve it. He got what he wanted. Now he's changed his mind. He's used to always getting what he wants. Not this time."

"He doesn't have what he wants." Nick shook his head. "Why can't you even try to see it from his point of view?"

"You want me to give him empathy? *Fuck*." Mase fisted his taped hands at his sides. He never thought he'd be so tempted to lift a hand to his brother. "Nick, I don't have time for this. I've asked you ten different times in ten different ways, as nice as I could, to let the 'Dad' thing go, yet here you are."

"I'm not trying to force you to go see him. I just want to talk about it openly. You shut me down before we can even have a real discussion"

"Like you could force me. You can't, and if you bring him here, you'll be fired."

"Just like that?" Nick asked.

Mase ignored the hurt in his voice. Sure, Nick was fitting in with the team, but it seemed he was there for all the wrong reasons.

"I've asked you. I've asked you to leave this alone, and you won't. That tells me a lot about why you're keeping in touch with me and why you're here at HC in the first place."

"I'm here because Bray—"

"Bray will keep in touch with you if you're not here. So will Ax."

"You didn't let me finish," Nick said.

"I don't need to. I don't want to hear your excuses, Nick. It's glaringly obvious where all your loyalties lie. That's fine. It's good to know, actually, but I'm not sure this is the best place for you."

"Why can't I have loyalty to our family? I don't want to feel like I'm being torn in two. What's wrong with wanting to bring our family together?"

"Because it's solely to Russell Hart's benefit and my detriment. You don't give a fuck about how I feel or what I want, as long as he gets what he wants."

"That's not true. I just don't understand why you can't hear him out, even if it's just to tell him you don't forgive him. He's dying, Mase."

"And if I'd died on any of my missions? If I'd died at seventeen when he kicked me out of the house? Would I have gotten to say a last word? Would he have even cared?"

Nick opened his mouth to respond, but Mase cut him off.

"Don't you dare tell me he would have cared. If he cared, he wouldn't have cut me off from my family. If he'd cared, he wouldn't have…"

Anger and regret and bitterness swirled inside him, making him sick. He shook his head. Part of him wanted to rail at his brother, and yet he'd been just as conceited before his father had shown him the real world in the harshest way.

"Nick, you have no inkling what it's like to be a loved, spoiled kid only to be tossed out on your own, completely unprepared for the real world. I had no one to turn to. I had nothing. I had no money and no experience, so I couldn't get a job, not with any hope of supporting myself. I had no way to make money, to pay rent, to feed myself.

"I had thought I'd been on the verge of being an adult, but I was completely coddled and suddenly twisting in the wind. If I hadn't joined the military, I might not be standing here today—or maybe I'd be working in some grocery store with just my high school diploma behind me."

"I think you're more intelligent and tenacious than that," Nick said quietly.

That was all the sympathy he got? He bared his soul and Nick came back with that.

"I realize it's hard for you as the golden child to sympathize—"

"I'm not the golden child. I—"

"The truth is that I can sympathize with you about as much as you can with me. I have no idea how you can stand there and say, 'Oh, it was just some little mistake Dad made so many years ago. Why can't you just let it go, Mase?' I don't know how to look at the world from that view, the one where tearing your child permanently out of your life is just some little mistake that can be swept under the rug."

"I don't think it should be swept under the rug. I'd never think that, and that's not what he wants. He regrets it. He regrets it every day. He can't pretend it never happened, but he wants to apologize."

"Good for him. I regret it, too. I have every fucking day of my life for seventeen years. The only side you're on is his. The only one you're fighting for is him. You don't see or care to see my perspective. You say you want a conversation, but all you want to do is defend him. I'm done here. There's nothing you can say to me that will make me forgive him, and you're aligning yourself right there next to him—like you were right there with him seventeen years ago, telling me to get the fuck out."

"Fuck you, Mase."

He'd kind of expected this from Nick, but it still hurt like a son of a bitch.

"There's that unconditional love our family's so famous for. If I won't do what you want, what he wants, I can just go fuck off. Good to know where I stand."

Mase shoved Nick aside and moved past him, but he stopped when he realized they had an audience. Ax was there, likely to meet Nick. Sam and Bray weren't far behind him.

"Mase." Bray took a step toward him, but Mase shook his head. He felt his throat close up. His nose burned as he hurried past everyone. He didn't even un-tape his hands until he reached his car.

He banged both fists on the hood a few times. Then he unrolled the tape, tossed it in his passenger seat, and roared out of the garage. If he couldn't beat something, at least he could get drunk.

Chapter Twenty

Jazz

He gave Mase a wide berth after that meeting. Instead of following Mase as he felt drawn to do, Jazz went back down to *Mémère's* apartment. It was the last place that Mase would go when he had murder in his eyes.

"Sorry we left," Jazz said when she answered the door. "Max found Kota."

"I know, *cher*. You need to bring that boy home."

Jazz smiled as he wrapped his arm around her. She saw all the guys as hers. Technically, Kota's home was with his father, but they all knew Mase would welcome him into HC with open arms, whether it was to live or work or both.

"Sit down, *mon petit*," *Mémère* said. "I think we need something harder than tea."

He huffed out a laugh and sat at her table. It was the scarred oak table she used to have at her house, the one *Pépère* had made for her when they were first married.

Jazz traced his fingers over the grooves and nicks. As a child, he'd colored there, made model airplanes with *Pépère* there, eaten so many homemade meals there. Why did those memories make him feel even more broken?

He stayed with *Mémère* for as long as he could manage to hold off those memories. Anger pulsed through him, just like it did with Mase. He'd learned to hide it better, but it still beat inside him like a drum. He didn't want any of it to spill out on the people he loved most in the world.

"I need to go check on Mase, *Mémère*," he finally said.

"When are you going to stop making yourself miserable?" she asked.

That's when he looked at the bottle of bourbon and realized that she'd probably had too much to drink. She never pressured him about things like that.

"I'm actually trying to save us from misery. I can never make Mase happy."

She reached up to cup Jazz's cheek. "*Pauvre ti bête,*" she whispered, just like she had when he'd been sick as a child. "No one *but* you will ever make that man happy."

He pushed that thought aside as he left her apartment. He had to get his laptop anyway, so he went up to the second floor. The moment he stepped into the bullpen, something felt off.

There were no jokes or barbs being volleyed about. No one called out to him, and everyone loved to remind him that his call sign was Woody. The name didn't bother him since Woodrow had been his great-grandfather's name and people had called him Woody for short as well. But guys—being guys—loved shouting it out when he entered the room.

The door to the war room was open, so he stepped over the threshold. Sam and Bray were inside talking quietly to Wade.

"What did I miss?"

Sam sighed. "Mase and Nick had it out in the gym after the meeting upstairs."

"Nick says he's going to quit, just like Mase told him to," Bray said.

"Mase fired Nick?"

"Not technically."

"He might, though, if Nick doesn't let it go, the talking to Dad," Bray said.

"Can't you talk to him?"

Bray looked at Jazz with a frown. "Not about this. I can't talk to either one of them about Dad. Mase and I pretend the problem doesn't exist, but Nick…? He can't have one conversation with Mase without bringing it up. I know it's because he sees Dad losing hope and deteriorating. Dad is going to die, but when he's gone, I'm worried that Nick and Mase won't have a relationship."

"What about Ax? Can't Ax talk Nick down?"

"Not about this," Ax said from the doorway. "And I feel like my loyalty is torn. I've gotten to know Russ. I really think he regrets what he's done. Like Bray said, Russ is dying. He's pretty damn sure that Mase is never going to forgive him, even if they do talk, but he wants the chance. He grills Nick every day about Mase, and I think that puts Nick on edge, like every minute counts."

"But he's putting off seeing Mom, too, because of all this," Bray said. "He'll email her, but he hasn't let her see him. I think he's afraid she'll try to talk him into seeing Dad as well."

"Nick's going to lose his own chance to be part of Mase's life if he doesn't let this go." Jazz rubbed his hands over his face.

"I know," Ax said. "We've all experienced some sort of flack for being queer. I was lucky enough not to have any of that shit in my own family, but what if he's really changed?"

"I hope he has," Jazz said. "Because then, the queer person he encounters next will hopefully be treated like a human being. Even if Mase never sees his father again, never forgives him, I know there's a part of him that's glad Nick didn't have to experience the same thing. That's why Russ should change, so he doesn't hurt anyone else the way he hurt Mase."

"Bray's given him that chance," Sam said. "That doesn't mean that Mase has to."

Ax's shoulders slumped, but he nodded. "Can someone at least tell Nick that he's not fired?"

"I'll talk to him," Wade said.

"And I'll talk to Mase," Jazz said.

It would give him a few other topics to cover so that hopefully they wouldn't have to talk about his sexuality.

Chapter Twenty-One

Mase

He sat on the cushy leather sofa of his condo. He'd considered breaking into Jazz's [;ace before drowning himself in liquor so that he'd still have the ability to actually break in. But he wouldn't be able to crash at Jazz's place, so he went to his own with his three new friends, Scotch, bourbon and whiskey.

If he never had to drink vodka or cognac again, he'd be a happy man. He started with the Scotch, though he regretted it as soon as the liquid hit his tongue. Scotch was what Russell Hart preferred, so when Mase had thrown a few bottles in his basket at the store, he'd automatically selected his father's preferred brand, even though not the stupidly expensive bottles his father bought.

Chances were that Russell wasn't drinking too much anymore. The alcohol soured in his stomach at the thought, so he pushed away the Scotch and opened the bourbon. The more he drank, the more pathetic he felt.

As he'd moved up in the ranks of the army, he'd pictured running into his father. He'd imagined his dad seeing him in his Ranger uniform. He'd pictured his dad regretting what he'd done once he saw that his son was one of the most elite soldiers in the army.

Even when he'd dreamed it up, he'd known it was a childish fantasy. Russell Hart was a trust fund baby. He respected what the army did to protect his freedoms. Seeing his son in a uniform wouldn't have made him as proud as a degree from an Ivy League school or to see Mase adding to his trust fund—the trust fund Mase hadn't known about until he'd turned twenty-five and it had been released to him.

Mase put a big dent in his trust by opening HC, but the building had increased in value, and Double-D was growing his bank accounts to a very healthy size.

Mase shook his head. He didn't want to think about his father. He didn't want to think about HC or his current mission. He didn't even want to think about Jazz. He especially didn't want to think about Jazz.

Sexuality was a complicated thing. He knew that. Sometimes finding the right label was impossible, and other times it took trying on a few to see what fit.

When his phone buzzed, Mase pulled it out of his pocket. It was Bray checking up on him. With a sigh, he told his brother he was home safe and that he just needed time alone.

Then, after closing out of the secure messaging app Max had installed on his phone, he went to the app store. He hadn't been with a man in three years.

While he'd been undercover, he'd only slept with women. It wasn't lost on him that he'd put himself into a position where he'd had to sneak back into the closet.

He was doing exactly what he told his father he wouldn't do.

Then again, he'd been mostly closeted in the army, too. Leaving his family for his principles hadn't lasted long when he figured out just how hard it was to support himself in the real world. But by then, he hadn't had a family to turn back to.

He could say he was doing it on his own terms and for an altruistic reason. While those things were true, he was sick of trying to find a replacement for what he really wanted.

Mase leaned toward women for the most part anyway, or at least he had for the last decade. Before that, he'd considered himself a four on the Kinsey scale, tipping more toward homosexuality.

But now, when he was with a woman, there was no pretending. He couldn't end up with someone who looked a little too much like Jazz but never quite filled that space. It wasn't fair to him or his partner if he spent most of his time wishing they were someone else.

His mind wandered to Blake as he poured himself another drink. Blake was more like Max than Jazz, with his full lips and delicate features.

"I really am getting desperate if I'm thinking about Blake," Mase mumbled.

He emptied his glass and poured another as he scrolled through the latest LGBT hookup apps. He didn't want to think about either Blake or Jazz tonight.

Blake would be much easier to push from his thoughts. What he felt for his ex was no longer any type of tenderness. Blake had abandoned him at his lowest point. Jazz, on the other hand, was never far from his mind.

Mase stiffened when he heard the quiet click of the front door. He had his gun in his hand before it swung open, but he knew who it was. He kept his gaze on the mirror in front of him, which reflected the room behind him.

"How drunk are you?" Jazz asked.

"Not drunk enough. I think you're on the wrong floor, Mr. Bernard."

With a sigh, Jazz closed the door. "Are we really going to do this?"

"No. That's the point. We're not doing anything. There's nothing between us. The CIA classified you as ace, remember?"

"Mase, don't act like a two-year-old."

Mase spun around. "I had a shit day. I'm in my home—temporary though it may be. I can act however the fuck I want. If you don't like it, leave."

"You definitely earn your name, don't you, Savage?"

Mase shrugged.

"I came to check on you *because* you had a shit day. I'm sorry that I played a role in it. I should have warned you, but..." Jazz shook his head. "You know me better than anyone else, Mase. Is this really such a surprise?"

Mase pulled over a second glass and filled it with bourbon. He held it as he walked over to Jazz, but when Jazz held out his hand, Mase just stepped around it. He walked until they were chest to chest.

Jazz looked up at him. There was no fear in his eyes, just confusion and maybe a little apprehension. Mase leaned down and lightly pressed their lips together—just a whisper of a kiss.

Mase pulled back only enough to say. "I bet you're already hard, and I've barely even touched you."

Savage

When he looked down, Mase saw that he was right. Jazz pushed him away as he took the drink from Mase's hand.

"Alcohol always did turn you into an asshole." Jazz sighed. "That doesn't prove anything. Ace people get turned on. Ace doesn't mean impotent."

"But do you want to do something about it?" Mase asked. "I don't care if you're ace or if the CIA classifies you as ace, do you want me or not? Once and for all."

Jazz's nostrils flared. "Do you know how many hours of porn footage I had to watch so that the Company believed I was ace?"

"What does that—?"

"With supervision, to make sure I didn't get even the slightest erection?"

Mase crossed his arms over his chest.

"Every kink from BDSM, to fetishes. I even had to watch pedophilia. They made sure nothing got me hard. Mostly it just turned my stomach."

"Should sex between consenting adults turn your stomach, even if you're ace?"

Jazz lowered his gaze to his drink, letting Mase know that he wasn't sure if that was what it meant either.

"You know I want to touch you, to be with you," Jazz said quietly.

The relief those words brought made Mase dizzy. Maybe the alcohol was really hitting him hard, maybe it was the crazy day getting to him, but Mase couldn't stop thinking about what Sam had said. He couldn't help but wonder... Mase lowered to his knees in front of Jazz.

"What are you doing?"

Chapter Twenty-Two

Jazz

The drink sloshed a little as his hand trembled. Jazz lifted the glass to his lips to cover it up and pretend to be unaffected. Mase's mouth was *right there*. There were certain fantasies that could turn Jazz on, certain fantasies that could get him off. He had no experience with getting a blow job, so he hadn't known how intoxicating it would be to have Mase's mouth so close to his dick.

And he was on his knees. Jazz looked down in time to see Mase lick his lips. He couldn't hold back the groan. When Mase leaned forward and nuzzled his cheek against Jazz's shaft, his dick pulsed against the zipper of his pants.

"Mase…" His mind spun with the pleasure of being touched by Mase.

Mase pulled back and looked up at Jazz. "That's not fear I see in your eyes. It's not disinterest, either. But if you don't want me, tell me to stop," Mase said. "Just one word and I will. Do you want me, Jazzy?"

"I just told you I do."

Mase leaned in and started to mouth Jazz through his pants.

"Or you could take out your cock and shut me up." The vibration of Mase's words against his shaft made Jazz's knees weak.

"We both know I'll freak out." Jazz's voice was a little too breathy for his liking.

"Bind me," Mase said.

That had Jazz opening his eyes. *When did I close them?* He never closed his eyes when he was vulnerable in any way, especially sexually. *Is it that I trust Mase?* The thought of Mase at his back still made him cringe and his erection began to flag.

Then Mase hummed against him. Jazz pulled in a breath and his dick was once again fully erect.

"You're drunk," Jazz said.

"I'm not. And even if I were, do you think I'll regret this tomorrow?"

Maybe. He had to regret all the times they'd tried anything sexual in the past, because Jazz inevitably pushed him away. Even in Texas, Jazz had freaked out when he saw how hard Mase was.

"Tie my hands," Mase said.

"What?" Jazz was sure he hadn't heard him right.

"If you tie my hands, then you'll know I'm not a threat."

Jazz set his drink on an end table nearby. Then he ran his fingers through Mase's hair and tugged on it until Mase was looking up at him.

"I know you're not a threat."

"Your logical brain does, but the anxiety that lives inside you doesn't trust it. What if I was at your mercy? What if there was no way I could overpower you, even if I wanted to?"

Why does that have my cock throbbing?

"Mase —"

"Do it, Jazz. What if this is a way for us to be together? I want to taste you."

"Without touching me?"

"You know I want to touch you, but more than that, I want to *be* with you."

Jazz's head was spinning with Mase's words and the pleasure his lips brought. Mase kept nibbling at him through his pants. If he didn't stop, Jazz was going to come. He opened his mouth, but only a whimper came out.

"I won't touch you with anything other than my mouth."

Jazz looked down to see that Mase had his hands clasped behind his back as if he were standing at ease in front of his CO, only he was on his knees.

Mase pressed his cheek harder against the underside of Jazz's length. He rubbed up and down, up and down. Jazz watched his hands as they clasped tighter and tighter, like Mase wanted to reach up but wouldn't let himself.

Jazz shuddered at the friction of Mase and his boxers against his cock. Mase hummed again, and that was all it took for Jazz groan and spurt into his underwear.

He panted as he hunched over Mase. This was where he normally freaked out, at the thought of reciprocation. As Mase stumbled to his feet, Jazz could clearly see the outline of his erection as it curved up and toward the right in his pants.

Jazz took a step back but stopped himself when Mase made no move to undress or even adjust himself. Then Mase swayed a little.

"How much have you had to drink?"

"Not anywhere near enough. I hate seeing that look in your eyes."

Jazz looked down to find that Mase was no longer hard — or at least no longer as hard. Jazz swallowed. In his mind, he wanted to know what Mase looked like, what he tasted like, but reality was another thing entirely.

With a scoff and a shake of his head, Mase stumbled toward his bedroom. Jazz followed at a distance.

He smirked as he watched Mase walk down the hall like a sailor who hadn't yet grown his sea legs. He kept pressing against the wall, then pushing himself upright.

Jazz could count on one hand the number of times he'd gotten drunk. He didn't like that loss of control. If he got drunk, he did it alone, just like Mase had done.

By the time he entered Mase's bedroom, Mase was passed out, face down on the mattress.

Why Jazz felt tenderness in that moment, he couldn't say. Mase was his Achilles heel. He was the only reason Jazz had ever strayed from carrying out the direct orders he was given. Mase was his sole distraction. In his own way, he was just as protective of Mase as Mase was of him.

He rolled Mase onto his back, then pulled off his shoes and socks. He was strewn slanted across the bed, his feet dangling off the edge.

Jazz leaned onto the mattress and unbuckled his belt. Mase mumbled something incoherent. Jazz unbuttoned and unzipped his pants, then tugged at them by the ankle cuffs. The pants weren't going to come off without a lot of maneuvering, so he let them be.

The master bedroom in the condo he'd assigned Mase was big and almost as luxurious as his. There was a sofa against the wall that looked out over the balcony. After stealing some of Mase's clean clothes, Jazz changed into some boxers, a pair of sweats and a T-shirt that were a little too big.

He settled onto the sofa and checked his email. His gaze kept straying to Mase. Finally, he set his phone down and scrubbed his hands over his face.

That was the second time Mase had gotten him off, only to have his dick deflate when Jazz freaked out. If Mase had any idea how much Jazz longed to touch him, to have a physical relationship with him... He shook his head. What would Mase do? Push harder?

He growled in frustration but cut it off when Mase stirred. This was why he stayed away from Mase. There was never even a temptation with anyone else.

In the beginning, when he'd first met Mase, he thought that maybe he was demisexual. He'd seen Mase around the base when he'd started Ranger school. And though he'd thought him attractive, it wasn't until Mase tried to protect him that Jazz's infatuation had begun.

It hadn't been the first time he'd been accused by teammates of being gay. The taunting and the fighting out in the open didn't really bother him. He just made sure no one ever caught him on his own in a place that was secluded.

Jazz had gotten a peek that day that had shown him exactly why Mase's call sign was Savage. He had no mercy. He'd come out of nowhere and had two of the three guys against the wall of the mess hall, the back of his forearms holding them here.

The look on his face had been cold. The third asshole had mumbled that this was probably just one fag protecting another. Then Mase's lips had spread in a smile. Both men he'd been holding had been wide-eyed and telling their friend to shut up.

"Don't think my girlfriend would agree with you," Mase had said.

Sam and Kota had both taken a step closer to him. The third asshole had closed his mouth then, and his Adam's apple had bobbed down, then back up.

"I'm always more suspicious of the ones who are always bringing up the subject of homosexuality." Mase's voice had been casual, but his eyes had narrowed. "They're usually the ones with latent tendencies."

Sam had nudged Mase then, and he'd stepped back, letting go of the two men he'd been holding. They'd both held their necks as they'd taken deep breaths. A moment later, one of the COs had walked by.

"Spew all the bullshit you want," Kota said low. "But if you touch him, we won't be holding Savage back. We'll be helping him."

When Mase had turned his back to the three men, he'd winked at Jazz. And that was when his infatuation had started.

Maybe it was because Mase had stood up for him. Maybe it was because Jazz had thought he was straight and taken. Subconsciously, that probably made him safe for Jazz to form a crush on.

His feelings had built and built over the next year. But then Mase had broken up with his girlfriend and admitted to Jazz that he was bi.

Mase groaned, bringing Jazz back to the present. "Fuckin' Jazzy."

Jazz couldn't help but smile at his grumpy tone.

Then Mase grumbled something that sounded suspiciously like "always want you."

That was the problem. Jazz always wanted him, too. He didn't want to torture Mase or himself.

As much as it killed him to watch Mase with someone else, Jazz did it, because trying to have something for himself only crashed and burned. Each time, he promised himself it would be the last time. He would back away and let Mase move on. Would this time be any different?

He couldn't stop picturing Mase with his hands tied behind his back or to a bed or... Jazz shifted on the sofa. He was getting hard all over again, and he'd just changed his pants.

He spent the next few hours considering Mase's offer while making sure the idiot didn't choke on his own vomit.

Chapter Twenty-Three

Mase

When he opened his eyes, Mase groaned before rolling over and covering his head with a pillow. It felt like the light was going to split his skull in two. How many drinks had he downed the previous night?

His phone buzzed on the nightstand. With a grunt, he turned and squinted at it. A new message from Wade. *Great.* He had to be at HC in one hour.

As he sat up, something on his nightstand caught his eye. There were two bottles of water and two pills. He huffed out a breath as his heart kicked up a little. *Jazz.*

He was tempted to toss it all in the trash, but he didn't. He swallowed the pills and drank one whole bottle before stumbling toward the bathroom and taking a long, hot shower. Then he drank the second bottle of water as he rode the elevator down to the garage.

Jazz's car was already gone, which wasn't surprising since chances were he'd be avoiding Mase for a while after what had happened the previous night. Whenever there was any sort of physical intimacy between them, Jazz needed space. Mase would be happy to give it to him if he didn't feel like he was starting from square one every time they ended up in the same room again.

As soon as he stepped off the elevator onto the second floor of HC, Mase knew that coming in with a hangover probably wasn't the best idea. All the noise and raucous laughter only made his head pound.

When he saw that Wade's desk was empty, he hurried through the bullpen and into the war room. But as soon as he opened the door, he locked eyes with Ax. All the words he and Nick had flung at each other came rushing back.

Mase's feelings toward Nick were too complicated to nail down when his temples were pounding into his brain. He loved Nick, but he just wished he had a fraction of Nick's loyalty and concern. He wished Nick cared enough in return to let Mase have a choice whether or not to see Russell Hart.

If Russell died without Mase seeing him, Nick would never forgive him. They would never move past it. Mase wouldn't give in to emotional ransom like that.

"Mase," Wade said. "Come on in."

With a nod to everyone, Mase sat at the end of the table. They were talking to someone he didn't know but who was dressed in street clothes.

"I wasn't an operator," the man said. "I never even applied for Ranger school."

"Neither did I," Ax said as he bumped shoulders with the dark-haired man.

"Well, we're employee-owned, but Mase has more shares here than anyone," Wade said, making Mase wish he'd been a few moments later.

This was an interview, and the recruit was obviously a friend of Ax's. Everyone at the table turned to look at Mase.

"This is Zayne Archer," Sam said. "He helped us out a little with an op—"

"Unknowingly," Zayne corrected.

"There are no military rank requirements," Mase said. "And I assume since you're on the second floor of this building that you have security clearance."

Zayne nodded. "The only job I've ever had was with the United States Army. I was honorably discharged—"

"With a Purple Heart," Ax interrupted.

"Due to an injury," Zayne finished, sending Ax a dark look.

"Your military record is flawless," Wade said, then looked at Sam and Mase, who both nodded—even though Mase hadn't actually seen his record.

"So there's a place here for you if you want to start our training program. There's a six-month probationary period. If you make it through that, you'll be a permanent part of the family."

"But...my injury..."

"Might mean fewer ops for you like it does for me," Wade said. "But you would still be a valuable member of our operation."

Zayne blinked a few times before looking around the table. He swallowed and nodded. Mase knew what it felt like for Uncle Sam to put you out to pasture before you were ready. Being labeled a hero could be an addictive thing. To be told you're no longer needed, to feel useless? It wasn't something a soldier could easily get used to.

"Why don't you show Zayne around, Ax? Max has already done his background check, so he's a go on all floors except number three."

Zayne's eyebrows lifted, and he looked around the room in surprise. "Don't you want to know the extent of my injuries?"

"You're not the only injured vet we'll have on the payroll," Wade said. "You're more than your injuries, soldier."

Zayne opened and closed his mouth twice before finally licking his lips and nodding.

"Now," Ax said, as he rubbed his hands together, "no more of this Zayne stuff. His handle is Saint, and the reason for that is—"

"Ax, shut your mouth."

Ax laughed.

"We'll call you whatever you want," Wade said.

"Saint's fine."

"Welcome to the team, Saint," Sam said.

Ax stood and slapped Saint on the shoulder. It took Saint a little longer to stand, then both men left the room just as Max stepped in.

Mase rubbed his eyes. The business side of HC made his head hurt, even when he wasn't hung over. He was surprised when Jazz followed Max into the room. He was even more surprised when Jazz met his gaze and gave him a nod with a ghost of a smile.

And just like that, Mase's spirits lifted. He spent the next hour watching closely. There was no avoidance at all. Last night was a little fuzzy around the edges, but he never forgot one moment when he was touching Jazz. Normally, that would mean two steps back, but maybe this time things *would* be different.

"That about wraps everything up," Wade said before turning to Mase. "I need to speak with you alone for a minute."

Mase sighed and gave a nod. It was likely more HC business stuff. When the room was empty, he slumped in his chair.

"If I give you more stock in HC, will you leave me out of these decisions, even when I'm Stateside?"

Wade chuckled. "We'll see what happens when you're Stateside as more than just part of your cover. That's not really what I wanted to talk to you about, anyway."

"No?"

"I'd appreciate it if you'd tell Nick he's not fired."

That caught Mase by surprise. "Can't you do that?"

Wade shook his head. "He knows he's not technically fired, but he thinks you don't want him here after what happened yesterday."

"I'll text him."

"Mase, you're not one to do things by halves."

"Maybe it wouldn't break my heart if he did quit."

"No? Well, think of it this way. If he leaves, chances are that Ax will, too. They're a package deal now. There's a reason we were stalled for six weeks when Ax went missing in action."

Mase scoffed. "He wasn't MIA. We all knew exactly where he was."

"He was mentally MIA. I wasn't about to drag him away from his family. They were reuniting with his sister after three years."

"I know that. I'm not saying you should have."

"Okay, well, it's easy enough to fake his death if he really needs to leave, but then it's a matter of building trust with all the contacts he was working with. He's been playing this role for two years."

"I know."

"And Nick's good. He has good instincts. He knew that Peter Thornton wasn't in on it with Campbell. At least that was his gut feeling."

"I know."

"And deep down, you like having all three Hart brothers working at Hart Consulting."

"Don't take things too far, *Lesley*."

"That doesn't work coming from you anymore, Savage. You desensitized me to that as soon as you found out what my real first name was. Think of it this way. I'm sure it's driving your dad nuts, knowing that Nick and Bray get to see you all the time but he can't even get into the building."

Mase smirked. Wade had as many issues with his own dad as Mase did. "Is he upstairs?"

"No, you have a reprieve. He's on R&R for the rest of the week."

Mase snorted because he knew exactly where Nick was spending his time off.

"But you can at least chat with Ax at some point this week when he's not showing Saint around."

"Fine."

"Good. Now." Wade clapped his hands together. "About Kota."

"What about Kota?"

"I have two attorneys working on his appeal."

"Already? This is exactly why you're better at running HC."

"It won't be cheap."

"I don't care how much it costs. Let's get him home."

"That's the plan. Now, go get some grub because we have more meetings this afternoon."

Mase groaned. More than food, he needed to get some coffee or he might fall asleep in those meetings.

Chapter Twenty-Four

Jazz

"We need you back in Europe, Monsieur Bernard. Clement is planning something, and I don't like it."

"I agree. It'll take me at least a week to wrap things up here and get back there. I trust you to keep everything going until I return."

That was all bullshit. René Barbier would love to usurp Lucien Bernard's position. René was the one feeding Clement information. The men in Greece were the ones he trusted — as much as he trusted anyone in Bernard's organization — though he had eyes on them all the time, as well.

"Of course."

Jazz rolled his eyes at the smooth way René said that. He pressed the button to end the call without saying goodbye. His time with Mase was coming to a close earlier than expected.

"You thinking about Mase?" Sam asked.

He and Sam had spent the afternoon in DC, meeting with one of their South American contacts, just the two of them.

Jazz huffed out a frustrated breath. "Why is everyone so intent on matchmaking?"

Sam shrugged. "Not so much matchmaking as..." Sam took a deep breath. "Similar issues?"

Jazz turned and watched his friend drive the SUV. Sam didn't look over at him, but his cheeks were a little pink.

"What issues, exactly?"

"Before I met Bray, I thought that I'd never have a real relationship. I had...some bad experiences as a teenager. It happened before I joined the military, but the effects were far-reaching."

Jazz's fingers were suddenly cold, so he curled them into fists and set them in his lap. It wasn't like he was unaware other men had been held down and used like he'd been, but he tried not to think about it happening to him, let alone think about it happening to someone he loved like a brother.

"No one ever took the time to even really notice my issues — or maybe I never let them see. Bray saw. It was humiliating, and I felt so exposed and raw, but I wanted him enough to try to do something about it."

Jazz licked his lips. He swallowed. "Seems like it all worked out."

Sam laughed humorlessly. "Now. At the time, any attempt I made failed spectacularly. I was surprised Bray kept coming back for more."

"He loves you," Jazz said, but then realized his mistake.

"Sort of like Mase keeps coming back?"

"It's not the same."

"No, I think it's even more special that Mase has been doing it for over a decade. Bray was ready to give up on me after a few months when I fucked up."

"Sam —"

"Don't cut me off. Don't block me out. I know you don't let your defenses down much, but you did when you got roofied, and, Jazz, Mase was the only one you called out for. He was the only one you wanted."

He'd always been the only one Jazz wanted. That was nothing new.

"I've been working with a therapist who specializes in sexual trauma."

"Sam —"

"I'm not going to force anything on you. I know Mase was pissed when you said you were ace. I know it's not really his business how you identify, however, ace and trauma are two different things. You can be ace and have sexual trauma. Only you can know what you are, but the more important question is, are you aromantic?"

"Why is that the more important question?"

Jazz looked out of the window while they talked. He watched the scenery as they made their way back to Virginia. He couldn't quite bring himself to look at his friend.

"Because even if you don't want sex, I know that you want Mase to wrap his arms around you — at least you would if it would cause comfort instead of distress. I know that, even if sex was off the table, Mase would want to hold you as well."

Jazz blinked against the sting in his eyes. He swallowed to soothe his burning throat. Mase had said as much, but that would be completely unfair to Mase to expect him to give up sex completely.

Did Sam think it was easy to keep walking away from the person he wanted more than anything? It was torture, but it was what Mase deserved, to find someone whole, someone he could have a complete relationship with.

"I'm going to text you her number. If you don't want to see her because she's my therapist, she can refer you to another specialist."

The rest of the drive was made in silence, but as soon as they parted at HC, Jazz's phone vibrated. It was like he suddenly had a ticking a time bomb in his pocket.

Maybe that was why he hadn't been able to get Mase's suggestion out of his head. Would it work? He wasn't fully convinced, but he was willing to give it a try, which was why he headed to Mase's condo instead of his own. When the door opened and Mase walked in, his stomach twisted with anxiety. What if it didn't work? He was sick of the push and pull. It only hurt them both in the end, unless…

"Don't worry," Mase said when he saw him. "I'm not planning on getting drunk again tonight." He continued past Jazz toward the kitchen.

"Good, because I wanted to see if your offer still stood when you're sober."

Mase stopped mid-step and turned toward Jazz. "Are you serious?"

"I think that's what I'm asking *you*."

"You know I'm serious. Even if I don't get to touch you with my hands, you know I want to have you — any way I can."

Jazz swallowed and fisted his shaking hands. "How would this work?"

"However you want it to."

It seemed that Mase might have overestimated Jazz's carnal knowledge. How was he supposed to admit that he'd made it to his mid-thirties with practically no sexual experience?

"Tell me what you need, Jazzy. There's no judgment here. Whatever it is, I'll give it to you."

"I need you to take over logistics, but I need to know how it's going to play out."

"Okay. I'm hoping this will last more than a few minutes, so I'd prefer you tie my hands in front of me while I kneel down in front of you."

Jazz let out a shaky breath. This would be the third time that Mase had gotten him off with nothing in return. That wasn't what he wanted. In Houston, he'd been surprised at how quickly he'd come and that he'd been able to come at all. Last night had been no different.

It had seemed like an accident. He wanted to know if he could do it on purpose. It was a step closer to being able to look at Mase while he was hard, so he nodded.

Mase gave him such a wide, wicked grin as he stepped up to where Jazz sat on the sofa. He lowered to his knees and unknotted his tie.

"Why don't we just use this for now?"

Jazz nodded and took the length of silk from his hands. Mase pressed his wrists together and held them out to Jazz. A lot of people might play at this, tying their partner up just for the excitement, leaving the knot loose enough that they could get out. That wasn't what was going to happen.

"Do we need a safeword?" Jazz asked.

"If you want one, you can choose one."

"I meant for you. You're the one who'll be tied up."

Mase held his gaze while he shook his head. "I'm not sure there's anything I would deny you, Jazzy. I'm confident enough in my skill that I know you can fuck my face and all it'll do is turn me on."

Jazz's cock flexed against the zipper of his pants, already wanting to break free. His gaze lowered to Mase's full lips, to the dark blond beard that surrounded them. How would it feel against him?

"You hold all the power," Mase said. "Whatever you want, whatever you need, I'll give it to you. You don't have to do anything but take out your cock."

Jazz shuddered. Mase's bound hands and the sofa at his back kept his anxiety at bay. He knew that Mase could easily stand with his hands like that. He could even fight off an assailant, but he wouldn't be able to overpower Jazz.

With a deep breath, Jazz let his shoulders relax. This scenario was perfect. He would have preferred Mase's hands behind his back, but he trusted Mase. This also wouldn't bring to light Jazz's lack of experience.

He didn't fool himself into thinking it didn't matter. It was part of what held him back every time Mase wanted to touch him, but it was only a fraction of what held him back. The bulk of it was the sheer panic that pulled the air out of his lungs when he thought of someone coming at him from behind.

Jazz stood. Mase looked up at him, hunger in his blue eyes. But before he unbuttoned his pants, he wanted to take pleasure in simply touching Mase. He carded his hands through the long blond strands of Mase's hair. The soft silkiness of it enveloped his fingers.

He ran his knuckles down the scruff of Mase's beard, along his sharp jaw. Mase nuzzled against him with his cheek.

This. This was what he regretted not having. It wasn't even the sex. He wasn't even sure he'd be able to enjoy anything sexual very much, but he wanted to touch and to be touched. Sam was right about that.

Jazz ran the pad of his thumb over Mase's lower lip. When Mase sucked the finger into his mouth. Jazz's lips parted on an unsteady breath. Okay, so maybe he did want the sexual part, too. If he could give that to Mase, maybe it would be possible for something to happen between them.

Mase pulled off Jazz's thumb with a pop. "Let me taste you, Jazzy."

With a nod, Jazz finally unbuttoned and unzipped his pants. He reached into his boxer briefs and squeezed the base of his cock. He'd never been so hard. Anticipation bubbled in his blood, along with a frisson of anxiety.

He'd fantasized about Mase's touch, jacked off to the very idea of it, even though it scared the shit out of him. What if he ruined it? What if he couldn't even have this much of Mase? And what if this was the point where Mase finally realized that he deserved someone a lot better than Jazz?

"Let me see," Mase said.

Jazz pulled himself free of his boxers. As soon as he did, Mase was on him, sucking the tip into his mouth. With a groan, Jazz gripped Mase's blond locks and flexed his hips forward the tiniest bit. He couldn't help it. Nothing had ever felt as good as Mase's warm, wet mouth.

His eyelids felt heavy, like they wanted to slip closed as pleasure burst from his balls up through his shaft. He wasn't going to last long.

Jazz looked down at Mase's arms. He could barely make out his hands, but he knew they were bound. He pulled back until his dick popped free of Mase's mouth. He hunched over a little and panted.

"I almost came."

"That's the point," Mase said. "Come back here."

"I don't know how I feel about you being bound."

"Well, if you look at the tent in my pants, you'd know exactly how I feel about it. I'll just have to get a little more creative when it comes to making you blow your load."

Jazz scoffed. Mase could sit there licking his lips and Jazz might 'blow his load'. He knew what it was like to be taken advantage of, to feel trapped and scared and helpless. He would never do that to anyone else.

"Maybe we need a safeword," Jazz said.

Mase laughed. "I'm hoping to have my mouth full of you. Even if I wanted a safe word, I wouldn't be able to say it."

Jazz's erection began to deflate.

"Jazzy," Mase groaned as he leaned forward and sucked the tip back into his mouth.

He flicked the slit with his tongue, making Jazz gasp and bringing his erection roaring back to life. He pulled away, panting.

"Jazz, my hands are tied in front. I can push away if I want to—but I don't want to. What I want is to taste your cum."

Jazz shuddered at the dirty words. And when Mase pulled him back into his warm, wet mouth, Jazz didn't argue.

Mase rocked back and forth on his knees, bobbing his head, taking Jazz deeper. When he gagged, Jazz stiffened for a moment, but Mase groaned and took him even deeper on the next pass.

"Mase, it's too good. I'm not going to last," he warned, but Mase didn't pull back or slow down. In fact, he sucked harder. "I'm going to... *Fuck.*"

Jazz's back arched and his hands fisted tight in Mase's hair to ground himself as he came. In his mind, it was the first time he'd really come with someone else. He wasn't counting what happened in Texas because he'd been half asleep, and he didn't count the previous night because Mase hadn't even known what he was doing. This was his first blow job, and he'd remember it for the rest of his life. Mase kept licking him until he had to pull back because he was simply too sensitive.

When Mase lifted his hands, Jazz took another step back. Mase was still hard. Fear swirled inside him at the thought of setting Mase free...until Mase smiled.

"I was thinking... If you wanted to experiment, you could tie me to the bed."

That was the last thing Jazz expected to hear. "Tie you to the bed?"

"Yeah. I was hoping you might want to touch me. I can jack myself off—or you could."

Jazz's dick twitched back to life. Mase's eyes were right there, and Jazz could tell by his soft chuckle that he'd seen it.

He'd be able to touch Mase all he wanted. He'd be able to taste him. Jazz nodded as he reached down to help Mase up off the floor.

Chapter Twenty-Five

Mase

He'd never seriously experimented with bondage. He could safely say it wasn't a kink of his, but he liked it, especially if it gave Jazz the freedom he needed.

More than anything, he wanted to touch Jazz, to run his hands all over his body. But if this was the only way he could have what he'd been desperate for, he'd happily let himself be tied to the bedposts for the rest of his life.

He was spread-eagled on his bed, his wrists and ankles each bound to a corner with silk ties from his closet. They actually felt good against his skin, and they wouldn't chafe as bad as rope might.

When Jazz stepped back after making sure his ankles were secure, he looked over Mase's body and licked his lips.

"What do you want?" Jazz asked.

Mase was the one tied up, but Jazz had never seemed more vulnerable. "Anything. Everything. What do you want?"

"I don't have a lot of experience."

"Jazzy. One swipe of your tongue might do me in. I don't care if you use your hands or your mouth or if you want to frot against me."

Because Jazz was hard again, Mase took great pleasure in knowing that Jazz wanted him almost as much as he wanted Jazz.

He couldn't remember the last time Jazz had looked like the kid he'd been when Mase first met him — unsure, looking for direction. At that moment, he did.

"Jazzy, show me what you like. Show me how you get yourself off. Do to me what you want me to do to you."

That had Jazz's lips lifting into a mischievous grin. He roved his gaze all over Mase's body, taking everything in.

Mase's cock was curving up toward his chest, dripping pre-cum onto his abs. And when Jazz noticed, his smile spread even wider.

"You're killing me here. Touch me, Jazzy."

Jazz climbed onto the bed, sitting at Mase's side. He ran his palms down Mase's chest, flicking his thumbs over his nipples. Mase arched his back, silently begging for more.

Then Jazz leaned down and sucked one coppery tip into his mouth and sucked…hard.

"Fuck." Mase grabbed onto the ties that bound his wrists.

Jazz circled one nipple, then the other, with his finger before experimenting again with his tongue, his lips and finally his teeth.

By the time he moved lower, Mase was humping the air, trying to get friction where there was none.

"I should have known you'd torture me, with your background."

When Jazz looked up at him, there was concern in his eyes.

Mase laughed and shook his head. "I meant that in the best possible way. You haven't even touched my dick. I'm so hard for you, Jazzy."

"Do you need a safeword?"

"Jazz, that's for people who won't stop if you ask them to. We don't need a safeword. We just need to trust each other."

"I do trust you."

Mase shook his head. "Not with sex, you don't. I don't blame you, but I trust you. I trust you completely. And I know that if I say 'stop', you'll stop. Everything else is just teasing. It's what I do. I want this. I'll do whatever it takes, for as long as it takes, so that maybe you can trust me, too."

Jazz nodded, but he still looked unsure as he reached out and wrapped his hand around Mase's length.

"Ah," Mase groaned. *Friction. Finally.*

Jazz stroked up and down, gently at first, but then he seemed to find his stride. He tightened his fist around Mase's shaft as he moved his hand up and down, faster and faster.

Mase tried to curve up a little so he could watch. After a while, his neck got sore, so he fell back and stared blindly at the ceiling. Then he closed his eyes as all his focus moved to the skin that Jazz was touching.

He dug his heels into the mattress and tried to lift his hips, to fuck harder against Jazz's hand. He had very little leverage, but his orgasm was coiling tightly inside him, anyway.

When he felt the wet rasp of a tongue along his slit, Mase tried to jackknife, but his bindings held tight.

"Holy fuck, Jazz."

Jazz chuckled at his predicament. Then he sucked Mase's crown into his hot, wet mouth. Mase didn't care if he broke his neck. He would hold himself up so that he could memorize this moment.

Jazz's soft, full lips were stretched wide around him and he flicked his tongue along the underside of Mase's crown, pulling an embarrassingly needy sound from Mase's lungs.

When their gazes locked, there was delight and such carnal satisfaction in Jazz's gaze that it took Mase's breath away.

"Jazz," he rasped in warning.

Instead of pulling back, Jazz doubled down and sucked him harder, bobbing his head faster. Mase groaned. His abs burned and his neck was getting tired, but he held there, watching.

"Jazzy, you're gonna get a mouthful if you don't pull back."

That stubbornness he knew so well was glinting in Jazz's brown eyes. Mase panted. He tried to pull back from the edge, but it was too good. Then Jazz hummed around him, and he was lost.

His vision blurred, his muscles contracted and Jazz choked a little as Mase's cock shot spurt after spurt down his throat.

It was more than he ever hoped for, and yet it wasn't enough. He wanted to be every single one of Jazz's firsts, even if he had to be tied up to do it.

Chapter Twenty-Six

Jazz

Was it stupid that pride burst inside him, filling his whole chest? He'd made Mase lose his mind, and he wanted to do it all over again.

"Jazz." Mase's voice sounded hoarse, "kiss me."

It was both a demand and a plea, and in that moment, Jazz wasn't capable of denying either. If life were a fairytale and love healed all wounds, he would have untied Mase and curled up in his arms, just like Mase's eyes begged him to do.

But the very thought of it sent a warning chill down his spine. If he tried it, he'd freak the fuck out, just like he would have yesterday or even thirty minutes before.

It wasn't a surprise. Maybe asexual wasn't the entirety of his sexuality. Maybe it was the right label, but he struggled with something more. It wasn't just sex that scared Jazz. It was the holding, the touching, the very things he wanted most that frightened him.

He had too many memories of being held down. But as he thought about it, it was the sex, too—at least bottoming. The thought of bottoming made every single muscle in Jazz's body clamp down tight.

Until this last week with Mase, being forced was the only memories he'd ever associated with sex, so he hadn't known that he could truly enjoy sex with someone else.

There was freedom in that, and that's what he reveled in as he leaned down and touched his lips to Mase's. He moaned when their tongues tangled, when Mase tried to dominate the kiss, even though he was ultimately helpless.

Maybe if this were possible, the rest was possible, too. That number Sam had texted him called to him like fresh cake sitting in the refrigerator. As much as he hated asking for help, he needed it to wade through the mess that was his mind.

When Mase groaned into his mouth, Jazz let that thought go for a moment. Mase demanded his undivided attention, and they didn't have much time left. Mase couldn't stay tied up all night, and as soon as he was free, Jazz needed to leave. As hard as it was, he pulled back.

"I have to go."

"You don't. What if we just lie here?"

Jazz shook his head.

"We're doing this again," Mase said.

Jazz couldn't help the smile that curved his lips. Mase sounded cocky, demanding. He wanted more. That made Jazz happy, so he nodded.

"As soon as possible," Mase said.

Again, Jazz nodded as he moved to release Mase's ankles first. He rubbed them, making sure to get the blood flow back into his joints. He did the same with Mase's left wrist, but by then, Mase was starting to get hard again. With one last kiss that was almost chaste, Jazz left Mase to untie the last knot and went up to his own condo.

Even though his body felt warm and relaxed, his mind was too keyed up to sleep. He sat on the sofa, looking down at his phone, knowing that the therapist's number was in there.

When his eyes started to blur with fatigue, he gave up the fight. Jazz found the number and pressed dial before he lost his nerve. He left a message, only calling himself Jazz, letting her know Sam had referred him.

He didn't use last names, because he didn't know if Sam had given her his real name or his alias. As soon as he hung up, his shoulders sagged with relief. If there was any chance that he and Mase could be together, this would have to be part of it.

Chapter Twenty-Seven

Mase

"What's up with you?" Wade asked as he stared across the table at Mase.

"What d'you mean?"

Wade narrowed his eyes. "You're smiling."

"Why is that suspicious?"

Wade snorted.

"He was whistling as he walked into the bullpen," Max said.

Wade raised one eyebrow at him.

"Fine. I'm in a good mood. It's not against the law. I would've thought you'd be happy about it."

"I would be if you'd spread some of that cheer to Nick. I don't want him to quit because you're being an asshole. He could be valuable to our team."

"Assholery runs in my family. Nick has been dishing it out just fine. Bray's the only one who got the nice gene from my mom."

"Yeah, well, you're at an advantage since you own the company. At least let him know you don't control the fate of his employment at HC."

Mase rolled his eyes. "Fine, but I'd like a little back up when it comes to leaving our personal lives at home. He can't corner me at work to talk about Russell Hart."

"That sounds fair. Now, speaking of your smile, where's Jazz?"

Mase shrugged. Maybe Jazz was sleeping in. He wasn't used to all that sexual activity. Maybe it had worn him out.

The door to the war room opened, and Sam and Jazz both stepped in. As hard as Mase tried to tame his grin, he just couldn't do it. And when Jazz returned the smile, it was like the fucking sun burst through the rain clouds.

"Sorry I'm late," Jazz said. "I had a last-minute meeting pop up this morning."

"Well, buckle in," Max said. "I'm pretty sure I know who paid the bartender to drug you, but I don't know why."

"Who?" Jazz and Mase demanded at the same time.

Max clicked a few buttons, and a face appeared across the monitors along the wall. The guy was blond, good-looking, but no one Mase had ever seen before.

"Levi Johnston, twenty-eight years old. He's a former drug addict, but I can't figure out how he ties in to this." Max said.

"Fuck," Wade groaned.

"I can't find a cell phone under Levi's name, so I haven't been able to track him. I can't find a recent address or home purchase under his social. No background checks for rentals, nothing. He hasn't paid taxes in years. He has no job to speak of. The last time I have anything on him is the rehab facility he entered almost five years ago."

"Okay, so he's a former addict, maybe using again?" Wade asked.

"I don't know."

"Does his family have money?" Jazz asked.

"No. His mother's dead. His father's an addict as well."

"Who paid for the rehab?"

Max turned to his laptop and started clicking away. Records from the rehab facility popped up on the screen. "Someone paid cash, upfront. Almost eighty thousand dollars for a ninety-day program."

"Keep digging," Wade said. "Start with the rehab facility, maybe a little before. Sounds like he's got a financial supporter who not only wants to remain anonymous but also wants Levi to be a ghost. We need to know how this ties in."

"I'm on it," Max said.

Mase watched Jazz. In their profession, you hid your tells, but Jazz was anxious. Mase could feel it as surely as he felt the tension in his own body. Was Martin Coleman the one who was bankrolling Levi?

"Try to find out if Levi's gay," Mase said.

"What are you thinking?" Wade asked.

"Could Coleman be the one supporting Levi?"

"Coleman thinks I'm dead," Jazz said.

"Is that what you found out in Texas?"

Jazz shrugged, but then his gaze sharpened. "It was Charles who thought I was dead. Martin didn't argue the point, but he wouldn't have. He'd want his father to think I was dead, even if he knew I wasn't. Mase is right. See if there's any link."

"You got it," Max said. "But I need you to answer a few questions for me first."

"Oh, here we go," Wade said under his breath.

"What questions?"

"How did you slip past my facial rec software? I've been perfecting it for years."

Jazz smirked. "Is that how you were trying to follow me? Good thing you tracked me instead or you never would have found me. The government makes facial recognition software, so certain government entities know how to get around it."

"Mine's better than the one the government has. I've used theirs. It's crap compared to mine."

"And yet, you still couldn't find me."

"How?"

"Since you're on my team," Jazz said, "I'll tell you. All it takes is a little makeup and some special glasses."

Maxes eyes went wide. "Reflection. Fuck. I need to adjust for that."

"It won't work, even if you adjust for it."

"It won't work running against the software, but if I tag anyone who has no recognizable features, I'll have an interesting list of aliases, even though I might not be able to recognize their face. I might even be able to nail down other body features."

"And that's why humans are still smarter than computers," Wade said.

Max opened his mouth, most likely to argue, but Wade barreled on.

"We've got a possible appeal date for Kota."

"Who can be there with him?" Mase asked.

"Depends on the date, but it'll have to be someone who can be seen supporting him in public. We might be able to send Chase, since he's met Chase. But it might have to be one of the guys he doesn't know. We can't send anyone who's undercover. There's going to be press on this for sure."

Mase's stomach twisted at the thought of Kota being in the courtroom alone. He knew what it felt like to face a trial and feel like the world was against you. He knew what it was like to be falsely accused.

"Whoever it is needs to visit him in jail," Mase said. "He needs to see a familiar face in that courtroom."

"Good idea. I'll make sure of it," Wade said.

Mase continued to watch Jazz through the remainder of the meeting. He was a mixture of emotions, just like Mase was. They still didn't know why someone had paid to drug Jazz. Mase wanted to ask Max about any intel they'd uncovered from the bugs Jazz placed in Coleman's house. Had Jazz admitted to Max that he'd bugged Coleman's DC home and office as well?

As much as Mase loved the physical trust Jazz was putting in him, he wanted Jazz to trust him with this, as well. He didn't need to know the specifics of what Coleman had done to Jazz. In fact, he didn't want to, not unless Jazz needed him to know.

He kept a tight lid on how he felt about Jazz's past. There was fury just waiting to be unleashed. Mase was deep undercover. Even though beating a congressman to death would probably fit his cover, it would bust open his true identity.

Besides, if he'd learned anything about Jazz, it was that he wanted to fight his own battles. He also had his own timetable, and Mase was determined to keep this thing between them firmly in Jazz's court.

Chapter Twenty-Eight

Jazz

He felt like a teenager. He'd looked at his phone every five minutes for forty-eight hours until he was tempted to block Mase's number, just so he wouldn't be able to check for messages.

What he'd experienced with Mase was…well, it was everything, much more than he'd thought himself capable of. He was sure Mase would be banging down his door every night, looking for more. Maybe it hadn't been as good for Mase as it had been for Jazz.

When he was called out of town last minute, having to drive up to Langley and stay the night, his handler had noticed he was distracted. It was the lack of…anything from Mase that had him on edge. So as he lay in his bed in one of the apartments owned by the Company, he dialed Mase's number before he could talk himself out of it.

"Jazz."

His name was a sigh from Mase's lips. It was said with a familiarity Jazz hadn't even known he'd longed for until he heard it.

"I just wanted to make sure you knew that I was out of town."

Jazz rolled his eyes at himself. That sure sounded like something a boyfriend would do. Was that what they were, or what they were headed toward? He found himself hoping it was, especially if Mase would continue saying his name like that.

Even though they were on the phone, he knew Mase was smiling. He didn't know if it was because there was a slight crackle through the phone that might have been Mase's beard moving over the microphone as he lifted his cheek, or if it was because Jazz's own cheeks heated.

"I heard. Though I do prefer to hear it from you directly. Maybe next time, you'll tell me *before* you leave."

"Maybe."

"What's the sigh for? Tough day?"

"What's that smile for?" Jazz groused.

"Who said I was smiling?"

"I know you are."

"You're calling. I'm usually the one to seek you out."

"Until we have sex. Then you go on radio silence."

"Is that what that tone of voice is all about? Jazz" — he sighed — "fuck. Maybe I should have said this two days ago, but I was blissed out when you left. This goes at your pace. I will never ask for more than you're ready to give. I was waiting for you to come to me."

Well, fuck. He should have gone back the next day.

"Is that fair? That I get to decide everything?" Jazz asked.

"You don't get to decide everything. I'm here because I want to be. I have no hesitancy about sex or cuddling or whatever you want to do. I mean, I have a few hard limits, but I don't know that there's much I would deny you. If we need to go slow, we go slow. What happened two days ago is already more than I thought we'd be able to have, so if you need me tied up, tie me up."

"I pictured you as more of a take control in bed sort of guy."

"I'm versatile," Mase said. "Any other questions?"

"So you want to do that again?"

"That and more. In fact, why don't you put me on video?"

"Mase, we both know how insecure a phone line is."

"I'm sending you an invite. It's end-to-end encrypted, even for video. Download it, then text me your username."

Mase hung up before Jazz could even respond. His phone buzzed in his hand. Mase sent him a link to a fairly popular messaging app that included video chats. After taking a deep breath, Jazz tapped the download option and waited. He hated picking usernames.

He usually reverted to a string of numbers because usernames were fairly public, and he didn't want anyone finding him. Once he signed up, he texted Mase.

Before he was ready for it, his phone beeped with an incoming video chat. Jazz sat up against the headboard before clicking the button to answer.

"There you are," Mase said. "I knew you'd have a frown."

"How did you know?"

"I know you, Jazzy."

Jazz rolled his eyes.

Mase laughed. "Are you getting ready for bed?" Mase asked.

"I'm already in bed."

"That's even better."

The smile Mase gave him had his heart—and his dick—kicking up. The video swayed for a moment. Then Mase was also in bed and bare chested.

"Why haven't we done this before?" Mase asked.

"What?"

"Video chat. It definitely gets around any fear you have of being touched."

"But don't you want to be touched?"

Mase's smile spread and turned wicked. Jazz had to swallow back a groan.

"I love being touched. But this could have been a way to ease you into being naked with me, being hard with me watching, watching me be hard. I feel like I should have suggested this years ago."

"I wouldn't have done it years ago."

Mase shrugged. "Maybe not the first time I suggested it but, eventually, you would have given in."

Jazz shook his head. "Do you have any idea how cocky you sound right now?"

"Confident. You might not want me as much as I want you, Jazz, but you do want me."

That sentence twisted Jazz's chest up into knots. How could Mase not know that Jazz wanted him more than almost anything, that he'd never wanted anything or anyone as much as he wanted Mason Hart?

"I've *always* wanted you," Jazz said.

"I know, but it was usually me making a fool out of myself. And I'm the one who kept coming back for more."

"Only because I didn't know how. I don't know how to flirt or instigate" — Jazz circled his head as all the sexual descriptions escaped him — "anything. I didn't know how to even let you know that I wanted you."

"I knew. I knew by how you'd lean in and give consent before everything from your past closed in on you. I know what that's like. I didn't want to push. And I didn't mean to be an asshole about the whole asexual thing, but it made me panic. It made me doubt all the times you leaned in to my kisses before your demons reminded you to pull away."

"I never meant to leave you high and dry. I know I did, but I never meant to. I told myself a million times to let you go, to stay away before anything even started. You do make me forget my demons, Mase, even if it's just for a few moments. And I never could resist you until the memories ripped me away."

"I always did wonder…"

"Wonder what?"

"Do you sleep naked, Jazzy?"

He huffed out a laugh. He wished he did, but fear had him making sure he always had at least boxers on. Sometimes, after a rough nightmare, he'd sleep fully dressed.

"No. I have boxers on."

"Maybe you should take them off."

"I knew this was where this was going to end up. You did a bait and switch with the deep discussion."

Mase shook his head. "I needed to get a few things off my chest, but this was always about seeing you naked, Jazzy. I didn't get to see nearly enough when I was tied to the bed."

"Do *you* sleep naked?" Jazz asked.

There was that wicked smile again. Jazz felt like it belonged only to him at this point.

"Yep, especially after you tied me up and wore me out. I didn't even get out of bed to brush my teeth."

"Show me," Jazz demanded.

Chapter Twenty-Nine

Mase

Mase panned the camera on his phone down to show his chest and torso. Then he got to the part that was tenting the blankets.

"That doesn't prove anything," Jazz said.

With a flick of his wrist, Mase flung the sheets away to reveal that he was, in fact, naked and very hard. When he heard a whimper make its way through the phone line, Mase tilted the camera back up.

"Does this freak you out?"

Jazz shook his head. "No, especially not now that I know what you feel like, what you taste like."

"You have no idea what you do to me," Mase groaned. "Your turn. I want to see everything."

"Hang on."

The screen was a whirl of colors, then nothing but textured white and a bright light. He figured he was looking at the ceiling. The picture jittered a little. Then

Jazz's face appeared once again. There was a click then Jazz moved farther away from the phone.

Mase did want to touch him. It would be a lie to say he didn't. He wanted to run his tongue over every delineation of muscle along Jazz's abs. He wanted to flick his nipples with his tongue, tug at them with his teeth.

He wanted so much with Jazz. He wanted everything. And yet if this was all he got, some video sex where he could see everything and in person sex where he got to see a little and touch nothing, he'd be so fucking grateful that Jazz was finally his.

When Jazz took another step back and Mase could see that he was fully hard, he groaned. Apparently, Mase's dick only scared him in real life—and if Mase wasn't bound.

Seeing Jazz like this, in his entirety and turned on, had Mase's pulse throbbing through his veins. He'd gotten up close and personal with Jazz's dick, and he'd seen him naked in the showers when they'd been in the military, but this? This was every fantasy Mase had ever had.

Jazz was gorgeous. He was slim but sleek with muscle. He didn't have any tattoos like Mase and most of the other guys did. He suspected it would be hard for Jazz to sit still for a long time with a tattoo artist holding him down so he could brand him with ink. His chest was lightly covered with hair, but no more than the hair on his legs and forearms.

Then there was that trail, the strip of sparse fur that started at his navel and thickened as it made its way downward. Jazz's groin was well groomed, his pubes cut short as his erection stood out, tall and proud.

Mase had to clear his throat before he could speak again. "Turn around, Jazzy. Let me see it all."

Jazz's brows lifted in surprise, then his expression turned wary.

"I like men's asses. I've been with plenty of guys who never bottom. It doesn't mean I don't want to look. Same with women. Many women don't like anal, but that doesn't mean I don't like looking at their ass. And you, Jazzy? You have a gorgeous ass."

"How would you know?"

"I've caught a glimpse or two over the years. Do you have any idea how many times we've showered together?"

"Countless times," Jazz said as he slowly spun so Mase could see his backside.

Jazz was in better shape than he had been in the military. He wasn't bulky, but there also wasn't any extra padding anywhere.

"Do you want me to bend over?" Jazz asked.

The thought of seeing Jazz's pucker made Mase's dick flex. If this was a test, he was surely going to fail, at least if Jazz saw his body's reaction.

"Nah," Mase said. "But maybe someday, while you have me tied up, you'll let me fuck you with my tongue. Then I'll get to see your hole real close."

Mase froze when Jazz's ass cheeks clenched tight. He wasn't sure if that was a good sign or a bad sign. Then Jazz turned around and Mase saw the hunger in his gaze.

"You'd want me to do that when you were tied up?"

Mase smiled wide, so wide he probably looked like the Grinch. "Just try sitting on my face and see what my cock does. But not until you're ready...*if* you're ready."

Jazz nodded. "My head wants it. I'm just not sure my body's ready — or maybe the other way around."

"I don't care what part of you likes it. I think if it turns you on at all, that's a good sign."

"Mase, lots of things turn me on, lots of things about you. I've had a pretty rich fantasy life. It's the real-world experience that's lacking."

"Not anymore. This is your chance. Show me what you've got, Woody."

Jazz groaned at the pun. Mase set his phone up on his nightstand so he had both hands free, and Jazz could see him as well.

"Show me what you like. I want to see you get yourself off."

Jazz complied. He moved his fist up and down his length, slowly at first. His eyes burned as he kept them on Mase. It was the hottest thing he'd ever seen. Jazz's muscles jumped, his stomach hollowing out when he twisted his hand as it slid up his cock.

Mase copied his moves, pretending it was Jazz's hands on his body instead of his own. Soon it was just their hands shuttling up and down their cocks as they both began to thrust into their fists.

Then Jazz sucked in a quiet breath when his thumb flicked over his slit, when his fist reached his crown. It was a quick subtle movement, one he probably used every time he jacked off, since it seemed so second nature. Mase followed suit and also sucked in a breath at how powerful the sensation was.

He groaned Jazz's name and was rewarded by seeing Jazz's cock jerk in response. He might have missed it if he hadn't been concentrating so hard on Jazz's groin. The idea that his voice, his groan, had a physical effect on Jazz had Mase's body coiling tight.

Heat built in his balls and at the base of his spine. He wouldn't last much longer.

"I'm close," Jazz groaned just as the same words moved through Mase's mind.

Even that had his insides wrenching tighter. He watched Jazz's hips rock even faster, his rhythm faltering as he became more desperate to come. They were so in sync. They belonged with each other, to each other. That was the thought that had the spark of heat zipping up Mase's dick. He arched his back, trying hard to keep his eyes open and on the phone when Jazz growled in response.

His vision was blurry with the strength of his orgasm, but he saw the moment Jazz came. He watched his neck arch and his muscles stutter and spasm. He watched the first ribbon of ejaculate spurt from his tip. Another wave of pleasure pulled Mase under as he continued to stroke himself. There was nothing sexier than watching Jazz come like that.

Jazz held on so tight. Watching him lose control was a thing of beauty. He wanted to do it again in real life. He wanted to feel Jazz's weight as he collapsed on Mase, totally spent and relaxed.

"We are *so* doing that again," Mase panted.

"Yeah?" Jazz asked, his wrinkled brow and tilted face full of insecurity.

"Oh yeah. That was one of the hottest things I've ever done."

Jazz's smile had a hint of shyness as his cheeks turned pink. "It was."

Chapter Thirty

Jazz

When Jazz woke in Langley, it was to the sound of his phone ringing, his HC phone. He blinked a few times and realized it was the therapist calling him back.

"Hello?"

"Is this Jazz?"

"Yes."

"Hi Jazz, I'm Marjorie Klein, Sam's therapist."

"I know who you are, Ms. Klein. Thank you for returning my call."

"I was calling to see if you had any time this morning to meet with me for your intake appointment."

"Today?" Jazz's heart started thumping like a rabbit in his chest.

"Yes. I had a cancellation, which is rare, so I thought I'd give you a call."

"What time?"

"Ten."

Jazz looked at his watch. That gave him two hours to throw up, then drive back to Richmond.

"Or if this is too soon—"

"No. This is what I need to do."

There was a pause, as if she was absorbing the dread in Jazz's words. There was laughter in her voice when she replied.

"It won't be that bad, I promise."

"I'll be there."

"See you at ten," Ms. Klein said.

Jazz rubbed his eyes and headed for the shower. It was going to be a long two hours.

* * * *

Not much made Jazz nervous—well, not much outside sex. Maybe that was why he was sweating as he waited to meet with the therapist. He was going to be talking about sex. That would be the main topic of every discussion.

"Jazz?"

He looked up from where he'd been blindly looking at a magazine to find a tiny sprite of a woman. She reminded him of a fairy, if fairies had short sleek brown hair and wore bright red lipstick. Her upturned nose and almond-shaped eyes were definitely fae-like.

"I'm Jazz," he said as he shot up from his sitting position.

"Please come in."

He wiped his clammy hands on his jeans as he followed her into her office. There wasn't a sofa as he expected. The office was large and divided into two sections. On one side was her desk with two chairs for guests facing that desk. The other side of the office was more casual, with a semi-circle of overstuffed leather chairs that looked softer than a cloud.

"Please take a seat." She waved toward the cushy chairs.

Jazz chose a seat and Ms. Klein left an empty one between them, which relieved him more than he would have thought.

"Thank you for seeing me so quickly, Ms. Klein."

"Feel free to call me Marjorie if you'd like."

He nodded. "Thank you, Marjorie."

"Sam told me he gave you my information, so your call wasn't a surprise, but he didn't give me any details about why you might like to speak with me. I just want you to know that his information is private and so is yours."

"Thank you."

"That's my way of asking you to tell me why you're here."

For some reason, that little aside paired with her conspiratorial grin put him at ease. He returned her smile.

Jazz opened his mouth but realized he didn't know where to begin. Did he start with the worst part?

"I've never had an intimate relationship." *At least, not until a few days ago.*

"So you desire intimacy?"

"Yes. I thought I was asexual, but..." Did he hand over Mase's name? It was both his real name and his alias. The only difference was that undercover, it was his last name...Mason. Did it matter?

"No need to overthink things. Tell me about why you considered yourself asexual and why you seem to be questioning that now?"

"I've never been a really horny guy. I mean, when I was a teenager, I…" Jazz cleared his throat.

"Masturbated? It's natural. It's also healthy for your prostate."

"Yes. I masturbated frequently. I had a crush on one of the guys at my school, but mostly because he was so nice. He was smart and funny and didn't make fun of me because of where I came from, but that was really it. I was younger than everyone else, so they thought I was a bit of a freak."

"How old were you when you graduated high school?"

"Sixteen. I finished college by the time I was nineteen. I started with a partial academic scholarship, but as soon as I turned seventeen, I signed on using an ROTC scholarship with the intention of serving in the army."

"And is that where you experienced your sexual trauma? In college?"

Jazz nodded as he tried to keep the memories at bay. "I was never a big guy. Part of the reason I wanted to join the military was to learn to defend myself. There were two guys in my dorm. They were ROTC as well, and juniors, so a lot older. One of them tried to flirt with me, at least I think he was. His friend, or boyfriend, I guess, seemed jealous.

"I didn't think much of it. It wasn't like I hadn't been teased or bullied before. I knew that I was gay. But it wasn't like I was going to advertise it. I didn't flirt back. I ignored it. Until one day, I was coming back from showering in the dorm showers, and I ran into both of them in the hall. The boyfriend shoved me into my room and onto my bed. He held me down and told his boyfriend to take me, that he knew he wanted…"

"Jazz," Marjorie soothed when his breathing started to kick up. "We don't have to dive so deep the first day. Can you follow my breathing?"

He nodded and did just as she asked. He pulled air in when she did, expelled it when she did.

"This happened repeatedly?" she asked

"Yes."

"For how long?"

"About four months. As summer approached, I knew I wouldn't come back the next year if I didn't do something."

"What did you do?"

"I recorded what they did. I didn't have a smartphone or anything, but one of the other guys had a small digital camera that took video and had a remote. I bought the biggest memory card I could afford and set it up."

"So you felt you couldn't report it, but the recording gave you power over them? You knew they'd stop if you kept the video?"

"One of them, the boyfriend? His father was powerful. He was one of the most powerful men in the state. I knew he wouldn't get punished, and worse, he'd want to retaliate when he got off scot-free."

"Do you still have the video?" Marjorie asked.

Her question surprised him. He thought she'd dig deeper into what they did to him. He nodded.

"When was the last time you watched it?"

"The day after it was recorded. I copied it, spliced it and sent them a clip. I told them I'd post it on YouTube for the world to see."

"So they left you alone after that?"

"For the most part. They never touched me again. They did break into my room, I assume, to take the camera."

Jazz bit back a smile. Even then, he'd been decent at predicting what people would do. He'd left a copy of the video on the memory card in the camera. They'd deleted it. They'd thought they were mostly safe. There was nothing they could do about the sent file in Jazz's email. It wasn't like he'd had a laptop. He'd only accessed his email from the school's computers.

"You don't seem upset about that," Marjorie said.

"No. I expected it. They only deleted a copy. I still have the original."

"So you used your wits to protect yourself."

Jazz scoffed. "After the fact."

"Do you know how many people would have just gone home and never returned? What you did took strength."

"But it broke me. Even the thought of sex made me break out into a sweat. If someone tried to flirt with me, I growled at them."

"That doesn't seem unusual in your circumstances."

"But I didn't want to be like that. I wanted to be normal, but I couldn't even stand to be touched. I became totally asexual—or at least I thought I had. Maybe it's sexual aversion. I don't know."

"Just because you have a sexual aversion doesn't mean you aren't asexual. Sometimes the two go hand in hand. Even if we help you move past your aversion to sex, you might not want it. I have some amazing sexual surrogates who can work with you to see—"

"I have a partner who can work with me."

"That can help as well, but he'll need some information, and I'd like him to attend a separate session."

"Oh. I haven't told him that I'm coming here. I didn't want to get his hopes up."

"Can we discuss the romantic side of your relationship with him? How are you coping with his sexual desire? Or is he asexual?"

"He's definitely not asexual. In the past, I backed away, but I didn't tell him why. I think he pretty much knows what happened to me, even though I haven't told him."

"And does he pressure you for sex?"

"Yes and no. He wants to be with me, so he tries to find his own way around the minefield that is my sexuality. I trust him. I've literally trusted him with my life when we were in the military, but I thought..." Jazz sighed. "I don't know what I thought. I guess I thought that if he was near me when he's aroused, I'm afraid that all his restraint might go out of the window and he wouldn't be able to stop, even if he wanted to."

"You said you thought that. What changed your mind?"

Jazz's cheeks heated as he thought about what happened in Texas. "He, he got me..."

"Aroused?" she asked.

"No. More than that. He's been able to get me aroused since we met more than a decade ago. But recently, he made me come. It was the first time I've ever come from the touch of someone else. But as soon as my orgasm faded, fear took over and I panicked. I thought it would be his turn and—"

"Take a breath," she said.

Jazz realized that his entire body was tight and stiff. His hands were fisted near his hips as his breathing once again spiked.

"I panicked," he said in a calmer voice. "I ran to the bathroom. When I came out, he wasn't aroused anymore. He said that the fear in my eyes took care of his erection."

"And in your experience, that's not the typical reaction."

"I don't have experience."

"Yes, you do. That's the core of what's driving this. You do have experience, but the only experience you've had was traumatizing. There are ways to move past this, but it's hard work. Your partner will need to come to sessions, and we'll have to work together to learn relaxation exercises. And if things go well, we would work to allow you to not only tolerate touch, but enjoy it."

Jazz was overwhelmed by such a powerful wave of want. What would it feel like to be wrapped in Mase's arms? To not only tolerate it, but to crave it?

"How would that work?"

"I've seen the most success with systematic desensitization. You'll learn some techniques to manage anxiety, and once you've mastered those, you and your partner will try something that might cause a small amount of uneasiness. We'll have to tailor it to you. Are there certain areas of your body that can and can't tolerate touch?"

"I don't like anyone at my back, which consequently was an advantage in the military."

"I'd like you to catalog specific areas. Imagine your partner touching your shoulder, the back of your waist, the nape of your neck."

Jazz pulled in a sharp breath. Marjorie nodded, as if she understood that was probably one of the biggest danger zones. If Mase grabbed the back of Jazz's neck, he'd probably tear him apart.

"Think about your body in small increments, say, four inches." Marjorie held out her hand, her thumb about four inches from her forefinger. "From your feet to your head, I'd like you to log how much anxiety each spot might cause if you were touched. Do a scale of one to ten—ten meaning causing the most anxiety."

"And I have him start at the spot with the lowest number?"

"I don't think you're ready for that yet. This is really just pre-work. The first step is learning techniques to manage anxiety and for you to start learning your own body."

"This sounds like a long road."

"It is. And you'll be doing all the work. I'm just here to guide the process. How are you handling intimacy and sex currently?"

"We've been circling each other for years, mostly because I can't—or at least I haven't been able to do anything until very recently."

"What changed?"

Jazz swallowed down the embarrassment that tried to rise within him. If this was going to work, he needed to be completely honest with his therapist, at least about his sex life.

"He asked me to tie him up."

Marjorie's eyebrows rose. "So this isn't typical behavior for him? It was a compromise to be able to be intimate with you?"

Jazz nodded, though he wasn't fully sure whether it was typical behavior for Mase. Jazz had imagined Mase as the sexual aggressor. He'd always been the one to instigate anything between them. He'd also backed off immediately whenever Jazz freaked out, which had been every fucking time until a few nights ago.

"That sounds promising. Imagine being able to untie him afterward and allowing him to touch you. That will be what we'll work toward at first. After he ejaculates, as we move forward, you can take advantage of the natural refractory period, which for most men is thirty minutes. I want you to imagine him touching you, even your back, as if there was no worry about sex because he was already sated. Would you like him to touch you for intimacy alone?"

Jazz's heart thumped heavily in his chest at the thought. "Yes," he said without hesitation. He'd love to let Mase touch him just for the sake of touching.

"Okay, then I want you to think about that, about your partner caressing you as a post-coital intimacy exercise. Even the thought of it will help prepare you for it. And if you get anxious, I'd like you to practice box breathing — in for a count of four, hold for a count of four, out for a count of four, hold for a count of four. Like we did before when you mimicked my breathing."

"So that's my homework?"

Marjorie smiled. "Yes. Assess your body for levels of anxiety. I'll send you a body graph that you can fill out so we can go over it. Then I want you to take a few moments every day to imagine your partner touching you with his hands. Imagine you've just finished having sex, and he's fully sated, completely flaccid.

"Think of him touching you, starting from the ankles up, and stop when the anxiety gets too much. Log how far you get each day. You can have him skip over any parts that are a ten on the anxiety scale. You'll want to share this with him, eventually. You'll need to be very open about these different zones. If you trust him and know he will pass over those areas, it will really help you manage your anxiety."

"I can try that."

Marjorie looked at her watch. It was the first time she'd done so. Jazz liked that he'd had her undivided attention. She tapped at her tablet and scrolled for a moment.

"I'd like to see you once a week while we work on your anxiety."

"I travel a lot for business."

"I'm happy to do virtual sessions. Just let me know before each appointment if it will be in person or if you'll need a secure link to log onto."

"So, once a week?"

"I'll send you a reminder that you can download into your calendar. For the first few weeks, the appointments will be sporadic as I try to fit you in to my regular schedule. If an appointment time doesn't work for you, just respond and let me know."

"Thank you for fitting me in so quickly."

"We'll see if you're still thanking me when you get my bill."

Jazz smiled but didn't respond as she stood and walked him to the door. He didn't care what it cost if it worked.

Chapter Thirty-One

Mase

The morning after his video call with Jazz, Mase woke yet again in a good mood. It lifted when he stepped off the elevator from the garage onto the first floor of HC, only to tank a few minutes later.

"Morning," Dee said as she stepped out of the kitchen, coffee cup in hand.

"Morning."

"I like that look on you, *cher*."

"What look?"

"The one that says you and Jazz are doing things I don't even want to think about."

Mase chuckled. "That obvious?"

"Only because you're both wearing the same smile."

"Is he back already?"

She gave a nod and a wink. "I must admit, his smile has an edge of wariness to it."

Mase wrapped an arm around her shoulder and leaned down to say quietly, "You work on him from your end. I'll work on him from mine."

"Mason Hart, I just told you that I don't want to think about what you're doing with your end."

Mase threw back his head and laughed. Dee's scandalized look was all for show. She knew everything that went on in HC, raunchy or not. She was the mother hen, and Wade was the drill sergeant. He had to admit that it was nice to have them both.

Being undercover was wearing on him. When this assignment was over, he'd give one of the other guys a chance at deep cover. Maybe for a few months he wouldn't have to pretend he was straight, and he could really be with Jazz.

Mase dropped a kiss on Dee's head and left her to her work. As he rounded the corner, he almost ran into Ax. They both took a step back and nodded at each other.

Mase moved around him. He was a few steps toward the gym when Ax said, "He didn't know."

There was no question who 'he' was, but Mase wondered what it was that Nick hadn't known. Had Russ finally admitted the whole truth? Curiosity got the better of him, and he turned around to face Ax.

"Are you saying he didn't know what an asshole Russel Hart is?"

"No. I think he had an idea about that." Ax smirked. "He didn't know your dad was moving here—or at least, he didn't know until it was a done deal."

Mase nodded, unsure what else to say.

"He fights with him, too...about you."

"Nick?"

"Yeah. Ever since I've known him, he's been fighting with Russ about letting you be. He did everything he could to keep Russ from moving here. He hasn't told him the address to HC. He's doing his best to protect you both, to give you what you both want. He feels stuck in the middle, and I have no idea how the fuck to help him."

"Tell him he's not fired."

Ax snorted. "That needs to come from you. He wants a relationship with you, Mase, but he does have loyalty to your dad. He's torn."

"How many times do I have to say no?"

"Nick isn't exaggerating about his health. He's not in good shape. You said you were glad he didn't turn Nick away. Imagine if he hadn't turned you away. Imagine you were Nick, and you'd never actually seen that side of him. Imagine he told you he loved you no matter what, just like you wanted him to, just like he should have." Ax put a hand on Mase's shoulder before continuing.

"Sure, you're pissed when you find out he didn't treat your brothers the same way, and you even stop talking to him for months on end because you're so angry. Then you find out he's dying. The dad who told you he loved you no matter what is dying, and his last wish before he dies is standing right in front of you. How easy would it be for you to let it go and not ask one last time? If Russ dies today, you might not regret refusing to speak with him, but Nick would regret it if he didn't take every opportunity to make that last wish come true."

Mase took one breath, then two. He'd asked Nick to be empathetic, but he hadn't been able to do the same.

"He knows he should keep his mouth shut around you. And each time he doesn't, he beats himself up about it. My fear is that Russ will die and Nick will feel like he did all he could for his dad, but then his guilt will turn to you. He'll realize that in doing that, he lost his chance to be your brother again. There's no way for him to win here."

"I feel the same way."

Ax nodded. "He doesn't expect you to actually forgive Russ."

"Why would I?"

Ax breathed out through his nose. "No one's asking you to. I didn't know Russ before, but I imagine he's a man who's always had a hard time admitting he was wrong. He's in a prison of his own making. He may still have money, but in every other sense, your situations have reversed. You've found love, and you've built your own family."

"So I should forgive him because I succeeded despite him?"

"No. You don't need to forgive him. But I don't think you've told Nick the whole story. Bray knows something that Nick doesn't, and no one will tell him. Make sure he has all the information, or all he can do is go with what he knows, what he sees. And what he sees is that his father has changed. And if we don't let people change, accept that they *can* change and grow, why should they try? If we permanently label people as bigots because they were ignorant, why should they try to become informed if everyone has already written them off? If there's no chance at redemption, why learn? Why grow? Why change?"

"I'm not responsible for my father's redemption."

"You're not. Like I said, I don't think Russ expects you to forgive him. And I'm not here on Russ' behalf. I'm here because Nick is hurting. When I first met Nick, I thought he was an asshole to ask it of you, as well. Then I heard him trying to hold your dad back. If it were up to Russ, he'd blindside you. He'd show up here or at your condo. Just remember that even though he's frustrated with you, Nick's protecting you as well. He's holding Russ at bay—and that's not an easy task."

"I can't talk to Nick if he doesn't come into HC. I'll let him know that I might have overreacted, but I won't seek him out at Russ' to do it."

"Fair enough. He's taken some time off this week, but I'll make sure he comes in next week."

"You're good for him," Mase said.

"I think you got that backward," Ax said with a salute before continuing down the hall in the direction he'd been headed.

Chapter Thirty-Two

Jazz

He blew out a breath before raising his hand to knock on the door. Mase had been totally honest when he said the pace of this thing between them was firmly in Jazz's hands.

Mase opened his door with a wide smile on his gorgeous face. He took a few steps back, swinging the door wider so Jazz could come in.

"I was hoping you'd take me up on my invitation. I was thinking we could relax, watch a movie, have some dinner."

"Is that what you want to do?"

"Don't sound so surprised. I don't just want you for sex. We've been friends a long time. You know me probably better than anyone else in the world."

Why did that make his heart stutter? That sounded an awful lot like being best friends, which was what they were — or at least what they had been before Mase left the military and went deep undercover.

"Why don't you relax on the sofa? I was making some pasta. I'll dish it up while you pick a movie."

When Jazz turned toward the living room, he stopped short. Mase had rearranged his furniture. The TV was on a different wall. His sectional had been moved to the corner of the room.

He darted his gaze to Mase, who was dishing food onto plates. Had he done this for Jazz? As he moved past the coffee table, Jazz plucked up the remote. He settled into the corner of the sofa, which was now firmly against the corner of the room. His body relaxed into the buttery soft leather as he pressed the button to turn on the TV.

"I should have known," Mase said when the movie started playing. "I haven't seen this in years. I couldn't bring myself to watch it with Ukrainian-dubbed voices."

They watched *Princess Bride* for probably the millionth time, quoting all the same parts, laughing at all the same parts—except one.

If you asked Mase what his favorite part of the movie was, he'd claim it was the sword fight between Dread Pirate Roberts and Inigo Montoya. But the part that always made him laugh—even though no one else usually did—was a little part that wasn't even a joke, just a silly rhyme from Fezzik the giant, "*Anybody want a peanut?*" Mase's laugh always made Jazz laugh.

And when that part came on, Jazz turned to Mase. He watched his mouth spread into a smile of anticipation. Then his lips parted as the laugh tumbled from him. Jazz realized he was smiling in response, chuckling like he always did. He also realized that this was what he wanted. It felt like a regular date—like more than a date, like a relationship.

Mase was careful not to move too close, not to touch Jazz as the movie played on. Jazz found himself watching Mase more than the movie. Was this sustainable? Could a relationship work if both people couldn't really touch, even if they both wanted to?

It was probably them both wanting to but not being able to that would crumble what was between them. Jazz shook off those negative thoughts and tried to enjoy the moment, enjoy Mase's laughter.

When the movie was over and the dishes put away, Mase gave Jazz a long look.

"I have a surprise for you," Mase said with a wink.

"A surprise?"

"Yep. Follow me."

Jazz followed Mase down the hallway and into his bedroom. Anxiety sparked in his gut, but he reminded himself of all the things Mase had done to earn his trust. In all the time they'd known each other, Mase had never done anything to break Jazz's trust. It was time to give Mase the benefit of the doubt.

Jazz stopped short when he stood in the doorway to Mase's bedroom. "You got a new bed?"

Mase's smile turned wicked. As sexy as that was, it made Jazz's stomach dip with fear. It was a predatory smile.

Then Mase did something that alleviated all Jazz's worry. He walked to the top corner of the bed and lifted a stainless-steel chain. At the end of the chain was a studded leather cuff.

"It looks less secure because it's leather, but it'll hold me."

Jazz nodded. He wasn't sure what he felt inside at that moment—grateful, touched, cared for? All he knew was Mase's thoughtfulness was more romantic

than Jazz thought he wanted or needed from a relationship. Apparently, he both wanted it and needed it.

"You don't mind?" he couldn't help but ask.

"Someday I hope you'll let me touch you while we're in bed, but I'm a patient man. I can wait."

For how long?

Instead of asking a question he didn't want the answer to, Jazz nodded again. Mase dropped the cuff behind the bed.

"Wanna watch another movie?" Mase asked.

"What?"

Laughter rolled off Mase and seemed to bounce like refracted light all over the room, warming everything it touched.

"Just because I bought the cuffs doesn't mean we have to break them in today, but by the look on your face, I'm guessing you want to."

"What do you want to do?"

"I always want to be with you...in or out of bed."

"No." Jazz shook his head. "I mean, do you want another blow job? I want to do what you want, not just what I want. The bindings are for me. What do *you* want?"

Mase took one step forward but stopped when Jazz stiffened. "I want you to fuck me."

Jazz was so shocked that his body swayed with it a little. "You...you want me to *fuck* you?"

"Why does that surprise you so much?"

"I guess I assumed you were a top. I mean, you obviously top with women."

Again, Mase's laughter bounced between them.

"Just because I'm bi doesn't mean I only top. For some, that's true. For many, it's the opposite."

"How would being bi mean you like to bottom?"

"Think about it. Like you said, I top all the time if I'm with a woman. Part of bisexuality is finding both sexes attractive. For me, another part is getting my prostate pegged."

"But you... I mean, some of the guys you've dated were definitely bottoms."

"I've dated men who like to bottom. I've dated men who don't like penetration at all."

"Is that why things didn't work out with Blake?" Jazz asked, even though he told himself not to.

"No, that's not why things didn't work out with Blake. He ghosted me once I got hit with the charges. Not that I would have married Blake, but it still hurt when he turned his back on me."

They needed to back away from this topic. It was quickly killing the mood, so Jazz brought them back around to the subject at hand.

"If you want me to fuck you, do you have condoms?"

Mase tilted his head to the side a bit and Jazz knew what was coming. It took him from semi-erect to fully hard and throbbing in the beat of a heart.

"I don't want anything between us. I want you bare inside me, Jazzy."

"But we just started... Don't you want to see test results?"

"No. I trust you, unless you need that from me, but I can show my results right now. I haven't been with a man for over three years. I couldn't risk it while undercover. I haven't been with a woman in about four months, and I was tested when I got back Stateside. I'm also on PrEP."

Jazz licked his lips. He didn't have much to say, but that was more because he didn't really have a sexual history to speak of, not one he wanted to tell Mase.

"I'll prep myself then you can cuff me to the bed."

Mase reached into a drawer and pulled out a bottle of lube. He pulled off his shirt, then reached onto the bed.

"Cuff this hand," Mase said as he put his free hand up near the headboard.

Jazz fastened one of the leather cuffs around Mase's hand, bending him over a little farther. Jazz watched as he tugged down his sweats. When his cock sprang free, Jazz's gaze snapped to Mase's cuffed hand. He took a deep breath, then helped Mase step out of his sweats.

"Can you squirt some lube on my fingers?" Mase asked.

"I'll do it," Jazz said.

"If I do it, it'll be quicker. You've never done this before, and I'm impatient."

Jazz wasn't sure how Mase was so sure of that. He wasn't wrong, but Jazz hated how confident he was that he was right. Jazz had tried to touch himself a few times, but never got farther than the tip of a finger inside him before memories swamped him. Both his erection and libido had waned at that point, so he'd stopped trying.

Jazz picked up the bottle of lube and squirted some onto the tips of Mase's fingers. Mase reached his hand behind himself then groaned.

"Let me see what you're doing. I'll never learn if I don't try."

Mase nodded. He turned and leaned forward, bending over the bed as he lifted one foot onto the edge of the mattress.

Jazz froze for a moment. It was sexy as hell, but he was a little worried that Mase was hurting himself. He had two fingers buried inside himself to the webbing. He thrusted them in and out while spreading them and stretching his hole.

"Jazz."

That pulled him out of his stupor, and he looked up into Mase's smiling eyes.

"Don't worry. It feels good once I get past the initial burn."

Jazz nodded, even though he couldn't comprehend that. He stopped that thought in its tracks before it could barrel into his past and ruin the moment. This was about Mase, about making Mase feel good.

Mase twisted his wrist, then thrust his fingers deeper. Jazz had a side view, so when Mase moaned and his cock jumped, he knew it was a good moan.

A drip of pre-cum fell from Mase's slit and started to glide down the underside of his shaft. Jazz collapsed onto the bed and used his tongue to catch that drop. When he pulled back, Mase's ass was at eye level.

Jazz picked up the lube and squeezed some over his hand. He reached out and coasted his glossy fingers around Mase's embedded digits. Mase shuddered and pulled his hand free.

Jazz circled him a few times before trying to press inside. As soon as Mase's heat enveloped him, Jazz groaned. He'd fisted his cock for years but couldn't even imagine what it would be like to thrust inside such tight warmth. His dick pulsed against his zipper, beating like a drum.

He pumped his fingers in and out experimentally, watching and feeling as Mase stretched to accommodate him. Jazz looked up at Mase's profile.

His eyes were closed, and his lips parted. Then he pressed back against Jazz's hand as if asking for more.

Jazz increased the speed of his hand until Mase swore. Jazz immediately stilled.

"Did I hurt you?"

"No. Do it again. You pegged my prostate."

Jazz slid his fingers forward until he felt the little bundle he'd grazed. Mase's ass clenched, and he bumped himself back until Jazz's fingers were once again buried inside him.

"I'm ready," Mase groaned.

"Are you sure? I don't want to hurt you."

"Lube up," Mase said. "It'll burn because it's been so long, but it'll hurt in the best possible way. I miss the way it feels."

Jazz couldn't comprehend how one could enjoy pain like that, but that probably had something to do with the fact that his only sexual experiences were filled with pain and no pleasure mixed in.

"Let me get you situated."

Mase moved onto his stomach and reached his free hand out to the other edge of the headboard.

"No. On your back. I need to see your face."

Mase gave him a smile that wasn't quite shy but wasn't as cocky as his usual grin. There was surprise and satisfaction in his gaze as he laid on his back.

Jazz uncuffed Mase's wrist, then re-cuffed it so he could lie on his back. Once the other wrist and ankles were bound to the bed, Jazz poured a puddle of lube in his palm. He spread it all over himself, then he added a little more, just to be safe.

The ankle cuffs had enough give that Mase could bend his knees and he spread them wide, giving Jazz the perfect view of his pink pucker. It was gorgeous, and yet Jazz felt a hesitation.

Mase made a sound that was so full of desperation, it could almost be described as a whine. "You won't hurt me, baby. I want to feel you inside me."

Those words pulled the air from his lungs. Mase had never called him any kind of endearment except 'Jazzy'.

Jazz lined himself up and flexed his hips forward. He watched his crown burst past that pink ring of muscle. All the air that had just disappeared from his lungs came back with a vengeance as Jazz gasped. Tight heat clamped down on the sensitive head of his cock. It was nothing like he'd imagined it would feel. It was more…so much more.

Then he looked into Mase's eyes and realized it was everything. He'd spent so many years avoiding any kind of physical closeness between them. It was hard not to regret that now that he knew what it felt like to be so close to Mase, to be inside him.

"Jazz, move."

He chuckled at Mase's demand but inched his way forward. When Mase sucked air in through his teeth, Jazz froze, worried that he'd hurt Mase. That thought had his erection flagging slightly.

Jazz looked down and saw that Mase was still hard, so hard that his dick curved up and leaked pre-cum just beneath his navel. He pressed forward, feeling Mase's tight heat surround more and more of him until Mase jerked and swore. Again, Jazz froze.

"Don't stop. Fuck. *Please* don't stop."

Mase's head was arched back. His eyelids were so heavy that Jazz could only see slits of his blue irises. But in those slits was desire, pleasure — pleasure Jazz was giving him.

Jazz pressed on until his balls were squeezed between their bodies. He slid his palms up to Mase's chest, tugging at his nipples. When he felt an answering spasm inside Mase's ass, he did it again.

Most of his weight was on his elbows as he hovered over Mase. He pulled his hips back and thrust forward. Mase hissed out a quiet, "Yes."

That gave Jazz the courage to do it again and again and again. He built a slow pace, keeping it steady, even when Mase demanded more.

"Don't stop touching me," Mase whispered. "I want to feel every inch of you against me, inside me."

Mase's words were too much. They brought Jazz to the edge too fast, so he leaned down and used his tongue to silence him. That just made Mase more demanding. He sucked on Jazz's tongue. He used the slack on his ankle bindings to squeeze Jazz's waist between his thighs. He tilted his hips up, chasing Jazz's cock when he tried to rock back.

He loved every part of it. He could see how people could get addicted to that feeling, that closeness, that intimacy. It only made him want Mase more.

"I'm not going to last," Jazz warned as he increased the rhythm of his hips.

"Then touch me. I'm almost there, too. I just need your hand on my cock."

Jazz reached between them. When he fisted Mase's length, they both groaned. Mase's ass locked down on him. Jazz swiveled his hips, causing Mase to keen and swear. Jazz was ready to stop until Mase said, "Do that again."

Jazz did.

"Again," Mase demanded.

Mase got even tighter. His shaft expanded in Jazz's hand. Jazz clenched every muscle below his waist to keep from coming before Mase, but it was a lost cause. Nothing had ever felt as good as being deep inside the man he'd loved almost since they'd met.

Lightning zapped up from his balls and split in two, one spark going up his spine, and the other up his dick. His eyes rolled back, and he made noises he didn't even think he was capable of.

That seemed to set Mase off, because his cock flexed and jerked in Jazz's hold, spurting between their bodies. Jazz shuddered as spasms caressed his over-sensitive cock.

When he collapsed onto Mase's chest, Mase tightened his legs around Jazz, as if trying to hug him. His body felt like it was floating. He wished he could fall asleep like that, with his cheek pressed to Mase's beating heart.

Mase rubbed his cheek back and forth over the top of Jazz's head. "You okay?"

Jazz had to swallow a couple of times before whispering. "I wish I could offer you more."

He leaned up to look down at Mase's face. His eyes were closed as he took in a deep breath.

"Jazzy, this is more than I ever thought we'd have. Maybe someday, you'll be able to curl up next to me on the sofa to watch a movie—or maybe you'll even be able to sleep in my arms. Even though those things would be nice, I don't need them. I'm a patient man when it comes to you. I'll take whatever you're able to give—happily."

But you deserve so much more, was all Jazz could think. By the time he was able to pry himself away a few moments later, Mase was asleep. Jazz uncuffed his hands and feet, rubbing his joints to make sure they had good circulation. Mase sighed but didn't wake.

After using a wet washcloth from the bathroom to clean Mase's chest, Jazz hesitated to leave. Mase had rolled away almost as soon as the wet cloth rubbed across his chest. Jazz watched the expanse of his back rise and fall with deep breaths.

He looked at his watch, remembering what Marjorie had said about refractory periods. Instead of dressing and going back to his own condo, Jazz slid back into Mase's bed and curled his chest along Mase's back. He closed his eyes and took long breaths, both loving the feel of Mase against him and hating the stiffness in his own body.

After a few minutes, when Mase didn't wake or even move beyond breathing, Jazz sighed. His body relaxed. He stayed until it had been thirty minutes. He was pretty sure Mase's refractory period was on the shorter end of normal. He pulled the top sheet up over Mase, leaned down to kiss his temple, then dressed and left Mase to sleep.

Chapter Thirty-Three

Mase

What a difference a week could make. That was Mase's first thought as he'd woken that morning. He'd taken to pretending to fall asleep immediately after sex. At first he'd done it because he wanted Jazz to feel safe and not judged as he high-tailed it back to his own condo.

As much as he wanted Jazz to know it was okay to leave, Mase wasn't sure if his face would betray his intense desire for Jazz to stay. Each night, Jazz massaged his wrists and ankles, then cleaned him.

Mase rolled away that first night because he was sure Jazz had no idea how thoughtful that gesture was, how rare it had been for someone to even think to take care of Mase. He'd willed his body to relax as he'd listened for the rustle of clothes.

But Jazz hadn't left. He'd stayed. Then he'd curled up and pressed himself into Mase's back. Mase was sure Jazz gave himself a time limit, because he'd felt

Jazz lifting his wrist multiple times, likely checking his watch. But it hadn't mattered. Eventually, Jazz had settled and their skin had pressed together in such an intimate way that had nothing to do with sex.

When Jazz finally did pull away, Mase had truly been on the edge of sleep. Then Jazz covered him and kissed his temple before leaving. He'd done the same thing every night since the first. And Mase would lie there, staring at the wall for at least another twenty minutes, smiling until he fell asleep.

"That smile's so big it's almost scary," Jett said when Mase stepped into the elevator at HC.

"I was thinking good thoughts."

"I need some of those kinds of thoughts."

Mase chuckled as they rode the elevator up together. When the doors slid open on the second floor, Jett stepped out, but Mase decided to head up to the fourth. He needed to talk to Nick. He'd let things go too long, at first because he was pissed at Jazz, then because he was too wrapped up in him.

When there was no answer in the apartment Nick shared with Ax, Mase texted Bray.

I was hoping to talk to Nick.

Bray responded immediately.

He's at a doctor's appointment. I'm picking Mom and Rosa up at the airport. I wasn't sure if you'd be up for seeing her…

Mase could practically feel the hope emanating from Bray's text. He was sure Bray wouldn't have told him their mom was in town unless Mase had texted him right then. Bray was trying to give him the space he'd asked for, so was his mom. She responded immediately to every email or text he sent but was careful about how often she reached out first.

Mase took a deep breath and responded to Bray's text.

Why don't you give her a tour of HC?

He was going to see his mother for the first time in over seventeen years.

* * * *

He knew she was in the building. He'd been in the bullpen when the chatter started. He'd looked over and Max had given him a nod as if to say, "Yep, she's here."

Mase blew out a breath and stood from his desk. He wondered what she was going to think about him. He didn't imagine she'd be disappointed in him since both his brothers had also ended up in the military. Would she like what he'd built here?

Even as he promised himself that he wouldn't care what she thought, he smoothed a hand over his hair then down his Oxford shirt. He figured he'd catch up with them as Bray showed her the gym, but as he stepped out of the elevator and turned to walk down the hall, he froze. So did his mom as she walked toward him, flanked by Bray and Dee. Behind them was a young woman who had to be Rosalie, the girl his mom had decided to adopt after Nick and Ax had rescued her from a trafficker.

They hung there for a second, no one saying anything. Mase watched the tears gather on his mother's lower lashes. Her nose turned pink as her mouth opened and closed. Then she was moving. She was moving faster than he knew she was capable.

He barely had time to open his arms before she was there, holding him so tight he couldn't get a breath in — or maybe that was because his throat was clogged as well.

"You're here," she whispered over and over as she sobbed into his chest.

Mase looked blankly at Bray and Dee, unsure what to do, so he wrapped his arms around her in return. That seemed to cause a new wave of sobs as her arms clamped tighter around him.

He finally had to look down, because if he kept his gaze on Bray and the tear tracks on his cheeks, Mase would be crying, too.

After a few moments, Mom took a shuddered breath, then leaned back to look up at Mase without letting him go.

"Look at you," she said. "So handsome. So grown."

At a loss for words, he nodded.

"I missed you," she said with a watery smile.

She said it the same way she had when he'd come home from summer camp. It was so familiar that it broke something inside him. Then he was the one pulling her close. He kissed the top of her head, unable to stop a few of his own tears from falling into her hair.

When Mase looked up, the hall was empty. He wasn't sure if he wanted to thank Bray or strangle him.

"There are a lot of things we've been tiptoeing around," Mom said. "Let's get the tough questions out of the way. Where can we talk?"

Mase led her down one of the side hallways to the library. As soon as the door closed behind him, she sat at a table and looked at him. She shook her head as if to clear it from a dream as she watched him.

"I told Gil not to come. I was sure you wouldn't be up for a visit. Bray was sure you wouldn't be up for a visit."

"Who's Gil?"

"My husband."

That phrase threw him. Bray had told him their parents had divorced. He'd probably even mentioned his stepfather's name. If he had, Mase didn't remember.

"It was almost like you died…all of you. It blew me away to see an adult Bray walk into my covert op. I almost broke my cover." Technically, he did break cover while Bray was in Kyiv, but his mom didn't need to know about that. "In my mind, I saw you all as you'd been the days before I left."

"Don't judge too harshly. Losing a child doesn't lend to aging gracefully."

Now that she was there, and he could see how much it had torn her up as well, guilt pounded on him like a hammer did a nail, until he was buried in it — up to the top of his head.

"Maybe it's selfish, but it felt like I was the only one who really lost anything."

She shook her head. "That's not selfish. You had the rug pulled out from under you."

"Why…?" Mase had to swallow before he could get the rest of the words out. "Why didn't you come looking for me before my birthday? On my birthday?"

"I thought you were both just cooling off. I thought your father had been insensitive, and you were angry at each other and went to your respective corners. Russ didn't tell me the whole story at first. He just said he'd fix things."

She huffed out a strained sound. Then she patted the table next to her. Mase smiled because she used to do that when he would pace, just like he was then. He sat next to her, and she took his hand in hers.

"He said you two had fought about you being bisexual. He told me a few of the insensitive things he'd said. I was angry at him for hurting you. If I'd known how long it would take to get you back, I probably would have punched him in the face right then and there.

"But I thought we'd all kiss and make up in a few days. I never thought your birthday would come and go with no word from you. I was angry at your father for a long time for missing your birthday with you. I was angry at how he handled the situation without even consulting me, at how he tried to use money and threats to manipulate the situation."

"When did he tell you about cutting me out of the family?"

"He didn't. Our lawyer did. He had no idea I wasn't included under lawyer-client confidentiality because I was named in the document. He assumed I knew and was in full support. He also didn't tell me the full extent. Once he realized I didn't know and had never signed the document, he clammed up. I had to demand it in the divorce proceedings before I knew he'd included a section about not contacting any member of the family."

"And that's when you left, after the lawyer told you?"

"Yes. I...I felt pity for your father. I could sympathize with him, but I couldn't forgive him. He knew he'd made a mistake in demanding you hide in the proverbial closet. He sent you that document to open a dialogue. He wanted to negotiate. He thought you'd stomp in there and throw it in his face, and he'd be able to back down without admitting fault. The one time he was counting on your rebellion, you fell in line."

That... That shocked Mase.

"By the time I knew the full extent of the damage, we had no idea where you were. It had been over a year without a word when I found out about the change in the family trust. I hired a private investigator. I found out you were in the army, but it's not easy to find someone's address in the military."

"Not if you choose to be unlisted," Mase said.

"Who were you hiding from if you thought we wouldn't look for you?"

"I knew at least Bray would come hunt me down and demand to know why I deserted the family. I knew Dad would put that label on me. I knew he wouldn't tell the twins what he'd done."

"I still don't think they know the full story."

"I told Bray the truth."

She nodded, looking down at the table.

"I'm sorry," Mase said. "I... I knew you probably wouldn't *want* to go along with what he was doing, but I thought you went along all the same. And I was bitter. I was *so* bitter. I joined the army because I was suddenly destitute. I found a family there, even though the organization as a whole tried to rip my guts out, just like Dad did. My brothers stood beside me, tried to defend me. Those are the same men I'm working with now. Those are the men who have my back."

"Sam?" She smiled.

"Yes. And Jazz and Wade and Mitch. There was also Kota. He's been off the grid for a while, but he's still my brother."

"And Bray and Nick, they're still your brothers, too."

"Bray, I get. Nick, not so much."

She smiled then. "I thought I'd lost him to your father for a while. It was really rough when Bray figured out what happened. He and Nick…" She shook her head. "It tore all of us apart."

"Nick wants me to see him."

Mase wasn't sure if he was looking for her to talk him into seeing Russell Hart or absolution for not seeing him.

"Only you can decide how long your father's penance needs to be. Your brothers have already made their choice. Maybe if you see how he's suffered alone, you'll feel he's done his time…maybe not."

"Will you see him while you're here?"

"I'm staying at his house, so the answer to that is unequivocally, yes."

"How does your new husband feel about that?"

She laughed. "It's strange to hear Gil referred to as my *new* husband. Gil knows that I still care for your father. How could I not? He gave me you three. But he's also the one who took you away, so our relationship is…complicated. Russ has a bit of a superiority complex, thinking he knows what's best for everyone. It tore our family apart. It tore me apart. Gil's gentle soul and unwavering love and support were able to put me back together—mostly. Besides, if you do decide to see your father, you'll understand why Gil has no fear that I'll have an affair with my ex-husband."

Chapter Thirty-Four

Jazz

As soon as he stepped into the HC building, Jazz was on alert because *Mémère* sat at her desk, dabbing at her eyes with a tissue.

"What's wrong?"

"Nothing, *Bébé*. These are happy tears. Mase is getting his reunion."

Jazz felt his shoulders wrench back and tighten. "What happened?"

"You should have seen it, *mon petit*. As soon as his mother saw him..." *Mémère* shook her head. "She practically flew to him and hugged him so tight."

"What did Mase do?"

"Well, for a minute, he stood there with his arms spread like he was getting measured for a suit. Then he finally wrapped his arms around her. There wasn't a dry eye in the house."

Jazz wasn't sure it was the fairytale *Mémère* was making it out to be. Mase had never spoken well of his parents. There had been a few times in the past when Mase would open up to him and tell him that he missed his brothers, that he wondered where they were and who they'd grown up to be.

So it hadn't been that big of a surprise that Mase had invited Bray to join HC. But the betrayal of his parents turning their back on him? That had cut Mase deeper than anything else ever had.

"Where is he now?" Jazz asked.

"We gave him the privacy he needed to be able to speak with his mother."

"Where?"

"Calm down, *mon petit*. They were talking in the library for a while. I don't know where they are now."

"Didn't it occur to anyone that Mase was bombarded? That he might not want to be left alone with his mom? She turned her back on him."

Mémère trailed behind him as he swiped his badge, pushed through the security door and strode toward the library. Before he could turn down the hall that would take him there, *Mémère* took his arm and led him farther down the hall and into her apartment.

When the door clicked shut, she pointed Jazz toward her dining room table and set about making tea. Jazz didn't sit. He was too restless. Instead, he simply stood next to one of the chairs.

"I don't know what happened between them all those years ago, but that woman was sobbing tears of love, joy and relief."

"My concern lies with Mase and how he feels about this, not the guilt his mom feels because she let his dad cut him off from the family. Didn't anyone think about what Mase needs?"

Mémère turned and walked to him. She cupped his cheeks in her palms like she had when he'd been a little boy. She looked deep into his eyes.

"Maybe that's your job, *mon petit*. Maybe he needs you to think about what he needs."

"I'm trying, *Mémère*. I'm really trying."

"I know," she patted his cheek. "I've seen that smile on Mase's lips — and yours, too. Just don't forget that you should get what you need as well."

Jazz nodded, but *Mémère* scoffed.

"You think I don't know when you're placating me?"

He pulled her in for a quick hug before stepping back. She gave him the sad smile that had become a habit after he'd gone away to college.

"I have a supportive family. You love me unconditionally. Mase has never had that, but he's been there for me, cared for me —"

"Loved you," she interrupted.

He couldn't quite acknowledge that, even though he knew without a doubt that he loved Mase. If he didn't, he would have stopped coming back long ago.

"I want to be there for him, too."

"Don't assume the worst. I've met both Mase's parents, and I can tell you that Vivian is a strong woman who loves all her sons without condition or reservation. Russell Hart is the one in need of redemption."

"Just because his mother loves him doesn't make her any less toxic."

Mémère gave him a sharp look. "Are you sure we're talking about Mase's mom?"

Her words made him stiffen, even though he felt as if they'd knocked him to the ground like a puppet with cut strings.

"We never talk about her, about what he did to her, about what she did to herself."

"What's there to talk about?" Jazz asked, every muscle in his body clamped tight.

"You deserve better. That man always did care more about money and power than what was really valuable," *Mémère* said as she brushed back some hair from his forehead so gently, as if he were the most valuable thing.

She knew what he'd been doing in Houston. He didn't know how she found out or who told her, but she knew all the same.

"She deserved better, too," Jazz said.

"Your mama fancied herself in love with him for about a minute and a half. Problem was, she was stubborn. She didn't want to admit defeat. Kept telling us he was getting ready to leave his wife."

Mémère shook her head as her eyes focused on something in the past. After a moment, her vision seemed to clear, and she gave Jazz a smile.

"She didn't want us to see how she was living. We probably wouldn't have seen you if we hadn't pushed our way in and just stopped by a few times a month."

Jazz could remember *Mémère* and *Pépère* bringing food and clothes and toys for him. His mother had given a quiet thanks and excused herself to put away the groceries, but she never came back.

His grandparents would play with him for probably an hour. When they left, they'd yell out their goodbye to his mom, who was probably hiding in her room. They'd leave him playing in that tiny living room, absorbed in whatever trinket they'd brought. His mom would come out a few minutes later, wiping her eyes, but she'd smile when he showed her his new toy.

"She was proud. She didn't want to talk to us about anything. We offered for her to move home. That seemed to offend her more than anything, so we stopped. Maybe if we'd just offered one more time…"

"It wouldn't have changed anything," Jazz told her. "She threw herself at him. Every time he'd come over, she'd fix herself up and hide me away in my room. She'd ask if he wanted to meet me and every time, he'd say 'What for?'"

Mémère shook her head in disgust.

"There were arguments, too. She'd tell him she needed money. He'd empty his wallet and tell her that was all he had. He'd tell her he'd bring more next time, but he wouldn't. Then finally, he told her he was going to stop coming around. That was the biggest fight they'd ever had. It lasted a long time. She told him she wouldn't be able to find a job, that she didn't have anyone to watch me, that she needed money."

"I figured it was something like that," *Mémère* said.

"She threatened to tell his wife. He went crazy then. Things crashed through the house, but it hadn't been the first time. He told her he'd crush her, that she couldn't prove anything, and he'd make sure of it. He told her he had money and power and she had nothing. He told her *she* was nothing. I guess she believed him."

They stood in silence for a few minutes as they remembered what had happened next. Jazz had been the one to find her in a bathtub filled with red water. He hadn't known his grandparents' phone number, but he had known how to dial 9-1-1.

"It kills me that she didn't call us," Mémère said. "She could have at least called us to come get you for the night. She let us do that a couple of times, remember?"

Jazz nodded. When he'd lived with his mother, his grandparent's house had seemed opulent with its soft sheets and towels, with pictures on the walls and curtains in the windows.

"That tells me she didn't really plan it. She felt desperate. She did love you."

Again, Jazz nodded. He had plenty of good memories of Mom. She'd take him to the park a lot because he didn't have many toys, and they didn't have a yard of their own.

"I think you always expected everyone to leave you like she did."

"No," Jazz said.

"Oh no? I remember the first time I met Mason Hart. I remember thinking, '*There he is.*' I thought you were lucky to have met the man for you when you were young and to have something like the military in common."

"It wasn't like that."

"*Oui, cher*, it was. He looked at you like you were the sun, moon and stars. And there you were, pushing him away at every opportunity."

"He did leave, *Mémère*."

She rolled her eyes. "If you push someone away long enough, they'll leave. Too long and it makes them feel like they're pushing something on you that you don't want. Mase would never do that."

"I know that."

"Why haven't you ever told me what happened? I was worried that sixteen was too young to let you go to school by yourself. I should have made you wait. I should have made you take a gap year. You were only sixteen."

Jazz stiffened. "A year wouldn't have made a difference," he told her.

Marty and Kevin would have been seniors if he'd come a year later, and they would have had even less fear because they'd have been at the top of the food chain. And maybe he wouldn't have thought to stop it. Or maybe he would have figured out how to stop it sooner, but that wasn't on *Mémère*. Still, there was no way he was going to tell her about what happened in college.

"More life experience might have helped."

He shook his head. "I'd already dealt with plenty of bullies by that point. I figured, 'what's one more?'" *Until it was too late*, but he wasn't going to tell her that, either. "I met some assholes. I grew up," he said instead.

"No. You fell apart and put yourself back together with a distorted view of the world."

"I disagree. I think my view of the world became more clear."

"What was it? I always assumed you had your heart broken by some asshole, but over the years, I wondered if it was something else."

"*Mémère*—"

"No. If we're going to have hard discussions, we're going to have them all. That boy has been pining over you for years, and you've been doing the same, all while trying to keep him at arm's length."

"I tried, *Mém*. Believe me, I tried. I'm not built for relationships."

"Well, I know that's not true. You've had a relationship with me since the day you were born — and look at all these boys here. You've known them for what? More than ten years?"

"That's different. That's family," Jazz reasoned.

"If you think your *Pépère* wasn't my family —"

"That's not what I'm saying."

Mémère opened her mouth to continue the argument, but Jazz's phone rang. She let out a frustrated huff when he pulled his phone from his pocket.

As he answered the call, Jazz kissed *Mémère's* head as he moved past her, out of her apartment, to look for Mase.

"Hello?"

"Just checking in because I'm on the East Coast, but I'll be heading west soon. You okay?"

Jazz smiled. He and Ghost had gotten closer over the years — or at least as close as two loners could get. Whenever Jazz was able to access his personal cell phone, there was always a message or two from Ghost.

"All good here. You need anything?"

Ghost snorted. "How long are you Stateside?"

"A week, two tops."

"Let me know if you have time to catch up in person."

"I can't today," at least not until he found Mase and made sure he was okay.

"No big. Let me know if and when."

As soon as he disconnected the call, Jazz checked the library, the bullpen, the war room, the gym and the firing range. Mase was nowhere to be found. He was about to give in and call him when Max passed him in the hall.

"Jazz, I wanted to talk to you about something."

"Sure."

Max looked over his shoulder, but there was no one else in the hall. "Can you come up to the third floor with me?"

"Sure."

When they stepped off the elevator, Jazz whistled. "This floor keeps getting more and more decked out. Soon, this will be the war room."

"Maybe." Max shrugged. "I've been continuing to look into what happened to you."

"Okay." Jazz wasn't sure why that needed secrecy.

"I also figured out all the code numbers of the listening devices you placed in Marin Coleman's DC office."

Ah, so that's it. Marty.

"I've been pulling all the feeds and trying to detect certain words, of course your name, Levi Johnston, any reference to drugging you..."

"I see."

Max's throat worked as he swallowed. Jazz had long ago learned to trust his gut, and his gut was telling him he wasn't going to like what Max said next.

"Martin Coleman probably didn't drug you."

"Why do you say that?"

"Because if he knew where you were, he wouldn't be trying to find the current whereabouts of Elodie Thibodeaux so that he could have a line to you."

Jazz's body went hot, then cold. *Mémère* owned a little beach cottage on Virginia Beach. She needed to see the ocean once in a while, but she lived at HC — and thank fuck for small favors.

"What does he know?"

"He's hired an investigator, but it must have been very recent because the investigator told Coleman that she's either renting the house or has sold it because he's seen Ax's parents living there. He's considering it a dead end after staking out the place for over a week."

"What did Coleman say?"

Max gave him a long look. "He said to keep digging. He said she would know where you are, and she'd be the key to getting you to give him what he wanted."

"Fuck."

"Jazz, whatever it is he wants, it sounds like he's really worried. I'm assuming it's a picture or a video, something he's worried you've made copies of."

"I have made copies. The video is seventeen years old. It would also be the death of his conservative political aspirations if it ever got out."

"I think you should let me have a copy."

"What? No. Fuck no. You're too young to see what's on that footage."

"I can encrypt it so that no one can see it, not without your code. But if anything happens to you, that video could mean protection for Dee."

"She doesn't know the video exists. She has no idea about any of this."

Max raised one eyebrow. "If you don't think she hears everything the guys talk about, you're kidding yourself. Dee's sharp. She's smart as hell, and you are her top priority. She knows more than you ever wanted her to. And if you want her to treat this building like the safe house it is until we lock this down, then you're going to have to tell her."

"So if you encrypt this video, and I'm the only one with a key, how is it insurance for *Mémère*?"

"We have a few options. You can talk to an attorney and will it to Dee. Or you can just fucking trust me and let me pixilate you out of the video and get it ready to blast on social media."

Jazz felt queasy. He had a fucked-up relationship with that video. He kept it close because it was a sort of protection, but he hated that it existed, that he'd let those two assholes use him over and over again.

"I assume you have a plan?" Jazz asked.

"You bet your ass I do. I'm going to send him an audio clip, just a snippet, and tell him to call off his investigator. From there, he'll do one of two things…"

"Back off or double down."

"Bingo. If the backs off, we simply keep listening. If he doubles down, we let him know we're listening. He'll assume his phone is bugged, which it is. You're welcome."

Jazz couldn't believe he was smiling. He knew this day would come, but he didn't know he'd have someone like Max watching his back.

"I'll bring you a copy of the video."

"I'll send him an email from a ghost account that he'll never be able to trace. Do you want it to come from you or just let him wonder?"

"The email doesn't need a signature. He'll know who it's from."

Chapter Thirty-Five

Mase

"We might need you to come back to Ukraine."

Mase's gut sank. Things had been going so well, but Oleksiy Kozak was supposed to be his boss, so if Kozak said he had to go back to Europe, he had no choice but to go.

"Fucking finally," Mase muttered, as if leaving to go there was his end goal.

Kozak chuckled. "You don't like being home, Mason?"

"I'm not home. I'm from the West Coast. And following Bernard around like a puppy serves no purpose. He's barely let me join him in any real meetings. I haven't made many new contacts. The man's paranoid."

"He's very interesting. He doesn't use any of the product he sells, and most of his men are loyal to him. Luckily, not all."

Even though he was on the phone, Mase kept his body still. He felt a tickle at the back of his neck, but he didn't rub it. He hid every tell, just like he was trained to do. And he kept his mouth shut when he wanted nothing more than to demand the name of whoever was betraying Jazz.

"Then grease his fucking palm and let's get this over with."

"It's not that simple. He's very high up in Bernard's organization. He's demanding a cut."

Mase huffed out a sigh. "Of course he is."

"He wants to take Bernard's place when we cut him out of his own pipeline, but he's smart enough to know that this will never happen."

"So he wants my job?" Mase asked.

"I think he's the type of man who wants all our jobs."

"Like Bagan."

Kozak growled at the name, just as Mase knew he would. This whole thing was turning into a cluster-fuck.

"Why is the up line so fond of Clement?"

Mase had been hearing code names more and more as he rose in Kozak's organization, but he'd never seen any faces to put with them. He wasn't sure Kozak had, either. But there had to at least be an enforcer, someone like Mase, who got his hands dirty for the big bosses.

The names he'd heard sounded a lot like military call signs — Thor, Dion, Rife, Car, Dair — but he didn't know who they were. He imagined that Thor was the hammer, the enforcer, but they'd never crossed paths.

"It is not fondness that makes them so determined to work with Clement. They can control him. They have dirt on him, and he owes them a lot of money. Bernard owes no one."

"Huh, who would've thought that owing someone money would keep you alive?"

"Only for so long, Mason. If I've learned anything, it is that no matter what, when you are no longer useful, The Wraith will make sure you are dead."

The Wraith. Was that another code name?

"I guess that's exactly where they want Bernard."

Kozak didn't respond.

Something started twisting inside Mase's gut, and it felt a lot like fear.

"If that's what's going down, then get me the fuck out of here. The US will extradite my ass if they think I'm in any way involved in a murder."

And he'd be able to gather a lot more intel to protect Jazz if he were surrounded by the men helping plan it.

"Don't be ridiculous," Kozak scoffed. "First of all, he's not a US citizen. But most importantly, we do not want to expose our ties to the US. Bernard might think he has a monopoly there, but he's about to take a fall. He will take the fall for us, as well. Then we can go back to business as usual, and the Americans will think they have rid the world of a villain."

That plan would be genius if Bernard wasn't Jazz, a covert operator. The US would definitely know they hadn't stopped any kind of trafficking ring if Jazz ended up dead — not that Mase would let that happen.

"You'd better not let anyone else know he's safe while he's on US soil. He might never leave," Mase said.

"We have strong insight into his operation, and they are leading him to come home. When he goes to France, you need to be back in Kyiv."

"Believe me, I don't want to be anywhere near him when they take him out."

As soon as he was off the call with Kozak, Mase called a meeting in the war room. Jazz and Max were the last to arrive. When Jazz walked in, he gave Mase a long look.

It was just like old times as they stood there, trying to assess if the other was going to turn tail and run or fight. Mase always wanted to fight for what was between them, but he'd taken his share of calculated retreats as well.

What had happened to make Jazz hesitate to give him a smile?

"I have some news from Kozak that we need to discuss, and Jazz will need to report it back to his handler."

"I have something I need to talk about as well," Jazz said.

Mase leaned back in his chair. He assessed each man before dropping the bomb. "Kozak's bosses want him working with Clement, even after what happened in Kyiv. They have leverage on Clement and think they can control him."

Ax snorted. "They're going to make Kozak work with Clement and probably Bagan? Those guys'll murder each other."

"Maybe that's the point," Sam said.

"Maybe," Mase agreed. "Eventually. For now, they're going to find a way to kill Bernard and let him take the fall. He was very specific about wanting to protect his US connections."

"The heat must be on," Wade said. "They figure if they hand over Bernard, that it'll take years for all our agencies to realize that he was only one piece of the pie."

"But he's the top of his organization. I don't even know how far down from the top I am, but he did mention a name today that I've never heard, The Wraith. Anybody know that one?"

Mase looked around the room as everyone shook their heads in unison.

"Is that a call sign?" Max asked.

"Probably. Can you see if there's anything you can find? There are a few other names I've heard tossed around when Kozak or Andreiko were on calls. I'll send them in a secure email, along with context."

"I'll see what I can do." Max nodded.

"Since we're talking about people who want to kill me," Jazz said, "we need to make sure Martin Coleman is still on the list. Max has some intel."

Mase lowered his hands from the table so no one would see his fists.

Chapter Thirty-Six

Jazz

Mase was pissed. There was no doubt in Jazz's mind that what Max had discovered added to the flame, but he'd been tense when Jazz had walked into the room. Did that mean the reunion with his mom hadn't been as beautiful as *Mémère* thought?

Jazz was tense himself, but for the first time in his life, he wanted to let Mase help him take out his aggressions in the bedroom. He was pissed and scared and horny, all at once.

His first instinct had been to run, to do what he always did when he got scared. When he ran, he didn't usually go too far. He'd find a gym and beat his own body into submission. His job required that he kept his reflexes sharp, but he went far beyond that.

His fear of being touched on the back had been very beneficial. It was like he'd developed a sixth sense. No one could sneak up on him, but it wasn't something he'd developed because of his job. It was instinct, as ingrained in him as filling his lungs with air.

What would happen when he retired? That wasn't far off. Being an operator was a lot like being a pro athlete. It required a lot of skills. If you weren't on top of your game, you got killed or put out to pasture.

When Bray had shown up in Ukraine looking for Mase, he'd unknowingly sped up a betrayal that had been in the works for a while. Andreiko had been working on getting Kozak out of the way long before Bray had come into the picture.

Bray had appeared to be Sam's weakness, and Andreiko had tried to exploit it, showing his hand. The problem was that Jazz had shown his hand as well, at least to a few people.

He'd disobeyed a direct order. His handler had told him to let Mase fend for himself, that Sam could save Bray, because it fit with the cover, but to leave Mase to the wolves.

He'd learned something about himself in that moment. He would sacrifice his career and possibly his freedom to make sure that Mase came home safe — even if he wasn't capable of being with Mase. Even if he couldn't give Mase what he needed, he'd protect him.

"I'm not sure I'll be good company tonight," Mase said when he walked into his condo and spotted Jazz.

"Because you're pissed? How did the talk with your mom go?"

Mase shook his head. "That's the last thing I want to talk about right now."

This was where some other boyfriend would offer to cook him dinner or cuddle on the sofa like they'd sort of done the other night. Jazz didn't fool himself into thinking they were boyfriends, but he could offer something, some intimacy.

"Why don't you go lie down on the bed and let me wear you out so you can at least get some sleep?"

Mase closed his eyes for a moment, then nodded. He started shedding clothes as he made his way down the hall. Jazz caught a glimpse of bare ass as Mase stepped into his room.

He was already hard when he stood from the sofa. He knew what to expect now, and that calmed him. Most nights, he laid Mase out on his back so that he could look into his eyes and watch them cloud with need as Jazz fucked him slowly. He drew it out, so he'd have more time with Mase, skin on skin.

When he stepped into Mase's bedroom, Mase was on the bed, face down, his ass in the air. Jazz couldn't get naked fast enough. He gave the ankle bindings a little more slack so Mase could stay in that exact position.

As soon as his wrists were bound, Mase pulled a pillow to him and scrunched it under his cheek.

"Hard and fast, Jazzy. I need it hard and fast. I want to remember you were deep inside me every time I sit down for the next week."

"How can you want that?"

The words were out of Jazz's mouth before he could stop him. Mase stiffened for a moment before relaxing.

"I don't want to talk about your past right now, but just suffice it to say that the pain can remind you of something bad or something good. When I'm sore, it reminds me of what it felt like to have you inside me, your breath on my neck, your chest pressed so tightly along my back that not even air can get between us."

By the time Mase was finished, Jazz's breaths were shallow and quick as lust filled him. He made quick work of prepping Mase, not that Mase cooperated. He wanted the pain.

Jazz couldn't bear the thought of hurting him, so he took full advantage of the fact that Mase was bound. He thrust his fingers deep inside, scissoring them wide. He pegged Mase's prostate at random intervals until Mase was desperate enough to whine and beg for Jazz's cock. Only then, when Mase was already a puddle of need, did Jazz line himself up and sink inside.

They groaned in unison when Jazz pressed his groin against Mase's ass. He rocked his hips back, only to punch them forward.

"Hard. Fuck me hard. Make me forget about today."

Jazz gripped his hips. He slammed into him over and over, watching himself disappear. Nothing had ever made him feel so possessive of Mase. Was there anything better than feeling the man he loved take him deep and squeeze him from the inside?

He felt the grip all down his length, adding friction and pressure to an already-tight hole. Mase kept egging him on, demanding he thrust harder, faster. He shut off the part of his mind that called himself a hypocrite for wanting Mase to feel him for days.

Mase had a lot more sexual experience. He knew what he wanted, and Jazz wanted to be the one to give it to him. He was quickly becoming addicted to being the one Mase wanted, even if Jazz had to come to Mase every time.

"Jazzy...touch me."

His grip on Mase's hips left no question that he was already touching him, but Jazz knew what he needed. He slid one hand down and gripped Mase's shaft. He fisted him and drug his hand up and down the thick length in time with his hips.

Mase tugged on his bindings. He reached up and wrapped his hands around the chain that attached to the bedframe. He moved up onto his knees and elbows so that he could press back, thrusting so hard that their skin smacked, echoing loudly in the quiet room.

He knew the exact moment Mase came. As soon as Mase's cock jerked in his hand, his ass gripped Jazz so tight that it flung him over the edge as well. The climax was so powerful, it arched his back, tossing his head back as he bared his teeth to the almost painful, sharp pleasure.

Fire burned from his balls to his tip as he came deep inside Mase, and Mase came in his hand. They were wrung out, panting as they recovered.

Mase tightened around him one last time, pulling a grunt from Jazz as his over sensitized crown protested. When Jazz went to pull out, Mase tugged at his bindings until they rattled.

"Not yet. Just... stay inside me a minute longer."

Jazz leaned down and pressed a kiss to Mase's shoulder. He wouldn't have much choice in a moment when his dick fully softened, but he understood that Mase wanted to keep that connection. Jazz did, too.

"I want to try something," Jazz said when he pulled free.

He rolled Mase onto his back. This caused all the chains to crisscross, giving Mase less slack. His eyes were heavy-lidded but curious. Jazz looked down at Mase's soft cock.

"You want me to lie in the wet spot?" Mase asked.

"No." Jazz reached up and unbuckled one cuff. "I want you to touch me."

Mase's eyes flared wide. "Are you sure?"

"I…" *Am I sure?* "I want to try it."

"Kiss me," Mase demanded, as if one of his hands weren't free.

Jazz leaned down and pressed their lips together. He felt Mase's fingertips along the back of his hand, then coast up his arm, leaving tingles and goosebumps in their wake. Jazz felt a warmth at the base of his spine. His dick tried to rally, but it was simply too soon.

When Mase moved his fingers up to Jazz's shoulder, he did his best to loosen his muscles and lose himself in their kiss. It worked for all of two seconds until Mase cupped the back of Jazz's neck.

It's Mase. It's Mase. It's Mase, he chanted to himself.

He could do this for Mase because of all the things Mase was willing to sacrifice to be with him. Mase deserved this, to touch him, to caress him, even if it felt like Jazz's skin was about to crawl from his bones.

He tried to pull in a deep breath, but his lungs felt frozen. His whole body felt frozen until he panicked, knocked Mase's hand away and crawled backward. Only then was he able to start filling his lungs. He sucked in air as if he'd just surfaced from a minute long dive underwater. Terror clawed at his insides as he scrambled back to the edge of the bed.

"Jazzy," Mase said. "Fuck. I'm sorry. I thought…"

Jazz didn't hear the rest of what he said because he was too busy picking up his clothes and running for the door.

He couldn't go back to his place. Mase would find him there, and even though the panic was what got his feet moving, it was shame and humiliation that kept him going.

There was a call he'd been putting off anyway, so as he pulled his car out of the garage, he dialed the number.

"Lucky for you I'm still on your side of the country," Ghost said when he picked up the phone.

"This is *your* side of the country, but it is lucky for me you're still here. I need a favor."

"I'm not joining that team, Jazz. You boys need to stop trying to recruit me by showing me how helpless you are."

"It's a personal favor."

"Then you're lucky I'm finishing up a job as we speak. I can meet you outside DC in about three hours."

Jazz looked at the clock. It was just after midnight. "Where?"

As soon as Ghost gave him the coordinates, he typed them into the navigation system in his car. It was an all-night diner. It would only take Jazz about two hours to get there, but he headed that direction, anyway. He needed to get away from Richmond, away from Mase.

He growled as he drove. He needed to get Mase out of his head. That was the problem. Mase was never far from his mind. It was selfish to try to hold on to him. Tonight proved he wasn't capable of giving Mase what he needed.

Jazz spent the whole two-hour drive beating himself up for trying too much. Doing things with Mase and talking with the therapist had given him hope. He'd learned a long time ago that hope was a joke.

After driving around the city for half an hour, Jazz finally pulled into the diner and ordered some much-needed coffee. He'd been sitting in the diner for twenty minutes with those same thoughts when Ghost appeared before him as if from thin air and sat down.

"You look like shit."

Jazz rolled his eyes. "How do you look so awake at three in the morning?"

Ghost shrugged as he flipped over the mug on the table, a sign that he needed caffeine as well. He looked so different now than he had when he'd been in the army. His dark sable hair was long, touching his collar, and his beard was in need of a trim. There were also a few silver streaks mixed in among the dark facial hair.

He hadn't known Ghost half as long as he'd known Mase, Sam, Mitch or Kota—and yet he felt the most kinship with Ghost, maybe because they were both such solitary creatures.

"What's this favor?" Ghost asked once his mug was full, and the waitress was far enough not to overhear anything.

"I need you to keep an eye on someone."

"Fuck, Jazz. I'm no babysitter. Is this about Diego Guttierez again?"

Jazz huffed out a laugh. Ax's little brother had snuck out to a party on the worst possible night. The HC team had been in the midst of rescuing Ax and Diego's sister when they'd found out that the man keeping her was also watching her family. Ghost had been in the area and had helped round up Diego before going on to save a boy from being trafficked.

"It's not about Diego. It's about *Mémère*."

"Who would want to hurt Dee?"

Jazz must have hesitated too long before coughing up the name, because as soon as he said, "Congressman Martin Coleman," Ghost hit right back with his response.

"He the one?"

"The one?"

Ghost smirked, shifting his beard with the movement. "Don't pretend everyone who cares about you don't know that someone fucked you over but good before you joined up. He the one?"

Jazz could only nod.

"You want me to manage the situation?"

"I just want you to watch Dee. She doesn't know, but I'm going to have to tell her."

"Is there a contract?"

"At the moment, he has someone looking for her. There was an investigator watching her house."

"Good thing she doesn't actually live there. What does he want?"

"Evidence. He wants it to disappear, and I think he's willing to use her to make sure that happens."

"If he's willing to use her, he's got to be willing to make *her* disappear."

Every muscle in Jazz's body tightened. He knew Ghost was right, but he hadn't been able to face that possibility. He couldn't lose the last piece of his family, not for something that he'd done.

Ghost sighed.

Jazz could hear the regret and the apology in the sound, even though no words were spoken. Ghost didn't pull any punches.

"I have three weeks free before I have anything booked, and I can delay that if needed. What do you need from me?"

"The guys at HC have been keeping tabs on me through trackers. I'll talk to Max, but I want you to watch *Mémère* the same way. She doesn't leave HC all that much, but when she does, I want you to watch her, to make sure she's safe—especially since I'll be going back to Europe soon."

"You sure you don't want me to make this problem go away?"

"I can clean up my own messes," Jazz said.

Chapter Thirty-Seven

Mase

Almost thirty-six hours. Jazz had disappeared for almost thirty-six hours and counting. Mase knew he was alive because he'd been in touch with Wade — not Mase — to say he was taking a day off.

"Max," Mase called as he stepped off the elevator onto the third floor.

"In here," Max called.

Mase followed the sound of his voice and found him in a large room with a soldering iron in his hand.

"I wanted to see if you were keeping an eye on Jazz since he's MIA."

Max didn't respond for a full thirty seconds. Then he put down the small item in his hand as well as the soldering iron. He looked up and gave Mase a sympathetic smile.

"I have a software tracking all his tags and his phones. If he gets within a certain distance of any of Coleman's known hangouts, I'll get a notification."

Mase nodded as he pretended to be interested in all the bits and pieces of wire and metal and plastic spread over the table where Max stood.

"Would it make you feel better if I tried to track him?" Max asked.

"Yes, but I won't ask you to do that because I wouldn't want him to do that to me. If he's putting himself in danger with no one watching his six, I want to know. Otherwise, he deserves privacy just like anyone else."

Max opened his mouth to say something but there was a buzz. Max looked at his watch, his brows furrowing. Then a ding came from the other room.

"Is that the alarm you were talking about?"

"No." Max pushed past him. "That's the alarm telling me someone is walking the perimeter of HC."

"What?"

Mase followed after Max, leaning over his shoulder as he sat in a chair that looked almost like the seat of a car. He scooted in to a desk that reminded Mase of a cocoon. It curved in almost a full circle. Five monitors touched edge to edge in what would be a hexagon, but for Max taking up the last spot with his chair.

Max started typing on a keyboard that looked to be broken in two, each tilted a little toward him. One by one, the monitors came to life, showing the HC building from different angles.

"Do we know who Coleman's investigator is?"

Max snorted. "I'll bet you a hundred grand he didn't find this place, but yes, I know who he is."

"How can you be so sure? You found it when you were helping Bray look for me."

"I don't mean to sound conceited or anything, but I'm probably worth more than you because of what our government has paid me. There's a reason for that. Not many people can do what I can do."

"Sounds a little cocky, and I thought you were so humble."

"When it comes to all things computer, I have no doubt in my skill. It's real life where I..." Max shrugged.

"Don't know your worth? I think we all struggle with that."

"Either way, that's not Coleman's investigator. Let me get a shot of his face and I'll tell you who he is."

Mase sucked in a breath when he looked at the monitor Max indicated. "No need. I know who that is."

"Who?"

"Blakely Kirkwood Moore, age, twenty-six, occupation, army specialist, or at least it was the last time I saw him three years ago. His specialty is computers, specifically machine learning. He's also my ex-boyfriend."

Max turned and looked over his shoulder for a long moment, his eyes wide.

"What?" Mase finally asked.

"Nothing. I just...didn't think he'd be your type."

"My type?"

"Yeah. I assumed that big buff army dudes dated other big buff army dudes—like Ax and Nick, Bray and Sam."

Mase shrugged. "There's a bit of a size difference with those guys as well. I've dated men and women of all shapes and sizes. Then again, if I were to say I had a type, it would be stubborn as fuck, emotionally unavailable guys who ghost me every time we make any progress toward an actual relationship."

"Sounds like you'll only find one of those in a lifetime."

Mase snorted. He wasn't sure if it made him lucky or unlucky that he'd fallen for Jazz. Sure as hell felt unlucky in that moment.

"Are you gonna let him in?" Max asked. "Because I'd really like to know how he found you. After I found all the documents about you buying this building, I buried them. No one should be able to find you now, machine learning or not—unless he's an actual genius who made a real AI. Only an artificial intelligence can hack better than I can."

"If he did, I doubt the government will look kindly on him using it to find me."

They watched as Blake finally located the gate and pressed the call button. With a few clicks on his keyboard, Max had a live mic feeding audio of Dee answering the call.

"Welcome to HC. Do you have an appointment?"

"Yes, I need to speak with Mason Hart."

"I'm sorry. We don't have anyone listed under that name. Is there anything else I can help you with?"

"What is HC?" Blake asked.

"The Habitat Council. We help re-home refugees and asylum seekers, so we're a very private organization."

Through the high-resolution camera, Mase watched Blake's face fall.

"Is there anything else I can help you with?"

Blake looked directly into the camera lens that was housed above the speaker. "My name is Blake Moore. Please let Mase know I'm looking for him. I think what I have to tell him is important—or not, but that's for him to decide."

Blake listed off a new phone number. Mase knew that Dee was writing everything down, even as it was being recorded.

"Just tell him..." Blake paused. He rubbed his forehead like he did when he couldn't solve some problem with his code — like he did when he threatened to give up altogether. "Tell him I need his help, and I think he needs mine, too."

Dee didn't give a reply. What could she say without repeating herself or giving something away?

"What're you gonna do? The dude looks a little...scared," Max said.

Mase took a deep breath. "I'm going to call him and see what it is he wants. Show me how to do that without being traced."

Max handed Mase a headset. As Mase put it on, Max typed furiously. White letters and numbers that might as well have been hieroglyphics scrolled up the screen.

"You ready?" Max asked after a moment.

Mase gave one stiff nod.

"Here we go," Max said as he pressed one last button.

Mase heard the bleating of the phone as it rang. He rubbed the back of his neck because this felt like a really bad idea, but Max was right. Blake looked scared. Even though he'd ghosted Mase, it was because he'd been scared then, too, scared to rock the boat.

Blake picked up on the second ring. "Mase, thank God."

"How did you know it was me?"

"This is a burner phone. You're the only person with the number."

"Why are you using a burner phone?"

"I need help, Mase. I think I did something stupid. I didn't know where else to turn."

He couldn't just trot Blake into HC. Blake was capable of making some of the same contraptions Max did.

"Come back to the gate. We'll talk. I can't guarantee anything, but I'll hear you out."

"Okay. I'm still here. I...I don't have anywhere else to go."

"I'll be right down."

"You're not bringing him in here," Wade said as soon as Mase took off the headphones. He wasn't even sure when Wade had arrived or how much he'd heard.

"No. I'm not. Max, I want you to record everything."

"Want me to try to tell if he's lying?"

Mase snorted. "Are you a human lie detector now?"

"No, but I can watch him through a thermal camera. Your skin gets hot when you lie."

"It gets hot if you're horny for an ex-boyfriend, too," Wade said.

Max shrugged. "No lie detector is one-hundred percent accurate. If he gets hot when talking about something mundane, we'd know he was lying. I'm no expert, but I have read about it."

Wade huffed and shook his head but told Mase, "Whatever you want to do."

"Just record everything."

Max nodded then was once again typing. Mase gave one last look at the monitor that showed Blake pacing back and forth in front of HC's gate. He kept looking around himself, running his fingers through his hair, his movements jerky. If Mase didn't know Blake as well as he did, he might think he was high.

As he trotted down the stairs, Mase made sure all his weapons were at the ready. He didn't expect an ambush, since Blake seemed to want to get inside, but he couldn't be too careful.

He walked quietly through the courtyard between the building and the wall that surrounded it. The gate was the only section not made of reinforced concrete. It was wrought iron, but so overgrown with vines that most people walked right past it, thinking it was just part of the wall.

Mase dialed in the code to unlock the gate and stepped out. Blake was pacing away when the gate clicked softly closed. He whipped around, his eyes full of…something. Relief, maybe. Then, all of a sudden, it was like a repeat of the reunion with his mother.

Blake ran to him, wrapped his arms around Mase and pressed his cheek to Mase's chest.

"I thought you were dead. He told me you were dead."

That caught Mase by surprise. "Who? Your father?"

Blake nodded, his cheek sliding up and down Mase's pec as he did.

"What's going on, Blake?"

Mase gently gripped Blake's shoulders and pushed him away under the guise of looking him directly in the eye. Blake couldn't possibly think that Mase had been pining for him for over three years. Blake had been the one who'd stopped returning his calls.

"It's a mess. I thought I was getting back at my father for what he did, but…" Blake looked off into the distance for a moment. "Either he's doing something so classified that I can't find anything about it or he's doing something illegal."

"What?"

Blake shook his head. "First, I wanted to make sure you were alive." Blake reached up and touched Mase's cheek. "I didn't mean to hurt you, but it would have been worse for you if I'd stayed."

"How did you find me?"

Blake looked up at him, his red hair like fire in the sunlight. He was a sweet, gorgeous kid and Mase had cared a lot for him when they were together. But having him pressed up against his chest felt a little too much like cheating on Jazz.

Mase gently grasped Blake's wrist and lowered it from his face. Blake wrapped his hand around Mase's. The move made him feel more trapped than cared for. Even though Mase wasn't allowed to touch Jazz, he didn't want anyone but Jazz touching him, not in such an intimate way.

"I've been keeping an eye on you since you got discharged — as much as I could, anyway."

"Since I was discharged?"

Blake lowered his gaze to Mase's chest. "My father played a role in having you discharged. He told me that if I let you be, he'd try to get you an honorable discharge. He lied."

"Big surprise."

"You were my first real boyfriend, the first one that I didn't hide from him — *couldn't* hide from him. I think he thought that if he got rid of you, that he'd also somehow erase the fact that I'm queer, and all his subordinates knew about it. I couldn't exactly walk away from the military. He threatened to get me demoted. I never would have made it as boots on the ground."

"I don't know," Mase said. "You made it through basic training."

"Barely, and only because of who my father was."

Mase scoffed. Blake was tenacious, obviously. He had wanted to join the army to prove himself to his father. He'd done it and had moved up the ranks quickly because he was brilliant.

"So after I got discharged, he kept you in line with threats?"

"I put my four years in. I was ready to walk away. I put in for IRR to move to the reserves. I didn't realize it would cause so much of a stir for me to be removed from active duty. Suddenly, I was called to the Pentagon."

Mase gripped Blake's shoulders tighter. "The Pentagon?"

"I've moved up since you left. I have some pretty high security clearance. I was working on some things that I can't discuss. I told them I couldn't work in an organization where my father could rule my life." Blake swallowed.

Mase's gut tightened. If Blake thought Mase could protect him from the government, not many could do that—and definitely not him.

"I guess they decided that I was more valuable than my father."

"What?"

"They told me that they were delaying my IRR request to give me time to think about it. Then, all of a sudden, they were pushing my dad to retire, something about budget cuts. But he knew it was because of me."

"How did he know?"

Blake shook his head. "I don't know."

"Did your father threaten you?"

Again, Blake shook his head.

"I heard him talking to someone, saying he wasn't done with what he needed to do. That he needed at least another year to complete the project, but they were pushing for him to retire in the next few months."

Mase looked up at the camera. He hoped Max was getting all this. He couldn't make Blake any promises because he'd likely be heading back to Europe soon.

"So that's why you bought a burner and came to find me?"

"No. I did a little snooping on my dad's computer to find out what he was up to, but he caught me. If he hadn't been with some of his men, I'm not sure what he would have done…" Blake's breathing became choppy and loud as his eyes clouded with fear.

With a sigh of resignation, Mase cupped the back of his head. "Deep breaths, in and out. Breathe with me, in when I breathe in and out when I breathe out."

Blake's nod was jerky, but at least he acknowledged Mase. He counted to four in his head as he pulled air into his lungs. Blake mimicked him. Mase held there for a count of four before exhaling slowly to the same count. When Blake's breathing was back to normal, Mase dropped his hands to his sides.

"So your father didn't do anything when he caught you?"

"His face turned purple, but I got out of there long before he would have had a chance to confront me about it. He was more pissed than I've ever seen him in my life."

"Because he knows what you're capable of."

Blake reached up and put his hands on Mase's shoulders. When Mase tried to take a step back, Blake squeezed tighter.

"I saw a file with your name on it."

"My name? But it's been over three years. I'm no longer the military's problem."

"It was a deleted file. He lied to me, Mase. He told me that he was the reason that you only got a dishonorable discharge and didn't end up in jail, but that's not true. They were trying to get you to take the fall. When you did your own digging, they allowed Captain Banning to take the fall instead."

"Tell me what you found."

Blake bit his bottom lip. "If you have a secure computer, I'll show you."

Once again, Mase looked directly into the camera. His phone rang in his pocket, and he wasn't surprised to see Wade's number on his screen.

"First floor only," Wade said. "And he agrees to a pat down."

Wade hung up before Mase could respond.

"Come on," Mase said. "I hope you're ready for the Spanish Inquisition. If you make it through, we can see what evidence you have."

Chapter Thirty-Eight

Jazz

It took him a while to build up his courage, but Jazz forced himself to walk into HC. He pressed the button for the second floor and took a deep breath as the elevator ascended. When the doors opened, he half expected Mase to be standing there, fuming, but it was Sam he saw pacing in front of the elevator.

"Good," was all Sam said when he stepped in and pressed the button for the third floor.

"We're going up?"

"Mase is fucking insane," Sam muttered.

That kicked Jazz's heart into high gear. "What d'you mean?"

"His ex is sniffing around HC."

"Blake?"

Sam nodded.

When the elevator doors opened, Jazz beat Sam off the elevator. There were only two people in the room.

Max sat at his desk. Wade leaned over his shoulder as they both watched the monitors.

Then, all the monitors on the wall lit up, all showing different angles of the perimeter security cameras. Jazz lost his footing when he saw Blake Moore stumble toward Mase and wrap his arms around him.

"I thought you were dead. He told me you were dead," Blake said.

Jazz's pulse whooshed in his ears as he fisted his hands at his sides. He'd never experienced anything like what was surging through him in that moment. Was it rage? Was it jealousy? He wasn't sure, but it made him feel more inadequate than he ever had in his life.

He watched Mase touch the man who used to be his lover. He gripped Blake's shoulders, he took his wrist. And when Mase cupped the back of Blake's head, Jazz felt his heart crack open with longing.

He shook his head as the longing morphed into that deep-seated fear. He wasn't sure he'd ever be able to let Mase touch him like that.

Something ugly twisted and grew inside him. It doubled and expanded until he felt it was all that he had room for. It was the realization that Mase needed this. He needed all the things Jazz was incapable of.

That look of adoration in Blake's eyes as he gazed up at Mase made him nauseous. No matter how much of that same feeling burst inside Jazz each time he looked at Mase, he could never express it like that. Even with Herculean effort, he'd never be able to wrap himself around Mase like Blake tried to do without thought.

"You're going to let him in here?" Max's voice was high with indignation.

"I said first floor only," Wade said.

"I get to see every file before he opens it," Max said.

"Bring a laptop we can grind to dust if needed."

"That's blasphemy," Max grumbled as he walked over to a table and plucked up a laptop.

"It was sure easy to pick one," Wade teased.

"This is one of the extras for new HC recruits. You think I'd be willing to get rid of one of *my* computers?" Max snorted as he made his way to the elevator. "This one doesn't even have all the basic HC software installed yet. It's as off the shelf as you can get."

"Good," Wade said. "Then you won't have wasted any time customizing it." Wade looked at Jazz. "You coming?"

Sam was already at the elevator, pressing the call button. Jazz had been standing there, watching everything happen as if in a dream...or a nightmare. He shouldn't go down to the first floor. He shouldn't sit by and watch Mase protect his lover. *Former lover.* But instead of declining, he nodded, giving in to his morbid curiosity.

When the four of them entered the conference room where Dee had led Mase and Blake, *Mémère* was in the doorway offering coffee and tea.

"No, thank you," Blake said. "Just water."

With a nod and a promise to be right back, *Mémère* slipped out of the room after a long look in Jazz's direction.

"What can you show us?" Mase asked.

Blake looked at Wade for a long moment. He swallowed. He looked at Sam, then Jazz, and finally Max. Physically, that was probably the order of intimidation. Wade was the tallest and widest of them all. And when he was frowning, like he was in that moment, he was intimidating even to Jazz, especially because the man knew how to fight.

"I don't exactly know what I have," Blake said. "I have deleted files I recovered from my father's work computer. There was a file on Mase, a file on Captain Banning and files on a few other men. Mase's file caught my attention, but so did a file called 'Timeline Transfer Blitz'."

"What's a 'transfer blitz'?" Wade asked.

"Blitz is Captain Banning's handle," Mase said.

"Fuck," Sam whispered. "You'd think they'd come up with a less obvious file name."

"My dad was never an operator. Plus, he's cocky enough to think that no one would ever hack his computer. I didn't open every file I uploaded to the cloud, but I did save every file he's deleted in the past five years. Mase's file was mostly full of dates and times. The 'Transfer Blitz' file was cross-referencing Mase's active duty assignment dates to Captain Banning's."

"The cloud?" Max said. "No way am I letting a stranger connect one of our computers to the internet so he can download something."

"You their tech?" Blake asked.

Max gave a stiff nod.

"I'll give you the location, and you can get the files. Then you can do whatever testing you need once you're disconnected from the internet."

"Will that work?" Wade asked.

Max seemed hesitant but nodded again. "I'll open a container first to try to protect the machine from any malware."

"If there's malware, it came directly from my father's computer. I didn't edit any files. I only accessed them."

As Max's fingers flew over the keyboard, Blake kept sneaking glances at Mase. He'd said something about thinking Mase was dead, so he was probably relieved, but there was still adoration in his gaze.

"What will you do if this can clear your name?" Blake asked.

"I'm doing what I was meant to do," Mase said.

"Where am I going?" Max asked.

As Max and Blake went back and forth, Jazz watched Mase. Was that really how he felt about everything? Was he glad he ended up working for himself rather than the government?

"These files seem innocuous," Max said. "I'm having a program go over them to make connections."

"What program?" Blake asked.

He stood from his chair and leaned over the table, but there was no way he would be able to see the monitor. He was at least an inch or two shorter than Jazz's height of five-ten.

"It's a program I created to find connections between data."

"Did you program all the algorithms?"

Max snorted. "Of course."

Blake narrowed his gaze. "What's your name?"

"Sin," Max said.

Jazz rolled his eyes at the moniker. Max had too much of a baby face to be roped with a name like Sin. Then again, Wade had told him it stood for Super Intel Nerd. That made the acronym much more understandable.

"I've heard of you," Blake said as he sat down. "I didn't know you were into machine learning. I thought you were more hardware with some white hat thrown in."

Max shrugged. "I only moved to hardware because no one made what I needed. Math is where I got my start."

"Do you work with any government entities?" Blake asked.

"Why?" Wade answered before Max could.

"I'm working on something for the army—or at least I was. I don't know what my dad's been saying about me for the last twenty-four hours. I was having a few issues. I didn't know if he had the security clearance to possibly help me." Blake nodded in Max's direction as he spoke to Wade.

"Whatever it is you're working on—and I think I know what it is—I probably already turned it down, so why would I help you?" Max asked.

Blake gave Mase a helpless look as if he expected him to come to his rescue. Mase, in turn, looked at Jazz.

"I'm already getting hits," Max said. "Looks like they were trying to verify that this Blitz character was with you on certain dates—mostly the dates leading up to when you were accused of sedition. Wait... Hello..."

"What?" Mase asked.

"There are old emails here. They were obviously trying to be as discreet as possible, but it looks like once you started turning over intel about your commanding officer, they covered their asses by making sure he could take the blame, then left a trail of breadcrumbs for you to find so they wouldn't be implicated."

Everyone turned to look at Mase. He rolled his lips and nodded his head as if this didn't surprise him, even though it likely pissed him off.

"Look for Sergeant Brett Stevens and Sergeant Jason Marshall's names," Mase said.

"Who are they, and do you have their call signs?"

Jazz answered for him. "They're the assholes who accused him of sexual harassment. Brett Stevens is call sign Shady, and Marshall is call sign Juice."

Max nodded and resumed typing.

"I didn't know about that," Blake said.

"Yeah, well, you can't expect to know everything that happens after you turn your back on someone," Jazz said.

"Jazz."

"Are you saying it's not true? He left you at your lowest point, let you face the wolves on your own."

"He had his own wolves to deal with," Mase said.

Maybe what he said was petty or immature, but Mase scolding him to protect Blake was the last straw. Jazz pushed his chair back, stood and strode from the room.

Chapter Thirty-Nine

Mase

"I'll be right back," Mase said as he hurried after Jazz.

He'd never known Jazz to be anything but empathetic and understanding when someone faced a situation similar to his.

Major General Anderson Moore was a bully. He was full of pride and bluster. He was a good old boy who thought he knew what was best for his son. He'd warned Mase away from Blake multiple times, but Mase had stood his ground.

Blake hadn't. Mase didn't judge him for it. He could see how Blake had meant to be selfless, but it had also been selfish. Blake wanted his father's approval, and there was nothing wrong with that. Mase had felt the same once upon a time.

But Mase wanted to come first. He deserved that. He'd cared for Blake, maybe even loved him a little, though he'd never told him that. He always held back on telling anyone that because, was it really love if it couldn't compare to what he felt for Jazz?

He caught up with Jazz in the hallway that led to the lobby. It was time to draw his line in the sand.

"Don't do this, Jazzy. If you run from me this time, when we know we could make it work—"

Jazz whirled on him. "But we don't know that. What we have now, it's not working."

"It is for me. I'm good with what we have," Mase said.

"No, you're not. You don't think I can see it in your eyes every time we're together? Your eyes beg to touch me."

"Don't you know that nothing will ever be enough with you? Fuck, Jazz. You could let me smother you and sleep on top of you every night and I would never get enough of you. Even if you let me touch and kiss and lick every inch of your body, I'd still want more."

"And I'll never be able to give you more."

"Bullshit," Mase spat. "That is utter bullshit. You've already given me more than I ever thought I'd have. And I'd rather have this with you than"—he waved his arms around as he tried to think of anything that compared to being with Jazz—"than anything else."

"I saw you out there with him. I saw you touch him and hold him as you calmed him down. I watched it on the monitor and thought, '*That... That's what he deserves.*'"

Mase huffed out a humorless laugh. "And I was out there thinking how wrong it felt to touch anyone but you."

"But you can't touch me." Jazz screamed. "Didn't the other night prove that?"

"I'd rather be tied up letting you touch me than be touching any other person."

"It's scraps. You're getting only scraps and pieces when you deserve the whole meal — the whole fucking restaurant."

"I should get to choose what's enough for me. *You* are more than enough for me. I won't lie and say that I don't want to have you sleep in my arms, but I hope that someday, you'll be able to share my bed."

Jazz shook his head through those last two sentences, and that's when Mase knew he'd never be able to get through to him. It's when he stopped fighting.

"Life is always trying to tear us apart, and it feels like you're more than willing to let that happen."

"I've never been as savage a fighter as you," Jazz said.

"I'm done playing tug of war, Jazzy. I want to stick with this, to take what we can get and watch it grow, no matter which direction it goes, but I'm done begging."

"You shouldn't have to beg," Jazz said as he walked away.

When the door swung shut behind him, Mase doubled over as if he'd been kicked in the balls. He couldn't get air into his lungs. How could words cause physical pain?

When a small hand landed on his shoulder, Mase gasped. He turned to see Dee standing beside him. There were tear tracks down her cheeks.

"Please," she said, "don't give up on him. I know it's hard. I know you deserve someone who will fight for you, but he doesn't even know how to fight for himself."

"He doesn't want me."

"Oh, *cher*." She helped him stand and cupped his cheek. "There's nothing he wants more than he wants you. But he's been letting fear drive him for as long as I can remember."

"Well, it's driving him away. And this time, I'm going to let him go."

"We all hide from the shadows of our past, Mason Hart…even you. I could kick that boy's ass for hurting you, but no matter how badly he hurts you, he hurts himself worse. You've tried to love other people. Jazz has known from the beginning if he couldn't open up to you, he couldn't open up to anyone. That's why he's never even tried."

Her words stung. He didn't want Jazz to suffer.

"I don't think me holding a grudge against my father changes anything about what's between me and Jazz."

"Our pasts shape us, *cher*. Sometimes, Jazz is like a child who tells his mother that he hates her because he doesn't know a healthy way to make sure that she'll love him unconditionally. I'm not saying it's right, but there it is. Think about it."

Mase nodded dully as she kissed his cheek and carried a bottle of water back into the conference room. When he turned around, he saw Sam and Bray standing there. Something inside him broke at the look of sympathy in Bray's eyes.

"Did you call him so he could come down and watch my humiliation?"

Sam slowly shook his head left then right one time, but it was more in tune with his words than a denial when he said, "Don't be Savage right now, be Mase. Don't close yourself off. When you were eighteen, you lost your support system. Maybe that's why you needed to be Savage, but you have a support system now."

"I don't need a support system."

"Yes. You do. If you need to be angry, that's fine. We'll go to the gym and beat the heavy bag until you wear yourself out. Don't go out and pick fights with strangers."

"Is that a thing?" Bray whispered. "Is that what he does?"

"*He* is right here," Mase growled.

As he walked closer, he noticed a few tears brimming along Bray's lower lids. Was his humiliation that sad? It wasn't the first time he'd begged Jazz not to run, and no matter what he said, would it really be the last? His cheeks burned with that realization and the fact that his little brother had just witnessed it.

"What do you have to cry about?"

Sam reached out and pressed his palm to Mase's chest. "You don't get to take this out on him."

"It's fine," Bray said, as he grasped Sam's wrist and lowered his arm. Then he turned to Mase. "You're my brother. When you hurt, I hurt, too."

All the anger drained from Mase. Bray didn't deserve his ire. No one did, not even Jazz. But he couldn't help but feel hopeless. Feeling powerless pissed him off.

Sam wrapped his arm around Mase as he steered him down the hall. Over his shoulder, he whispered to Bray, "Tell Wade Mase is out for the next few hours at least."

* * * *

When Mase stepped out of the shower and into the gym bathroom, he stopped to look at himself in the

264

mirror. He shouldn't have said what he had. His anger would just make Jazz stay away from HC longer. He rubbed his hands over his face as he thought about what Sam had said.

Jazz ran, but so did Mase. They blasted away from each other and Mase tended to be the last to come back to the fold. Maybe it took longer for him to lick his wounds, since Jazz was always the one turning him away. Maybe deep down he was hoping Jazz would open up to someone, even if it wasn't him.

"How're you doing?" Bray asked.

Mase looked over at his brother. "What am I supposed to do?"

"I don't know. I've never seen any two people more in love and more determined to protect each other from themselves than you and Jazz."

"Love's not enough."

Bray gave him a sad smile. "Mom said that when Nick and I asked her why they were getting a divorce."

"Too bad she went back home. Maybe she could give me some advice about walking away from someone you love."

Bray opened his mouth, then closed it without making a sound.

"Go ahead, out with it."

"I didn't want to be like Nick, but I was actually thinking Jazz is the one who keeps walking away. Maybe Mom's not the one who has the same experience."

Mase huffed out a laugh. "You think I'm in the mindset to talk to him after all these years?"

Bray shrugged. "The love of his life walked away, but not far enough. They're tied together. They're still a big part of each other's lives. Knowing how I feel about Sam, I can both understand why he still wants to see her and am floored by his ability to do it."

"I'm not sure there's anything about him I can respect at this point."

"No, I can see why there wouldn't be. But maybe in exchange for having those few minutes of your time he's been vying for, maybe he can give you something in return...perspective."

Mase looked at himself in the mirror for a long time. He saw parts of his father in his own face sometimes. Was he ready to face his old man?

"If I do this...Nick can't be there. I don't mean to be cruel, but—"

"I get it. He'll want it to go the way he thinks Dad wants it to go."

Mase nodded. He didn't want to always question if their father was the real reason Nick was there, but that was how it felt.

"It would probably be best if we surprised him—not a 'make him jump' surprise, but not a lot of warning. He'll just work himself up, and...it also gives you wiggle room to change your mind."

Mase turned and looked at his brother. "I'm glad you found me."

"What?"

"I'm glad you did all those stupid things and even risked your life to find me. I'm happier you didn't get yourself killed, but I'm glad to have you back in my life."

Bray's mouth dropped open as Mase pulled him in for a hug. When he stepped back, Mase cleared his throat and wiped at his eyes.

"Let me get dressed. If we're going to surprise him, we might as well do it before I lose my nerve."

Chapter Forty

Jazz

"I'll be heading back overseas," Jazz said.

"Well, let me know what the time difference is and I'll rearrange some things to make sure you get your appointments," Marjorie said.

He continued to stare out of the window.

"Jazz?"

"I really appreciate you fitting me into your schedule, but I'm not sure —"

"I tend to add more patients than I should. I love it when I'm able to help someone. This job is full of meaning for me, so I don't mind the extra hours."

He nodded. "Do you think people should confront their aggressor?"

She took a deep breath. "That's a loaded question. Can you tell me what brought this on? Are you considering pressing charges?"

"I freaked out the other night with Mase."

He closed his eyes. He'd been keeping everything to himself for years. Now that he had someone who listened, who was paid to listen without judgment and help him find solutions, he couldn't seem to keep his mouth shut.

"Why did you freak out? You said you were binding him to feel comfortable having sex?"

"He had a rough day, personally and professionally. I wanted to comfort him. I wanted to offer him something of myself. I want him to be the only one who gets to touch me — everywhere."

"Jazz, that takes time. No matter how much you love him, your body's reacting to the trauma, not to Mase. This is not something you can jump into with both feet. I assume you panicked and now you're beating yourself up about it?"

He shrugged.

"Did you prepare him? Did you tell him the areas he couldn't touch?"

Jazz shook his head.

She gave him a look of sympathy. "You're not setting yourself up for success this way, Jazz. I was hoping you'd bring Mase with you so we could make sure he has some tools to help you deal with anxiety and so he knows what to expect. How can he support you blindly?"

"He won't be supporting me anymore. We...broke up, I guess. I don't really have enough experience to know for sure, but he said if I walked away, that was it. And I walked away. I lost my chance."

"I'm willing to bet he doesn't know about our sessions at all?"

"No. I didn't want to get his hopes up."

Marjorie chuckled. "So instead, you dashed them?"

When Jazz didn't answer, she continued.

"I gave you my card, Jazz. There's an emergency number on the back. They can get in touch with me on nights and weekends. Why didn't you call me when it happened?"

"It wasn't an emergency."

"If you panicked and ran away from someone you love and trust because of past trauma, that qualifies as a mental health emergency. If you're going to do something drastic, call me."

"I was thinking about confronting the man who raped me. That's drastic. So I'm telling you."

"In court? It can be a very difficult thing to do."

"No. Just face to face."

"Is this about the other night? It's understandable, even expected to be angry about all he's taken from you."

"I need for him to lose his power over me. I was sixteen when it happened. I'm thirty-two now. For half my life, I've lived in fear. How am I not past this?"

Marjorie sighed. "Ignoring something doesn't make it go away. If you had been working with a therapist for sixteen years and still had made no progress, I'd understand your frustration, but you haven't. You've tried to ignore it, so it festered. Now, you have to view it as if today is the day after it happened for the last time. That's your starting point. You have to allow yourself to move through all the emotions that you haven't really let yourself feel."

Those words tried to suck Jazz back to that day when he had been sixteen and helpless.

"Mental health takes effort and must be learned," she said. "It's not an instinct like breathing. It's learned, like speaking, like writing. Unfortunately, we don't teach it to our children, so most people go through life thinking they have something to be ashamed of if they face anxiety or depression. We shame people instead of teaching them coping skills. Coming here, working through this when you could just continue on ignoring it, that's the bravest thing you can do. It's why I'm willing to come in at six in the morning, stay late or even work weekends. It's why I take late-night calls, because I know what it's like to be in your shoes."

"Did you face the person who hurt you?"

"In court, yes."

"Did it help?"

"Yes...and no. There were people who didn't believe me, even after the conviction, so it didn't end simply with me getting justice. But I spoke up. I trusted myself to speak up so that I knew I wouldn't be a victim again. I sought out therapy, and I knew he wouldn't be able to do it to anyone else ever again."

That was why Jazz did what he did. He might pretend to be a monster, but in the long run, that was his goal...to protect others.

"I didn't tell Mase that he couldn't touch my neck because I wanted him to be able to. Then I freaked out, as if it were his fault. I can't keep doing that to him."

"Then bring him here. I'll help you find the words."

Can she? If Mase is willing, can she help me find the words?

"And confronting the man who raped me?"

"Jazz, we're only a few sessions in. Give yourself time to look at this from a different perspective other than fear. If you confront him now, you might revert back to exactly what you felt the last time he assaulted you."

"The last time he assaulted me, I felt vindicated in a way."

Marjorie pulled back, her brow wrinkled with obvious confusion.

"I recorded it. I egged him on. I fought harder than I had since the first time it happened. I knew I'd be getting my revenge."

"Justice and revenge aren't the same thing. You deserve justice and the ability to move on. Would you like to press charges against the man who assaulted you?"

Jazz shook his head. "No. I don't want to drag this through court. His family has too much power. It would be dismissed before I even finished filling the charges."

Marjorie looked at him for a long time. "Revenge is something that usually brings more pain than healing. Regardless of what happens between you and Mase, I'd like you to continue our sessions. I can help you, Jazz."

* * * *

He tried to assimilate Marjorie's words, but the longer he thought about it, the more rage started to pulse within him. It had always been inside him, ever since the first time Marty had held him down. It had grown each time he'd run from Mase.

Hatred and bitterness grew inside him until he hadn't been sure there'd been anything left. Then Mase had come back from Ukraine and things had changed. They'd kissed, they'd touched, they'd made love. Mase had rearranged his fucking living room.

Still, none of that mattered. He'd lost Mase again — not that he could blame anyone but himself. And even if he kept going to therapy, even if in a few years, he might be ready for a relationship, it wasn't fair to put

Mase through that. Because what if in a few years he wasn't ready? What if he never was?

It was easy for Mase to say this was what he wanted, because it was all new. He wouldn't feel the same about being tied up every time they had sex in a year or five years. It would get old. He'd start to regret that he couldn't cup Jazz's face like he did with Blake.

Martin Coleman didn't deserve to have this much power over him, not after so long. He'd taken up way too much of Jazz's time. After driving around Richmond for a few hours, Jazz had calmed down a little.

When he stopped to get some coffee, he saw an encrypted message from Max. Coleman hadn't heeded his warning. He had called his investigator, asking him to double the manpower looking for *Mémère*.

All the rage that had settled into a dull buzz inside him came roaring back to life. He knew what Marty wanted, and maybe it was best for both of them that Jazz gave it to him, but he wasn't stupid enough to go alone, so he made a call.

Chapter Forty-One

Mase

Mase smirked when Bray pulled through the wrought-iron gate of a large home. They were in the ritzy Windsor Farms area, just about five miles from HC. The house wasn't as grand as the one Mase had grown up in on the Pacific Coast, but it was a gorgeous Georgian house made of dark brick. Each window was highlighted by bright white shutters. Three tall chimneys rose higher than the two-story pitched roof.

"Guess he's planning on staying a while," Mase said.

"Considering he put in an elevator, I'd say he plans to stay."

An elevator?

"Do you want to stay here while I make sure Nick's not around? Ax said he was going to call him and make an excuse."

"So Ax knows?"

"He knows that I want to have a private discussion with my father. I didn't mention you might be here, as well."

Mase nodded. Bray was giving him a lot of wiggle room to back out. And yet that seemed to make him more determined to go through with it.

"You wait here. I'll text you when I find Dad."

"No. I'll come."

Bray gave him a long look with raised brows. "You sure?"

With one curt nod, they made their way to the front door. Bray didn't knock, just walked right in. After all these years, Mase could barely remember that feeling of constant welcome.

"He's usually by the pool or in the sunroom."

Mase heard voices as they approached a room with an open door.

"You haven't seen him?"

His dad's voice wasn't as commanding as Mase remembered. It was slow and partially slurred. His tone also wasn't demanding, but Mase still remembered his voice.

"No, Dad," Nick said. "I've told you he's avoiding me now, as well. I defended you one too many times."

"I didn't mean for you to hurt your relationship with him."

"And yet you moved yourself out here when I specifically told you not to."

"I *have* to be here, Nick. What if… What if at the last minute, right before he heads back to Europe, he decides that he would talk to me if he could?"

"Then he could call you." Nick sighed.

"This is not the type of apology that can be given over the phone. I guess I hoped if he knew I made the first step…if he knew I was willing to overcome any obstacle to see him, that maybe…"

"I'm not sure it's going to happen regardless, Dad."

"I know you tried, Nick. I just… I guess I pushed us both too hard."

"I'm sorry. Now he's not even talking to me. He thinks I only joined his team to be your mole or something. Bray made it sound like he was having this breakthrough in his relationship with Mase, so I followed. I thought maybe… But then every time we talked, you kept hoping…and I kept pushing…and now…"

"You wanted a relationship with Mase, too. You missed your brother. I understand," their dad said.

"Sometimes I wonder how you would have reacted to my coming out if Mase and Bray hadn't done it first. I mean, I was just the coward who came out last, and I seem to have been rewarded for it."

"That's not what happened." Dad said.

"Isn't it?"

"No…and I love all of you. I'm just not good at showing it, and I have a hard time when things are outside my control. I won't lie and say it wouldn't have been easier on all of us if you hadn't all been straight as an arrow. Things would have been much easier, but that doesn't mean they would be better or that I don't love you. I just didn't handle the hard times as well as I thought I would…or could."

"I want to ask you something. I've wanted to for a while, but I didn't want to cause you more stress. What happened on Mase's eighteenth birthday?"

"He didn't tell you? I'm not sure if I'm grateful or not. Mase's eighteenth birthday was the biggest mistake of my life, second only to turning him away when he came out to me. I'd done everything I could to force him to come home. I cut off his credit cards, his phone, his car insurance, repossessed his car. He still dug his heels in."

"Don't you think he would have been more likely to come back if you would have continued paying those things, so he knew you still wanted him to be safe and have the ability to call?"

"It's easy to look back now and know it was all a mistake, but then, it was about changing the situation to my advantage. He'd have to come home and negotiate with me if he had no other means."

"Or he'd do something desperate like start selling drugs or worse."

"You'll be a better father than I was if you think about that. All I thought was that if he just came home, he could have everything back, and I'd be able to plead my case for him staying quiet about his sexuality. So instead of backing down, I made the worst decision of my life. I stayed the course. And I did it without your mother's knowledge."

"What does that mean, you 'stayed the course'?"

Mase stepped past Bray and into the room.

"It means instead of reaching out, even though he knew I was living in a shithole in Garden Grove, he sent a courier to the rundown, drug-infested apartment complex. He sent a courier with a document formally cutting me off from my family — not just financially, but telling me not to contact you in any way."

"What?" Nick turned and looked at their father for confirmation, his eyes wide with horror.

"I was worried that by telling you and Bray what I'd done, I'd lose you, too. I'd already lost your mother because of it."

Mase missed part of Nick's response as he took in their father's appearance. Nick's tone was scathing. That did ease a little of the hurt he'd felt at Nick constantly coming to their father's defense.

Their dad looked about eighty years old. He'd lost too much weight. Mase could see the bones in his wrists and his skin seemed almost translucent. His hair was gray and thinning a little. His face looked emaciated and loose-skinned.

This stranger was not the father he remembered, but looking at him, Mase could see why Nick and Bray had done what they'd done. Their father wasn't just sick, he was heartsick. It didn't suddenly open Mase's heart with forgiveness.

Maybe it made him an asshole, but it made Mase feel better to know that his father had at least suffered a little for the decision he'd made. It also might have made him the tiniest bit more willing to listen to the words that were sure to come from his father's mouth.

"I can't believe you didn't tell me that!" Nick said. "I can't believe I was acting like you were just ignorant when you went full hog and were an asshole to your own son."

"Nick—"

"No." Nick shook his head. "I...I just can't right now."

"I was wrong, so wrong. I was conceited and stubborn." Russ looked back at Mase with tears in his eyes and his lips curved up. "You look...so tall, so grown up, so...so..."

Mase had to look away as a tear slid down his father's cheek. Russell Hart didn't cry. Mase had never seen the man cry.

The anger seemed to melt from Nick as he tried to comfort their father. He reached over and placed his hand over Russ's. Mase watched as his father struggled to place his left hand over the one Nick had comforting his right one.

Bray had told him about the stroke, but it was a different thing to see the aftereffects with his own eyes. The man who had been so full of life, the man who had been in such control of those around him, was now out of control. It was sad to see, even if there was some justice in the sight.

"Give us a minute. There are some things I need to say to your brother."

Nick nodded. He turned to leave but paused in front of Mase. "I…" He sighed.

"Maybe I should have told you," Mase said. "Explained why."

"Or maybe I should have believed you, that you had your reasons."

Mase nodded.

Nick patted his shoulder and left the room. When he turned, he saw Bray follow Nick out. Mase took a fortifying breath before turning to face his father as the door closed with a quiet click.

"Now that you're here, I wish I'd written everything down. There's so much I planned to say."

"I'm not sure how much I'll be willing to listen to."

Dad nodded. "I'm sorry, Mase. I was so wrong. What I did, it was so wrong. It was paradoxical intentionality. I was trying to squeeze you to come back home, but I just pushed you farther away."

"How did you expect me to get that from you telling me not to contact the family?"

"I guess I thought I knew what you'd do. I thought you'd do what I would do. You were so much like me — hotheaded, a little entitled. I thought you'd come home and demand what you were owed."

Mase snorted. "If I learned anything, it was that you didn't owe me anything."

"I thought you'd fight for your birthright, your inheritance."

"I don't give a shit about money. You turned me out. *Me*."

"I guess I should have known that if you were stubborn enough to walk away that you'd never come back. It's probably good that you didn't. If you had, I would have used that to force you to stay in the closet. If I'd done that to you, Nick and Bray would have followed suit. They would have known you weren't being your true self, and they would have learned not to be theirs. You always protected your brothers, even in leaving."

"I don't know if I can forgive you. If you'd just reached out…"

Mase shook his head and walked to the floor-to-ceiling window of the large sunroom. He could see the James River. He watched it ebb and flow in the distance.

"You forget where you get your stubbornness from. I'll give you a hint. It's not your mother. Don't hold it against her. She had no part in it."

"I know that now. I spoke with her."

"You did? She didn't tell me. She probably didn't want me to be jealous or do something stupid to try to get my chance to talk to you."

Mase looked out over the few acres of land between his father's house and the river. Of course, his father would find one of the rare properties with riverfront access.

"It's still weird to think that you two aren't married anymore."

"For you and me both. I'm sure you'll meet the lawyer soon enough if you're talking to your mom."

Mase shook his head at the bitterness in his father's voice. He thought about what Bray had said.

"How did you move on? When she left. How did you get past it?"

Dad snorted. "I didn't."

"But she stayed with you when she was here."

"Mason, I fucked up. I know that, you know that, your mom knows that. Maybe I'm a little delusional because I didn't learn from the mistake I made with you. When your mom left, I was sure she'd be back. She's the love of my life. I was the love of hers. What else was she going to do?"

"Find someone else?"

Dad shrugged ruefully. "I didn't see that one coming. I was too proud to grovel — with you or with your mom. Instead, I tried to manipulate the situation. When that didn't work, I dove headfirst into work, letting it take over even more of my life than it had when you were kids. But what else was there to do when I was all alone?"

Mase could think of a lot of things he could have done.

"I could kick my own ass for taking so long to learn these lessons. I live every day of my life in regrets and what-ifs. What if I'd just hugged you when you told me you weren't straight? What if I'd just reached out to you instead of trying to force you to make the first move? What if I'd begged your mother to come back? What if

I'd tried to force my way in front of you fifteen years ago when I realized that my knee-jerk reaction might cost me everything important in my life?"

"What if things had still ended up here?" Mase asked.

"Then at least I'd know I tried. That's why I moved here. I wanted to die knowing I'd done everything I could."

Why were Mase's eyes burning at those harsh words? It was obvious that his dad wasn't well, but he seemed so matter-of-fact about his life being over. And how did this equate to his relationship with Jazz? Mase hadn't been the one to walk away. That was Jazz's MO in their relationship.

"If Mom tried to come back, would you take her back?"

Dad huffed out a laugh that sounded more like a wheeze. "Ask a question you don't know the answer to."

"Why didn't you grovel? When she left, why didn't you chase after her?"

"Pride. My pride had superpowers. It was really, really hard to kill."

"And if she kept leaving, how many times would you take her back?"

"You can't count that high," his dad said.

"Even if it hurt every time she walked away?"

Mase finally turned to his father. He was seated in the same position. His face was a contradiction. His mouth was curved up in a smile as tears pooled in his eyes.

"If there's anything I've learned, it's that you can't control anyone or anything. Thinking you can is just you fooling yourself. I hope I've finally learned what it is to love unconditionally. I never stopped loving you, Mason. I simply wanted you to fall in line. It was unfair, but I felt I had the right as your father to lay down those demands. I was wrong. I was wrong about a lot. But there is one thing I've learned, one thing I know is true."

"What's that?"

"You don't turn away love, even if it doesn't look like you expect it to. I love you, but I wanted your love for me to look a certain way. I wanted it to be marriage to a woman like your mom, grandchildren, taking over my company. But I shouldn't have cared if it looked like you being married to a man, still hopefully with grandchildren. It shouldn't have mattered. I was so lucky to find happiness with your mom. I shouldn't have cared if you found happiness with a man. I should have just wanted you to be happy. I *do* want you to be happy."

Mase turned back to the window because he couldn't bear to watch his father cry.

"Who is he? This man who has you tied up in knots?"

"Jazz."

He said the name without even meaning to, like he couldn't keep it inside. Was this what Jazz's love looked like? Not being able to be touched? He could easily live with that, if only Jazz would stop running.

"He's a lucky man to have your love. Have you told him?"

Mase opened his mouth only to close it. He'd been about to say that, of course, Jazz knew Mase was in love with him, but did he? Had Mase ever said it out loud?

"I think he knows," Mase said as he looked over his shoulder at his father.

"That's another lesson I've learned. Never leave anything unsaid. I don't expect you to forgive me, Mase, but thank you for coming here. Thank you for seeing me. And please, don't blame Nick. I pestered him, and I knew that his concern about my health would push him to push you." Dad shrugged and gave a self-deprecating smile. "Maybe I'm not fully reformed."

Mase smiled despite himself. "I don't know what I feel. I'm too twisted up inside to figure that out right now. I'll probably be heading back to Europe soon, but maybe when I come back —"

"Don't make any promises. I'll keep my hopes up, regardless, but don't make promises out of guilt. Your anger will surge back once you leave and I'm no longer deteriorating before your eyes."

"Maybe," Mase said, but he didn't think so. Ax had been right. If we don't let people change, accept that they *can* change, why should they try?

Chapter Forty-Two

Jazz

"I meant did you want me to sneak in and kill the fucker, not have a conversation with him," Ghost grumbled as they watched Marty's house.

"I know what you meant. I also know that I need to look into his eyes. I can't let him have this much head space."

"I get that. That's why I didn't walk away when you suggested this. But we can't kill him if you talk to him. I can see the security cameras from here." Ghost squinted. "It's not the best setup but not the worst. I already see holes and blind-spots I could use to go in unseen."

"I don't want to kill him—not today, anyway. Max helped me get everything set up. If anything happens to me, all my evidence goes public. He'll never be able to shut that down like he will a court case."

"What are you looking for here, Jazz?"

"I want to see fear in his eyes."

Ghost huffed. "That's easily doable. But will that help?"

Jazz sighed. He didn't answer because he just didn't know.

"Well, we know his wife's not in town. He's alone in there. Let's go."

Jazz nodded and pulled the lever to open the car door.

"Are we knocking on the front door or going in the back?"

"Back," Jazz said. "Let's use those blind-spots. You can show me why they call you Ghost."

With a dramatic roll of his eyes, Ghost motioned for Jazz to follow him. "This is child's play, and don't even pretend you haven't already been in there."

Jazz smiled.

In less than two minutes, Ghost had them in. Marty's DC house was nowhere near as luxurious as his house in Texas. It was less than three-thousand square feet, which made it quick and easy to find him. Marty was in his office, staring at his computer monitor.

Ghost stayed back where he'd remain unseen. He had Jazz's back. Knowing that helped Jazz cross the threshold into Marty's office, even though his hands were sweating and he felt a little light-headed.

"Why are you looking for me?"

Marty jumped and yelped in a high-pitched tone that reminded Jazz of a chihuahua. His hand went to his chest as Jazz stepped out from the shadows.

"My father thinks you're dead."

Jazz shrugged like it didn't matter.

"I knew that couldn't be true."

"Why? Because then you'd feel relief? Because you'd never get caught for what you did to me, for what you did to Kevin?"

"I didn't do anything to Kevin. He did that to himself. I got your email."

"I wondered, since you haven't heeded my warning."

Marty leaned forward. Jazz held back an eye roll when he heard the slow quiet grinding sound of wood against wood. Did he really think Jazz wouldn't know?

"Reach for your gun all you want, Marty. You can't kill me."

With a smirk, Marty pulled his gun out from under his desk. "You're trespassing. I didn't let you in my house and my security cameras will prove it. This could relieve my problem forever."

This was something Jazz was familiar with. He'd had guns pointed at him many times. And like in that moment, it was having the upper hand that had saved him.

He looked at Marty, really looked at him. He'd been too scared to do that when he'd been hiding behind a curtain in Texas. They'd both had birthdays, and there had always been four years between them, but Marty looked older than his thirty-seven years. Maybe that benefited him in congress, but it wouldn't help him now.

It was apparent by the fullness of his features and the extra layer under his chin that Martin Coleman had softened with age. He was no longer that buff ROTC cadet. He was just an average-looking middle-aged man with graying brown hair and brown eyes.

It wasn't this current version of Marty who struck fear in Jazz's soul, it was the Marty of the past.

Something inside Jazz shifted. He wasn't sure that he and his body had come to an understanding that would allow him to accept touch, but at least his conscious mind knew that Martin Coleman was no longer a threat.

"You have no idea what I've been doing since I left the military, do you?"

"It doesn't matter." Marty cocked his gun and pointed it at Jazz.

"No? I may not have the connections your daddy does, but I know a thing or two about electronics now. I know all about making copies of video files."

Marty lowered his weapon the tiniest bit. "How many copies?"

"Wouldn't you like to know? If you think I would leave my grandmother unprotected, you're dumber than I thought."

"How did you know I was looking for your grandmother?"

"You might work for the people of the great state of Texas, but I work for the federal government—in a capacity in which they keep tabs on my friends and family."

Marty's face hardened. His eyes lost focus on Jazz as if he were lost in thought. "CIA?"

Jazz shrugged.

"It's either CIA or FBI. They're the ones who recruit from Delta Force."

"Awe, you followed my military career."

"Don't flatter yourself. I didn't give you a moment's thought until Kevin started making noise about feeling guilty."

"And your dad took care of that, too, didn't he?"

Marty stiffened but didn't respond.

"Leave my grandmother alone. And you better pray she lives to a ripe old age, because if something does happen to her, I might just send these videos out into the wild."

"Unless I just kill you now." Marty raised his gun again.

Jazz smiled. "You think I'd come here without accounting for that? No wonder Daddy had to buy your way."

"That's. Not. True."

"And he still pulls all the strings, doesn't he, Marty?"

"If you were so smart, you'd know it's time to shut your mouth."

"If anything happens to me, those videos will not only be sent to news outlets, but they'll also be posted on social media as well. That wouldn't do well for your political aspirations."

Marty's hand fell a little, his elbow hit the desk with a loud clunk. Thankfully, he'd taken his finger off the trigger.

"What do you want?" Marty asked.

"Nothing for now except for you to back off."

"For now," Marty repeated.

"That's—"

"Put the gun down."

Jazz huffed out a breath at the sound of Mase's voice. Marty didn't put the gun down. He swung it toward Mase, which made Jazz's stomach dip and churn. If Mase got hurt because of Jazz...

"What are you doing here?" Jazz said through clenched teeth.

"I'm watching your ass, like always."

"Ghost has my back."

"Then why is he down the hall and not in here making sure this rat's ass doesn't blow a hole in you?"

"He'd be a lot worse off if he did."

"How much will it take to get all the copies of the video?" Marty asked.

When Jazz flicked his gaze to Mase, he watched his face turned to stone. It locked down like it did before he went apeshit, before he turned savage.

"You get nothing," Mase growled. "You deserve nothing. The only reason you're alive right now is because Jazz hasn't given me the go-ahead to end you. But make no mistake… When you die, it will be by my hand."

"Savage! Stand down."

Mase gave one sharp shake of his head.

"We should probably be heading out anyway," Sam said from somewhere outside the room. "You done here, Jazz?"

Jazz looked at Marty, whose eyes were wide as he listened to voices coming from down the hall.

"You keep your money, Marty," Jazz said. "I have more than you now, anyway."

Marty's mouth dropped open to match his wide eyes, but he didn't say anything as Jazz turned and left.

Chapter Forty-Three

Mase

He didn't follow Jazz. He stayed where he was and looked at the man who'd ruined Jazz's life. At least a little of what he felt must have broadcast on his face, because Coleman inched his hand down to the desk, where he loosened his grip and set the gun against the wood with barely a click.

Mase kept his gun on Coleman. His eyes narrowed as he assessed the older man. He imagined that sixteen or seventeen years ago, Coleman was probably in excellent shape. He must have been, because Jazz would have been able to fight off this slender man who was thick around the middle.

"Are you his boyfriend?" Coleman asked.

"You don't have to worry about what I am to him. You only need to worry about what I am to you?"

"And what's that?"

"I'm your grim reaper."

"If you kill me, you'll end up in jail, and you won't be able to protect your precious Jasper."

"Jazz doesn't need protection—not from you, not anymore. He could rip you in half. And I'm going to make sure that any tiny corner of his mind where you're taking up space is blasted to hell, which is exactly what's going to happen to you the next time we meet."

Coleman's Adam's apple bobbed as he swallowed down those words.

"How does it feel? How does it feel knowing that something's coming without knowing when or how bad it will be? Maybe it'll give you a little taste of what you did to Jazz all those years ago. And maybe, when I finally come for you, it'll be a relief."

"Savage!" Sam called from around the corner.

His index finger twitched against the smooth trigger behind it. He wanted to kill the man so badly. But if he did it then, he might bring down everyone he loved. It wasn't easy to kill someone with Coleman's connections, and it wasn't something you did spur of the moment.

When Mase lowered his weapon, Coleman pulled in a stuttered breath. Mase used his gun to salute him.

"Till next time, Coleman." Mase turned away but then turned back. "And don't forget, I'll be watching you." Mase strode away.

"Coleman's already on the phone, sounding the alarm," Max said through the comms. "Get the fuck out of there. *Now.*"

Mase followed Sam out through the back of the house to the van they had a few houses away. When he climbed in, Max was still swearing up a storm, complaining about how many cameras and security systems he was going to have to clear of any evidence.

"I don't know if I can get through all this before the cops are there and pulling the recordings. He's a congressman, for fuck's sake."

Mase wasn't sure how the rest of the meeting went with Blake since he'd ducked out to let off some steam. Wade had let him know that Blake's intel was good, and he seemed on the up and up, which was why he made a suggestion.

"If you're worried about it, Blake might be able to help. If you think we can trust him."

Sam turned to look at Mase as Mitch drove the van back to HC. "Do you think we can trust him?"

"I'm the last person to ask. Too many feelings involved." Anger, hurt, disappointment, resentment. "I'll leave it up to you guys. I'm just saying he has the skills."

"I checked him out," Max said. "He's clean."

Mase wasn't sure exactly what that meant, but he hoped for both his and Jazz's sake that it didn't mean that Blake wanted to be part of the team.

By the time they got back to HC, Max and Blake were working furiously at their keyboards.

"Cops usually do a radius, probably a mile or so," Max said. "That means we need to do two more than that because he's a congressman and his dad's a senator."

"If we know the route they took, we could technically follow them and erase everything from start to finish."

"I fucking love having someone who speaks my language," Max said.

Wade's back stiffened as he hovered over the pair of them. Mase set a hand on his shoulder.

"Everything okay?"

Mase motioned to Blake with his head, but Wade's gaze was on Max.

"Everything's fine if you think a shitfest is fine."

"It's all under control now, Lambchop," Max said.

Mase looked at Max, his brows lifted and turned to find half of Wade's mouth quirked up.

"I see Ax strikes again," Sam said. "I don't know why he has such a hard-on for call signs."

Mase snorted. "Easy, he has a decent one, but he knows at least half of us got ours because of some stupid shit we did in basic."

Wade grunted in response. He had been a SEAL where most of the other guys at HC came from the army, so they didn't know what Lamb stood for, only that the way his teammates said it meant he got it from something stupid he did as well.

"Max is just pissed that he can't find out more about my past. He's been wheedling intel from some of the guys, putting together his own HR files, since we don't have electronic files on anyone that he can hack."

"I can hear you, y'know," Max said.

"I know you can, Lambchop," Wade replied.

Mase chuckled when Max's ears turned pink as he grumbled that Wade was Lambchop. Somehow, he doubted it truly bothered Max to have Wade using such a lovey-dovey term of endearment.

It reminded him of Jazz and how he grumbled when Mase called him Jazzy. As if reading his mind, Sam shoulder-checked him as he walked with him toward the elevator. "So what are you going to do about Jazz?"

"What can I do?"

"You can tell him how you feel."

"You think that's going to make a difference when me chasing him and crawling on bended knee hasn't worked?"

Sam shrugged. "Some men love the chase. He's watched you blaze through a lot of relationships since he met you."

"Yeah. There's a reason for that."

"But does Jazz know he's the reason?"

How can he not? How can he look into my eyes and not see how deep my feelings run? How much more can I cut myself open, only to have Jazz turn away?

"Ultimatums don't work when you're running on fear," Sam said.

"How did Bray get through to you? How did he do in days what I haven't been able to do in years?"

Sam gave Mase a crooked grin. "I don't know exactly what Jazz has been through, but I know it's worse than anything that happened to me. My no-go area was a much smaller section of my body. But the thing is, it didn't matter how much I trusted Bray. It didn't matter that my mind was telling me there was no danger, my body reacted as if there were."

"But you got past that."

"No. I'm moving past it...very slowly, with the help of a good therapist and Bray's unconditional love."

"It's not *my* love that has conditions." It seemed to be his pride that had conditions.

"You two have a pattern. Until one of you breaks it, you'll just go round and round."

"I wouldn't say it's a pattern."

Sam snorted. "You stay apart until you either can't resist each other or you get thrown together again. When you're near each other, it's like there's this static electricity in the room or like you're magnets, and we can all feel the force pulling you together." Sam brought his hands together.

"But then suddenly you're like magnets repelling each other. Jazz runs off out of embarrassment and probably fear. You run off and try to find someone to make you feel whole when you know that no one else can. He watches from the sidelines, his heart cracked open wide because he knows that someday, you might find someone who fills that space he wants to fill but doesn't know how."

"That'll never happen."

"I know that, and you know that, but Jazz doesn't know that."

"You sound a little like my father."

Sam rolled his lips together.

"Go ahead. You can ask."

"How did it go? Bray said there was no screaming, and you were calm when you left."

"He said everything I knew to be true and everything I wanted him to say to me when I was seventeen."

"Too little, too late?"

"It would have meant everything to me then. Now, it only made me feel a little vindicated, and as much as I hate it, a little sorry for him."

"Then don't wait until it's too late for you and Jazz."

"You keep talking like I just need to reach out and grab it. Jazz is the one who keeps running. Are you sure I really mean that much to him if he can just keep walking away?"

Sam shook his head and gave Mase a pitying look. "First of all, he's running from his reaction to you and the fear that it will make you turn him away. Second, what's the one thing in life that matters most to Jazz besides Dee?"

Mase scoffed. "His job."

"There's one thing about Kyiv that I didn't tell you. At first it was because I thought the order came from Jazz's handler and the chain of command. Jazz risked everything for you the day Kozak's men took Bray."

"What? How?"

Sam looked around. They were still standing by the elevator since neither of them had pressed the call button. But no one came onto the third floor unless they were looking for Max. Sam scrubbed his hands over his face.

"When I found out Bray was gone, we were headed back to Kozak's compound. I was ready to tear the place apart. I let Jazz know what had happened. I asked him what to do if your cover was blown. He told me to get you out by 'any means necessary'. If things had gone differently, if we'd had to shoot our way out of there, Jazz would have lost his job and his reputation. And we won't even mention the few bits and pieces that slipped past his lips when he was drugged."

Mase rolled his eyes. Poor Jazz was never going to hear the end of that.

"You might charge in like the savage that you are, but Jazz works behind the scenes. That's why he's one of the best covert operators. And maybe, just maybe, he thinks that when he walks away, he's protecting you then as well."

Chapter Forty-Four

Jazz

He had the world's worst timing. He and Ghost sped away from Marty's house, trusting that Max would work his magic and delete everything, since he'd obviously been tracking Jazz.

When his phone rang, he pulled it out immediately. He thought it might be Mase calling to read him the riot act. Mase had shown up to watch his back. Even though Jazz had freaked out, even though he'd walked away, Mase had still come.

They needed to talk. Mase had proved over and over again how much he cared for Jazz. It was time Mase knew how much Jazz cared as well. And the first thing he needed to do was to take Mase's word at face value. He needed to tell Mase everything.

Only the call wasn't from Mase. It was from his handler. After answering and going through security protocols, Jazz advised his handler that he wasn't alone in the car but was with a trusted associate of HC.

"We have your private jet ready to go. We need you at the Richmond airport in the next two hours."

It would take almost that long to get back to Richmond.

"I might need a little more time. I'm heading back to Richmond from DC."

"You have two hours, Jazz. We have a flight plan. Call back when you're alone."

So much for a heart-to-heart with Mase. Ann, his handler, wanted him to confront René and get as much info from him as he could before agreeing to anything. Things were heating up.

His gut told him this was going to be a sketchy situation. Maybe Mase being pissed at him was a good thing, just in case he didn't come home this time.

"I'm on a flight back to Europe tonight."

"I heard," Ghost said.

"Will you keep watching *Mémère* until we figure out what Coleman's going to do after our visit?"

"This is the most boring job I've had since leaving the military."

"I know, and I hope it stays that way."

"At least I can do a lot of reading."

"Think of it as a paid vacation."

Ghost snorted. "Except I'm not getting paid. I turned down a paying gig to be here."

Jazz rolled his eyes. He knew how much Ghost got paid per 'gig', and it was plenty.

"It's paid. I may not be able to offer you millions like some of your other clients, but I'll pay you for your time."

"It's a favor, remember?"

"It can be a paid favor," Jazz said.

"Nope." Ghost popped the P. "I'm going to sit my ass outside HC until you're sure your Dee's safe. Then you're going to owe me one, big time."

Jazz sighed. "You might think calling in a favor with me would be great, but I really don't have that much pull with the government."

"It's not the government I'm after. This wasn't the first time I've seen how your boys come together at HC. You didn't even call for backup, and they were there. They must have lit out of there as soon as we got to DC."

"I should have known they'd track me somehow." Jazz hadn't been as careful. Maybe subconsciously that was what he'd wanted.

"I may not be a joiner, but if I ever need someone at my back..."

Jazz smiled. "We'd be there, even if I didn't owe you a favor. That's what friends are for."

"Yeah, well, I don't have many friends, and I don't trust just anyone to have my back."

Jazz knew how that felt all too well. He wondered if Ghost liked it better that way. Jazz sure didn't, even though he seemed to do everything in his power to make sure it stayed that way.

"You're going to run again, aren't you?"

The question caught Jazz off guard. It was Mase's question asked in Ghost's voice.

"What d'you mean?"

Ghost flicked a look at Jazz before returning his gaze to the road. "In general, I'd say you're a tenacious guy, Jazz, and smart, very smart. But there's this one tender spot you have. It's also a blind spot."

Mase.

"Army Ranger, Delta Force, picked up by the Company." Ghost shook his head. "Not much you can be afraid of when you face death all the time. Then again, maybe it's the living you're afraid of."

He couldn't very well deny that it was fear that drove him away from Mase.

"You have to stop doing this to yourself, Jazz."

"Don't you mean to Mase?"

"No. I might not have been in your division, but we knew each other. I've watched you cut yourself into pieces about a dozen times over the years."

Jazz sighed. "Usually you're more original than this. You're not even the first person today who's been on my case about it."

"Yeah, but I know you better than everyone. Well…almost everyone. You're not going to move on until you make up your mind one way or the other. Because every time you cut yourself off from everyone who cares about you because of Mase, you make a new cut over an old scar."

"I give him space when I realize I can't… I just can't."

"No," Ghost said. "You forget I know the same people you know. When you walk away, you cut off your friends, too."

"Mase's friends," Jazz corrected without thought. If he were talking to anyone else, he might try to backpedal, but this was Ghost. "They were Mase's friends first. And if I'm the one backing away, he should be the one who gets the support."

"Bullshit. They're grown-ass men who are mature enough to support two friends who want different things."

That was the problem. Jazz didn't want different things. He just couldn't get out of his own head.

As if he'd read Jazz's mind, Ghost said, "Or maybe it's that you don't want them to remind you that you want exactly what Mase does — and that you deserve it, too."

"I'm not running this time. I'm going to talk to him."

"From Europe?"

"If I have to."

"Good."

As soon as Jazz got to the airport, he called Wade to let him know he was heading out. He'd have to meet Sam in France since his handler had his plane scheduled to touch down in Greece so he could check up on the newest part of his operation.

He suppressed the urge to call Mase and tell him that he was going. Wade and Sam would let him know. And if, when they were back in the same room, he would give Jazz another chance, Jazz would tell him about the therapist. He'd invite him to an appointment to see if they could make things work. No more running.

Jazz had just boarded his flight when his phone rang. His heart skipped for just a moment as his mind turned once again to Mase. When he pulled his smartphone out of his pocket and saw that it was René, his shoulders sagged as he answered the call.

"I'm on the plane," Jazz said.

"Oh, good. We have an issue. Vladyslav Bagan wants to meet with you and Kozak."

"Bagan? Where did you get that information from?"

There was a slight hesitation. "Kozak."

"I've had one of his men on my ass since I've been in the States. Why is this coming through you?"

"I'm not sure."

"Bullshit. You and I are going to have a long talk when I get back to Paris."

"Yes, sir. Will you be here tomorrow?"

Jazz didn't like how René was trying to nail him down. "No. I'm going to check up on a few points of the operation before I get back to Paris. When is this meeting supposed to happen?"

Another little hesitation. "Bagan's been asking to meet for a while now. I've been pushing it off since you were out of the country, but I think he and Clement are taking advantage of the fact that you're not here."

First it was Kozak requesting, now it was Bagan?

"But you're there, René. You were so sure you could handle business in France while I was out of town. It sounds like that's not the case. I also wonder why you haven't mentioned this request from Bagan until now."

"I can run things. I have been running things."

"And yet you keep calling me with issues, keep telling me to come back home. And not once in all those calls did you mention Bagan, only that you didn't trust Clement."

Jazz could hear the click of René's tongue over the phone. It was one of his tells, dry mouth. "Clement and Bagan are working together."

"Yes, I know. Why haven't you been investigating that further?"

"I have."

"Good. I'll expect a full and thorough report when we're face to face. I'd like you to check on the operation in Greece. That's our biggest priority right now."

"Yes, of course, Lucien."

Jazz disconnected the call before René was even finished saying his name. That was one of the reasons

Jazz had promoted René above the others whose loyalty he questioned. René thought he was tough. He wasn't. He was just smart enough to get himself into trouble, and he loved himself a little too much to let himself be used as a scapegoat.

When he landed in Greece, Jazz met with the two men who were handling the operation, Alain and Emile. They were the two men he trusted most — or at least that Lucien Bernard trusted most. They were simply in it for the money, not the power. People who were there for the money simply wanted a piece of the pie. Give them a big enough piece, give them motivation to keep things growing and they would give you their loyalty.

Jazz kept his word. For most of his men, that was enough. René wanted more. He wanted the power, the control, the recognition — at least within certain groups.

"René said you told him to come look over our shoulders," Alain said.

"No. I told him to come check on the operation because I need to talk to him without giving him a head's up."

Alain nodded. He was a big, burly man who was a quiet, straight forward enforcer. He'd been Lucien Bernard's bodyguard for a while until he'd been promoted when the Greece operation took hold.

"Is that why you're here without giving *us* a head's up?" Emile asked.

"I don't like people to know where I am or what I'm doing. I put you two in charge of this new area because I trust you. That's all you need to know. Don't break my trust."

"René will be here tomorrow," Alain said.

"Good." That worked out perfectly for Jazz. "Don't tell him I'm here."

* * * *

Jazz was working in the office he used while he was in Greece. He'd spoken with his handler about his concerns but had been advised to go forward with the meeting with Bagan. He hoped they weren't planning to use him as bait for something. He could never tell where loyalties swayed, even with other operatives that were on the same team.

It was mid-afternoon before René burst into the office as if he owned the place. He froze when he saw Jazz sitting at the desk.

"Lucien."

"René."

"I didn't expect you to be here, or I would have knocked. You wanted me to come check up on Greece?"

"Yes. I wanted a chance to speak with you." Jazz gave him a smile that was in no way warm or welcoming.

"Of course."

"Sit down, René."

As soon as René was seated across from Jazz, he began to sweat.

"Do you know why you're here, René?"

"Because you asked me to be."

"You've been having a lot of conversations with Vladyslav Bagan."

Jazz felt a surge of both anger and satisfaction when a look of fear flashed in René's eyes before he schooled his expression into confusion.

"What do you mean?"

"Oh, don't be coy, René. Do you think I don't watch my own operation, my own men? I would have been willing to promote you in time if you'd proven your loyalty."

"I am loyal to you. I have been. And yet you put Alain and Emile in charge of the 'highest priority' and left me in Paris."

"I left you in Paris to be in charge in my absence, but let's not forget you had begun discussions with Bagan long before Greece was up and running."

"That's not true."

Jazz gripped the gun he'd set next to his keyboard on the small pull-out shelf of his desk. He held up his weapon, making René blanch.

"Lucien."

"I need the truth, René."

Even from across the desk, Jazz could see beads of sweat pop out along René's hairline.

"You never trusted me, Lucien."

"I never trust anyone, not until they've proven I can. Do you think I don't have eyes on this operation as well?"

"I thought I was your eyes on the operation."

Jazz shook his head as he slid his finger onto the trigger. He didn't technically have authority to kill men randomly, though the CIA would look the other way if he could convince them it was self-defense.

He'd killed men, men who thought they worked for Lucien Bernard, but it had all been planned. It was laid out like a chess game to either make him look tough, push toward his ultimate goal or just move pieces around to give himself a better chance of winning the game in the end.

"Start from the beginning. Did you reach out to Bagan, or did he reach out to you?"

René licked his lips. Both of his hands gripped the armrests of his chair. "He contacted me. He'd been injured in an attack on his home, and he was sure it was you who'd done it."

Jazz held back a snort. It had been Sam who'd taken the shot, but it had been directed at Ruslan Andreiko, Kozak's former business partner. Jazz had given the go-ahead, but only because his handler had told him it was approved.

"But you've been working for me for years. You know that I didn't call a hit on Bagan. If I had, he'd be dead."

"He's not going to believe anything I tell him."

"He might have if you hadn't agreed with him to betray me."

"I didn't."

Jazz laughed.

"He said that you could keep France. He wants Greece."

"Of course he does. All the poverty, all the refugees... So what you're telling me is that *you* want Greece. I didn't give it to you, so you made a deal with Bagan to take it from me. You realize he has no intention of handing it over to you or letting you live. As soon as you've served your purpose, he'll kill you."

René shook his head. "I know your organization in and out. I'm as valuable to him as I am to you."

"This is how valuable you are to me, René."

Jazz shot him in the shoulder. René gasped, groaned and slumped down in his chair. Alain burst through the door, his gun drawn. When he realized what was going on, he smirked at René.

With a shake of his head, Alain backed out of the room, muttering French curse words before quietly saying "*Trou du cul*," and shutting the door.

Jazz couldn't agree more. René was an asshole. René writhed and groaned, rolling from side to side in his chair.

"Now," Jazz said, "I want the full story. Don't leave anything out, and I'll know if you do. You're a horrible liar, René. It's no wonder you're shit at poker."

Chapter Forty-Five

Mase

"I'm not any happier about it than you are," Sam said.

"I knew he was pissed. I knew he would run, but going back to Europe with no one on his six—"

"Don't act like he doesn't do that all the time," Sam said.

"Not to mention you're doing the same thing when you step on that plane," Ax said.

"I don't have anyone gunning for me specifically, not with all this stuff converging. Both Lucien Bernard and Jazz Thibodeaux have people after them."

"Mase, I can see that look in your eyes. You head to Ukraine, and the rest of us will head to France and watch Jazz's back."

"I need to talk to him. Last night you were all 'go talk to Jazz before it's too late'."

Jett and Ax laughed at Mase's impression of Sam.

"I still think you need to talk, but taking more risks with this op isn't the answer."

"I'll just have Max build it into my flight like a regular layover."

Sam snorted. "I don't think many people want to fly almost to their destination, only to backtrack."

"I don't know," Jett said. "I'm sure people don't want to, but airlines'll do crazy shit to save money and fuel."

Sam grumbled about traitors. "You better clear it with Wade and you better damn well tell him I'm against it. He'll want to talk to the higher ups and—"

"Fine," Mase conceded.

He might not be employed by the government anymore, but he technically still worked for them. If he ruined a multi-year deep-cover op because he couldn't wait a few weeks—or months—to talk face to face with Jazz, all the sacrifices he made might be for nothing.

When they parted ways at the airport, Mase couldn't help but feel that he'd made a mistake. He still felt that way more than forty-eight hours later when he finally strolled back into the secure compound where he'd spent most of his time the past three years in Kyiv.

He'd spent even more time there since he'd taken over all operations in Ukraine. It was like living in a goldfish bowl. No one really trusted anyone, and everyone watched what everyone else was doing.

Mase had been careful. He only had a few secrets formed in Ukraine, and they all involved helping queer people emigrate to the US. He refused to use slurs to fit in with the other guys, but he didn't contradict them, so Kozak's men thought he agreed with their views.

Most of the men were ignorant and naïve enough to think that the majority of people agreed with them.

They thought his restraint was what had him rising so fast in the ranks. He knew it was more than that.

Knowledge was power, and Mase had some knowledge about Kozak that few in the world did. So, as Kozak had ascended the ranks, he pulled Mase along with him — partly because of the intel Mase had, partly because Mase hadn't used that information, so Kozak trusted him.

He was at his desk, looking over logistics and trying to figure out whose hands to grease to get a shipment out of the Black Sea through Istanbul when he heard shouting. He only paused a moment because Kozak's men fought about everything from sports to women.

Then a shot rang out and another. Mase pulled his firearm from the holster at the base of his spine. He clicked a few buttons that turned his computer monitor into a mosaic of security footage. Every screen showed chaos.

Men were in hand-to-hand combat with the random flash of gunfire. There was so much movement that Mase could hardly recognize anyone. But there were way too many people. They were under attack.

Mase unlocked a secret drawer in the desk and stuffed all the contents into his pockets. After Kozak had been shot and almost killed, he'd had a panic room installed.

That was before he'd been promoted and moved to Spain. Still, Mase was glad he'd done it. He moved around his desk. *More shots.* The floor shook with the reverberating pound of heavy footfalls.

Mase silently opened his office door so that anyone who searched that room would think he'd left. He heard a familiar voice, a voice he hadn't heard in almost a year, not since Bray had showed up at that very compound, risking his life to look for Mase.

Sergiy.

Kozak had cut him loose after he'd had a few of the guys pick Bray up and bring him to the compound against Kozak's orders. They'd found out too late that Sergiy had been acting under orders from Kozak's partner at the time, Ruslan Andreiko.

Since Andreiko had betrayed Kozak in favor of working with their rival, Vladislav Bagan, it made sense that was where Sergiy had landed, even though Andreiko was dead.

Mase was punching in the code to open the panic room when someone stepped into the office. He swung around, raising his weapon, but it was too late. Heat blazed through his left side, but he still aimed his gun at Sergiy and pulled the trigger. Sergiy sunk to the ground, blood pouring from his stomach wound.

"Should I open all your old wounds?" Mase asked.

"Is that why you didn't aim for my heart?"

Mase had aimed for his heart, but he'd pulled the trigger while his body was still off center from being shot.

"So Bagan's making his move? Finally finishing what Andreiko couldn't?"

"Fuck Andreiko. This is bigger than all of you. Bagan's taking over all of Europe. Kozak's American friends are helping Bagan now because they want to deal with Clement and Bagan. Bernard and his gay watchdog just got blown up, along with Kozak. I'm just here to clean up the rest of you riff-raff."

Mase's knees gave out.

Jazz.

Fuck. Sam, Ax, Mitch and Jett were with him.

His hand reflexively jerked, pulling the trigger and shooting Sergiy in the face. He knew Bagan was gunning for a meeting, but blown up?

Mase's stomach roiled. His heart pounded. Beads of sweat popped out along his hairline as he swallowed to keep from retching. Gunfire reminded him that he had to move.

He turned away from Sergiy's body and moved into the closet just in time. He punched in the code a second time, this time with trembling fingers. He slipped through the narrow door into the panic room, closing it behind him without a sound.

The first thing he did was turn on the computer and pull up all the security feed. Then he took the burner phone from his pocket and started typing. The room was supposed to be soundproof, but he was taking no chances while he was so outnumbered.

There was only one phone number programmed into the phone and Max set it up so that it would be relayed through many different countries before reaching his computer.

10-33 Mayday. I'm injured. Woody and team are in danger. Did the meeting go through?

He tapped his fingers impatiently in a quick tattoo on the tiny desk. Woody, Jazz, Jasper...even Lucien. All Jazz's names ran through his head in a loop as he begged the universe not to let anything happen to him.

Would he feel it? If Jazz died, would his heart shatter like it did every time he thought Jazz was gone for good?

While he waited for a reply, Mase opened the small emergency first-aid kit he'd taken from the drawer in his office. He pulled out the two packets of combat gauze that was covered with a coagulant. He ripped one package open with his teeth.

The long-folded strip stretched out like an accordion. Mase pressed it against his wound and hissed when it stung like a motherfucker. It wouldn't help any internal bleeding, but clotting what he could would help keep more blood inside him, which he figured was the goal. His phone buzzed as he reached for the second packet.

What's your status?

Are we secure? Mase asked in response.

Anonymous but not secure.

Bullet wound to the abdomen. Completely surrounded. Was advised they're blowing up our whole team. Coordinated multi-sight hits. Explosion for other operators. Get them out. Now.

Checking on status of team. Stand by.

Mase watched as men gunned each other down. He put on headphones and plugged them into the computer, clicking on random cameras to try to hear what was being said.

It was madness. He wasn't sure how the men could tell each other apart. He also wasn't sure he'd last in there if they exploded the building. Was that their plan? The walls had been reinforced with steel to protect against bullets, but depending on how close to him a bomb went off, it might break through.

He had to count on the fact that no one except him, Kozak and the construction team he'd brought in, knew about the panic room. All the other men simply thought that Kozak didn't want to work in the office where he'd been shot, so he'd changed buildings—but only once construction on the panic room had been completed.

That was why Sergiy had had such a hard time finding him. It was probably what saved his ass. When he felt the desk vibrate as his phone buzzed, Mase silenced the video feed and picked up the burner. What he read knocked the wind out of him.

Unable to communicate with other team. Tapping into surveillance at your location. Requesting backup. Stand by.

Mase huffed out a breath. There was no backup. He'd known that from day one. He was alone. He found himself happy that Jazz wasn't.

"Jazz," he whispered.

Chapter Forty-Six

Jazz

"He only said it was a trap. They didn't tell him how they were planning on killing us. That would have been stupid of them to give him all the details."

Sam gave a disgusted snort. "They were stupid not to realize you're a paranoid motherfucker and that you'd latch on to the fact that there was a traitor in your midst. You said he's a bad liar."

"I've known his tells for a long time, but René didn't know he had telegraphed his dishonesty so well. Bagan and his people haven't known him long enough to see it. René has illusions of grandeur. He probably just bragged, and they believed him. Bagan got Andreiko to turn on Kozak, and they were true partners. Why wouldn't he believe he could turn a man who considered himself my right hand?"

"I don't like how remote this is," Mitch said.

Ax maneuvered the SUV around a big curve in the road. Jazz didn't like it, either. He'd agreed to the meeting last minute, so there would be very little time to plan. He'd refused to meet at their first choice of location, which had also been fairly remote.

"You said this is Kozak's place?"

"One of them," Sam said.

They'd landed in Malaga and taken a helicopter to Algeciras. They were driving along a coastal road, the navigation system telling them they were only a dozen kilometers away.

They didn't have a firm plan because they had no idea what they were facing. Sam, Ax and Mitch had been to the house once before with Bray in tow just over six months before, so they knew the lay of the land somewhat.

About two kilometers out, they dropped Jett off. He pulled the case containing his long-range rifle out of the back, closed the hatch and gave the car two pats.

Ax didn't pull away immediately. They watched Jett move off into the high grass and weeds that swayed in the ocean breeze. Jett's call sign was Hawkeye. He was a precision shot at almost any distance. The army had been sad to see a natural born sniper like Jett go. He was happy to laugh and flirt when he was with people, but the man could also lie perfectly still for hours on end if needed.

Soon Jett disappeared over the crest of a hill.

"Jett, do you copy?" Mitch asked into his ear comm.

"Copy that."

Jett's voice was staticky, but still there. Max had been trying to improve their comm systems range, but he'd only been able to increase it from approximately four-hundred feet to about six hundred.

That would probably be enough to keep track of Jett, especially since cell reception was almost nonexistent in certain areas. Jazz pulled his satellite phone out of his briefcase and sent an encrypted text to Wade with their timetable.

Bagan, Clement and Kozak were the targets. Jazz's handler had approved their deaths. Jett knew it was shoot to kill if he saw the opportunity.

After about five minutes, Ax started driving again. As they made their way to Kozak's beach home, Mitch kept trying to signal Jett. When they approached the long driveway, Jett came crackling back over the comms.

"Lots of activity. The front of the house is calm as a duck on the surface, but there's frantic paddling under the water."

"Do you have a line of sight on either target?" Mitch asked.

"Yes. Tango Bravo. You give the word."

Bagan.

"Don't do anything until you have eyes on all three."

Ax turned. The car crunched over the dirt driveway. When they crested a low hill, a small villa came into view. The building was stark white with a red clay roof. Behind it was a breathtaking view of the Strait of Gibraltar.

"Hang fire," Jett said.

Ax slowed down around a small curve in the driveway, but didn't fully stop because that would signal they knew what was going on. The windows were already open, letting in the sea breeze and letting them listen to what was happening around them. It wasn't as if a window was going to protect them from a bullet, anyway. The broken glass just made the situation worse.

"There's a tense situation inside the house."

"Between who?"

"Standby," Jett said. "Tango Bravo and Tango Kilo."

"Any sign of Tango Charlie?" Mitch asked.

"No sign."

"Roger that."

"What's the next move here?" Ax asked.

"Keep inching forward," Jazz said.

As they pulled up onto the paved driveway behind a line of SUVs similar to theirs, Jett started swearing.

"Something's wrong. Guns are out."

Mitch, who was in the front passenger seat, had his gun out and aimed toward the house before Jazz could even register Jett's words. There was a reason his call sign was Flash. They all sunk low in their seats.

"Get down." Ax pressed the accelerator, jerking the car forward before spinning it around so that he and Jazz were facing the house. That way, Mitch could crawl out and cover the rest of them as they did the same.

Mitch opened his door, set one foot on the ground, and took aim over Ax's lowered head. "What's my approval here?" he asked.

"Targets are first priority," Jazz said, "but so is our safety. Jett, do you have a visual?"

"Negative," Jett said.

"Fuck," Jazz grumbled as he pulled out his weapon, slid out of the door, then took aim as well.

The front door flew open. In his peripheral vision, Jazz watched Mitch tick his gun from target to target, assessing danger while looking for the highest priority kill.

Kozak burst from his house, surrounded by three of his men. He was running away, so he must have figured out he was on the hit list, too. He was down the path heading to another car when he spotted them.

"Sam," he called out, then violently shook his head from left to right while waving his arms. "Go!"

That had them all confused. He was warning them? That little stunt probably saved Kozak's life because it made his head a moving target for Mitch and Jett.

A half dozen of Bagan's men flooded from the front door, their guns drawn. But they didn't assess the threat. They just started shooting.

The SUV shook as bullets pierced the car near the engine. Kozak's right shoulder jerked forward, a crimson stain spreading over his shirt as he fell to the ground.

Bagan stepped from the house, flanked by two men. All three had their guns drawn. Bagan didn't make it three steps before he dropped like a stone. More men filed out behind him, but they paused when they realized their boss was dead.

"Tango Bravo hit confirmed." Jett's voice came through the earpiece. "Still no visual on Tango Charlie."

Then something burning hot grazed Jazz's cheek.

"Open fire," Jazz said

Jazz only got a few shots off before there were more than a dozen bodies crumpled on the stone path and paved driveway in front of the villa.

"I see two men still inside," Jett said. Glass shattered in the distance. "Correction. One tango remaining."

"Try to get him alive," Jazz said. "We'll see what intel he has."

They moved as a unit, two aimed front, two watching behind them. It was as if they'd never left the army. They crouched and moved through the house.

"He's running out the back," Jett said. "Do you want me to stop him?"

"Without killing him," Jazz said.

That's when they saw a man running past the infinity pool. On the next step, his leg slipped from under him. He fell and gripped his calf.

Sam and Jazz went to talk to Bagan's man while Mitch and Ax cleared the rest of the house.

Jazz didn't speak much Ukrainian, so when Sam snorted at the words flowing from the man, he figured it was mostly slang, probably swear words.

Sam hoisted the man over his shoulder in a fireman's hold, and they all moved back into the house.

"We need to check the car situation," Sam said.

"Jazz, you got something on your face," Ax pretended to wipe food off his face as he came out of the back door.

Jazz rolled his eyes. His cheek stung where the bullet had grazed him, but he didn't have time to deal with that now.

"House is clear," Mitch said.

"If Clement and his men are on their way, the last thing we need is another shootout. And if they see bodies out here, they'll either come in with guns blazing or turn tail and run."

"Clement," the Ukrainian man spat. Then he was off in Ukrainian again, but most of it Jazz understood.

Clement didn't like to get his hands dirty, so no one was too surprised to hear that he'd refused to attend the meeting, opting instead to pretend he'd be there and let Bagan handle the rest. Apparently, Bagan had been pissed. He'd wanted Clement out of the deal all together, but his American contacts held firm that

Clement would be over the Mediterranean, everything from Portugal to Bulgaria.

Mitch went out of the front door first, his gun aimed down at any of the men who might still be alive. Sam followed with their lone survivor, followed by Jazz and Ax.

The man was muttering about what he called stupid names. He listed a few names Mase had mentioned, Dark Horse, Dion, something that sounded like Rife.

They walked toward the car with Jazz and Ax walking sideways, facing the house, when there was a quiet groan. They lowered their gun's muzzles toward the bodies on the ground, assessing any threat.

"Sam?"

One of the bodies jolted. That's when they realized that one of Kozak's men had fallen on him. Kozak was trying to get free. Jazz and Ax moved the body. Kozak was face down, trying to push himself up with his good arm while the other one lay in a pool of his own blood.

The *rrr-rrr-rrr* of a car trying to turn over had Ax turning toward their SUV.

"This car isn't going to start," Mitch said.

"If you take me with you, you can take any of my cars," Kozak said.

"Looks like I'm savin' your ass again, Kozak," Sam said. "But you're the reason we're here, so this is the last time."

"I'm done," Kozak said. "I want you to sneak me into America. I won't be shot one more time."

Sam looked over his shoulder at Jazz with raised eyebrows. Jazz shrugged. He'd ask, though he might get shut down.

"I guess he did try to warn us," Jazz said.

"Yes. I remember how you saved me," Kozak told Sam. "They were going to get rid of all of us. Bagan let it slip when he found out Clement wasn't coming, which was right before you drove up."

"Seems like we still have one loose end," Ax said.

"If we blow this place up, we can pretend Kozak died," Mitch suggested.

The man Sam was carrying started talking a mile a minute. Jazz and Mitch looked at each other, but Ax started to chuckle.

"Looks like Bagan and his band of assholes did the heavy lifting," Sam said. "That's what they were doing in the back, rigging this place to explode, and Bohdan here can help us set it off if we get him to the US, too."

Jazz huffed out a breath. "I'm not making any promises. I'll have to contact my handler. We'll need two cars unless Kozak has an SUV that can seat seven. Ax, get the code to the garage from Kozak, then check it out to see what we're working with. Mitch, you're good with demolition. Take this guy with you and check out the back of the house to see how easy it will be to detonate. Sam, let's get these bodies in the house. Jett, start making your way down to us."

Even though they weren't in the military anymore, it was easy for them to fall in line. Not only was Jazz's cover to be the number one, he was also the highest ranking officer among them.

He and Sam lugged body after body into the house. He lost count after fifteen. If the explosion was big enough and with that many bodies, the police would have a hard time identifying everyone. It might be the perfect opportunity to claim Kozak and Bohdan had been killed and sneak them into the States.

Jazz would see what his handler could do. Neither man would have the lifestyle or cash flow to which they'd become accustomed. The US government would also keep a close eye on them for the first five years or ten years to make sure they didn't do anything illegal, but if they really wanted a clean slate, this was their chance.

"We've got a group of SUVs approaching," Jett said through the comm. "Not sure if they're going to turn up the driveway, but how common is that on this little coastal road?"

Sam and Jazz looked at each other.

"Ax, any of the cars in Kozak's garage look like the three Bagan brought?"

"Yeah, one, but wouldn't it look better if we had two? More like Bagan's lighting out of here before the house explodes?"

"My thoughts exactly. Mitch, what's the situation?"

"Found the detonator in the hands of Jett's last kill."

"You didn't happen to find any car keys on him, did ya?" Ax Asked.

"Nope, but a few of these guys must have some."

After backing an SUV out of the garage, Ax tossed a key fob to Jazz, who caught it mid-air. Then Ax trotted inside to find another key.

"This thing has a timer, which makes sense, since Bagan hadn't been planning to die. I'll set it for three minutes. Can someone come get Bohdan in the car? Let me know when you guys are loaded up. Just leave a door open for me."

"Jett. Get your ass down here. Let's GTFO," Sam said.

"On it, boss. The SUV caravan has stopped on the side of the road."

"Guess we know who it is," Ax said as he stepped out of the house with one arm supporting Bohdan and the other holding a key fob up for everyone to see. He clicked a button on it and one of Bagan's SUVs beeped as the lights flashed.

Ax put Bohdan in the back seat before getting into the driver's seat. Sam went to the second vehicle and put Kozak in the back seat before climbing into the front passenger seat next to Ax.

Jazz's instinct was to get into the driver's seat of the second car, but after he took his satellite phone from their SUV, he got in the back seat with Bohdan.

"Don't leave without me," Jett said as he trotted up.

Ax leaned out of his window and pointed at Jazz, "Key's in the car. Let's head out."

After storing his gun bag in the back seat, Jett climbed into the driver's seat. Jazz handed up the key and Jett started the engine.

"Jett, you start heading toward the exit. We'll leave a door open for Mitch."

Jett pulled away without argument. Behind them, Ax turned his car around and popped the back door open.

"Okay, Mitch," Jazz said. "It's go time."

"Roger that."

Jazz turned to look out of the back window. Less than ten seconds later, Mitch came running out of the house and jumped into the back seat. Before his door was even closed, Ax was pulling away, catching up with Jett.

"All right, Flash," Sam's voice came over the comm from the other car as he teased Mitch. "You see the target, you shoot."

"If you see a muzzle, you shoot," Jazz corrected. "We're not taking any chances today. Jett, let Ax pass you so they can take the lead."

"Roger that," Mitch said as Jett pulled onto the weeds beside the groomed dirt path.

Ax gave them a salute as he passed.

"We've got two minutes," Mitch said. "But we're already far enough away that the worst that will happen is our windows break, so keep yours down."

They turned onto the road, heading back the way they came, toward Algeciras and in the direction that would have them crossing paths with Clement.

Jazz pulled out both his phones. He used his satellite phone to send a coded, encrypted message to his handler.

"Fuck," Sam said. "Jazz, we're getting a text from home. Savage is injured. He knows about the bomb. He's under fire. All the messages must have come through when we passed through a spot with reception. I have eight texts."

Jazz pulled out his phone. He had eight as well, mostly asking if they need backup, not that there was really any available, not unless the CIA had agents close by that they were willing to deploy.

Jazz already knew they wouldn't be willing to do that, not for a group of five operators, but they might be willing to send someone to help Mase.

Up ahead, they saw the two large SUVs pulled over onto the side of the road. As they got closer, the windows rolled down.

"Get down," Jazz told Bohdan as he shot off text after text to both his handlers and anyone he knew who might have sway.

He'd walked away. He'd walked away from Mase in HC, and if Mase died, it would have been the last real interaction between them. Mase would die knowing Jazz had chosen his fear over Mase.

Maybe his therapist could help him, maybe she couldn't—maybe Mase would stay regardless of Jazz's progress, maybe he wouldn't. But Jazz's fear had held him back from even taking the chance.

They had something that was working, but Jazz had pushed himself too hard and fucked it up. Mase had been steadfast and true, always keeping to his word.

And it was the man in the SUV, along with Bagan, who'd given the order to wipe Mase out. Jazz did something he'd never done before. He let his personal feelings take over. He didn't wait until he saw the muzzle of a gun. He simply started shooting.

He leaned over Bohdan, who'd crouched down and shot out the windshield of the first vehicle. He knew Clement would be in the second car. One paid security to take the lead. But once he started shooting, so did Mitch.

Glass shattered.

Metal pinged as bullets tore through.

Return fire rocked the car on its wheels as they continued forward. Like two pirate ships crossing on the seas, they emptied their weapons.

Jazz released his empty clip, letting it thud to the floor of the vehicle. He quickly pulled one from the inside pocket of his suit and slotted it into his gun with a click just as they approached the second car.

Clement's SUV shook with both the velocity of the bullets and the men likely scrambling inside. But they were too late.

"Jazz," Sam shouted, but Jazz just kept shooting.

The driver of the second car tried to pull out, slamming against the driver's side and throwing Bohdan toward Jazz.

"Jazz!" Sam shouted again.

He didn't take a breath until the second clip was empty. He turned to watch the car veer off the road and tumble down the steep hill toward the ocean. If Clement was in that car, Jazz didn't hold out much hope he was alive.

It took Jazz a moment to realize that the car had stopped. Sam hopped out of the other vehicle along with Mitch, who aimed his weapon at the car still on the side of the road.

Sam wrenched Jazz's door open. "How many clips did you just empty?"

"Now's not the time," Jazz said as he picked his phone up off the floor of the car.

Boom.

They all turned in the direction they'd come from. Smoke already billowed up into the air. The shock wave hit next, rocking the car on its wheels much like the bullets had and jerking Jazz's hand, sending his satellite phone flying. He and Sam both turned to watch it bounce down the steep hill and land in the ocean.

"Fuck!" Jazz shouted.

"This car's clear," Mitch called out. "Do you want me to climb down and check the second?"

"No," Jazz said at the same time Sam said, "Yes."

"We don't have time," Jazz argued.

"We have all the time in the world to make sure Clement is dead."

"You can stay if you want, Sam, but I'm going to the heliport."

Sam yanked Jazz out of the car and slammed the door shut. He pulled him far enough down the path that Bohdan wouldn't be able to hear them, even with the windows open.

"Don't do this," Sam said through gritted teeth. "You'll ruin years of his work."

"If he's dead, it won't matter. None of this will matter." Jazz's throat burned. "I always made sure he had backup so this wouldn't happen."

Sam's brows furrowed. "He never had backup."

Jazz looked out over the ocean.

"Did you put someone else in Kozak's organization? Someone to back up Mase — because if you did, call him right fucking now."

"Not exactly."

Chapter Forty-Seven

Mase

His side still burned like a son of a bitch as he watched the chaos die down. Bagan's men had won. No one was beating down the walls to get to him, so Mase tried to stay calm. He unmuted the monitors, trying to listen for any intel on when they might clear out. He wasn't in any kind of shape for a physical fight.

"Where's the man in charge? Andrew Mason."

The words were spoken in English, words with a British accent. Mase narrowed his eyes as he scanned all the monitors. Then he found him, the man who knew his alias. He was about the same height as most of the other men. He wasn't bulky enough to be muscle, so he was likely the brains.

Then one of the men answered him, also with a British accent. "Sergiy said he knew right where he'd be, but that building was basically deserted. He went haywire, and I haven't seen him since."

"Sergiy's dead," another man answered, this time with a Ukrainian accent. "And Mase is gone."

"What do you mean, gone?"

"Unless he's one of these bodies. We'll have to check."

The man in charge seemed to expand by a few inches. "You guys promised me that you knew what you were doing. With Kozak dead, we need someone who knows this operation."

"Sergiy knows this operation."

"Yes, well, Sergiy's dead, as you so rightly put it. And now the man who was actually in charge may be dead as well. I need a list of contacts. I need to know how shipments move, where shipments move, dates, times, things Sergiy would be far removed from since he's been out of the loop for so long. Do you have that?"

"No," the Ukrainian said.

"Then find me the man who does, dead or alive. I need to know his status."

"Yes, Thor."

The hairs on Mase's arms stood straight up like little soldiers as a chill ran down his spine. Thor, the hammer. Not muscle like Mase had expected, but an enforcer, all the same.

Mase watched closely as the two Brits moved through the hallways. They stepped over bodies, looking at each face as they went, looking for Mase.

"Bagan's overconfident," Thor said, "in his ability and his importance."

"Well, we don't have to worry about him for much longer. Rig won't put up with his incompetence or his demands."

"No. He won't. He wants more territory, but we need someone to make a smooth transfer or it will take too much time to get up and running. We need this Mason character."

"And if he's dead?"

Thor fisted and unfisted his hands. "Then there will be hell to pay—and not just from me. I'm not going to get stuck cleaning up Bagan's mess."

Mase had a choice to make. Did he stay in the safety of his panic room, or did he trust that these men really did want him alive? He waited another forty minutes as they combed through all the bodies and started gathering the men they had left alive—mostly wounded—into one area of one building in the compound.

He wasn't sure what he was waiting for, and he kept checking his burner to see if he had any updates from HC. There was still no word from Jazz or any of the team.

Wade was trying to get boots on the ground, but the closest contact he had was in Warsaw, so it would take them time to get there. And it was two guys, so they couldn't exactly take on all of Bagan's men.

Any word from Woody? Mase texted for what felt like the millionth time.

No word.

Mase hung his head as he slumped in the chair. He was running out of energy. He needed medical attention. He couldn't stay in that room forever. His wound was too big to heal on its own. Once the decision was made, he dialed Wade and went through security protocol.

"Hotel charlie 146373 sierra alpha," Mase said quietly when the line picked up.

"Hotel Quebec 487432 lima alpha. The line is secure," Wade said.

"I'm going to take a calculated risk."

"What calculated risk?"

"They're looking for me. I'm still valuable to them. They want me alive."

"The fuck they do. If they did, you wouldn't be injured. What's your injury?"

"Bullet wound. Lower left quadrant of my abdomen. I sealed the wound, but I'm losing energy. There might be internal bleeding."

"Savage, I have men headed your way."

"They won't be here in time. And they won't be able to get past all Bagan's men. There's a man out there I've never seen before. He's using code name Thor. He's British. I'm going to send you screenshots. Find out who he is."

"Savage, I don't like this. I don't like this at all."

"Still no word on Woody?"

There was a long pause. "Is that what this is about? If he's gone, you're going to risk yourself?"

"I would have thought I'd feel it if he died. I mean, every time he walks away, there's that little spark of hope inside me that he'll come back, that we'll get another chance."

"He never wanted to leave in the first place. That man runs on fear like most people run on caffeine."

"Either way, I'm doing this because I think it's my best chance to survive. If he's gone, I won't rest until every motherfucker who killed him is dead, too. I'm going to go right up this chain of bottom feeders."

"Okay. Okay. Keep this phone on you. We'll track it so we know where you are."

"Roger that."

Mase disconnected the call. He stood, but his left leg gave out. He leaned heavily on his right side, dropping the phone and pressing his hand onto the desk to stay upright.

After a few deep breaths that made the pain in his side worse but seemed to help his legs stand firm, he picked up the phone and stuffed it in his back pocket. If they took it from him, there wouldn't be much he could do.

Mase took his weapon, just in case. He might not make it out of the compound, but if they were going to kill him, he'd take as many of those assholes down with him as he could.

Since his body was numb and on fire all at the same time, he wasn't able to be as quiet as he had been slipping into the panic room. As soon as he stumbled out, the closet door flew open and the British man was there, the one who wasn't Thor.

Mase lifted his gun and aimed it at the man. The man stepped back, his hands up. His eyes remained on the barrel of the gun because it was shaking.

"Are you Andrew Mason?" the man asked.

Everything started spinning. Mase dropped his gun as he fell to the floor. Pain exploded inside him, radiating from his side out to his limbs.

"Fuck!" he shouted. "That hurt."

"Thor!" the man called. "This must be him. This one's American."

Mase's vision clouded, and he was worried he was going to throw up from the pain.

"If you killed him..." Mase couldn't finish the sentence.

"Shit," Thor said. "He's been bleeding out this whole time. I will not be responsible for his death. We still need him alive. Lift him."

Chapter Forty-Eight

Jazz

"You have no reason to be there," his handler said.

"Then fire me."

"Jazz, you know it's not that simple."

"Sure it is. Bernard died in the fire just like Kozak, just like they planned."

"You're too good. They're not going to want to let you go."

"Are you saying I can't quit?"

"You can quit, but not in the middle of a deep-cover op. You know that. And no one's going to fire you. If they were going to do that, they would have done so after the stunt you pulled in Kyiv, which luckily didn't come to fruition."

"Then find a reason for me to be in Ukraine, because if you don't get me a flight plan, right now, I'm going to do it myself...or fly commercial."

She paused so long, he thought she might have hung up.

"Let me see what I can do."

Jazz tossed his phone onto the seat of the car. The plane was gassed up, ready to take him back to Paris. He needed to go a lot farther than that.

"This is crazy," Sam said.

"What would you do if it were Bray?"

Sam rolled his eyes. "I didn't say don't do it or that we don't have your back. I just said this is crazy. Especially..." Sam shook his head.

"After I left."

Jazz looked at his friends. They were waiting for help from the US Naval Base in Cadiz. Wade had worked his magic and gotten approval for the medical staff there to take a look at Kozak and Bohdan.

Jett would go with Jazz as a bodyguard because that was his current role. Sam, Ax and Mitch would stay with their new charges to see if approval came through to smuggle them into the US, most likely via a flight from the naval base. Ax got out of the car to stretch his legs and check on Mitch and Jett, who were looking after their charges, leaving only Sam and Jazz.

"I've been talking to Marjorie," Jazz said.

Sam tilted his head as he turned back to Jazz. "Why do I get the feeling she didn't tell you to do any of the things you did during your last forty-eight hours with Mase?"

"I might have taken things a little faster than she suggested."

"It works, Jazz. It's not a fast solution, but it works — at least it did for me. I'm still not where I hope to be. Maybe I never will be, but Bray and I make it work."

"Don't you think Mase deserves someone whole? Someone...normal?"

"Who's whole? Who's normal? Mase isn't. I'm not. Bray's not. We might be different levels of fucked up, but we're all fucked up, Jazz. You think Mase deserves someone whole. But do you know what I think Mase deserves?"

"What?"

"What he wants. And there's no one he wants but you. He needs you. If he deserves so much, then you should be the one to give it to him because your effort will prove your love more than anything else ever could. Even if you never have the sex life you think he deserves, he at least deserves your effort."

* * * *

A flight that would normally take about four and a half hours took about six by the time Jazz got approval for the flight plans. As soon as they touched down in Kyiv, he was on the phone with Max, who was tracking Mase by following the burner phone he'd used to contact HC.

"We could be walking into anything here," Jett said.

"Considering the phone's at a private hospital where expats prefer to go, there's a good chance it's exactly what it seems," Jazz said as he dialed HC. "What do you have for us?" He asked after going through security protocol.

"Andrew Mason was admitted to the hospital," Wade said. "We verified that, but we don't have any other updates."

"I'm working on it," Max said, letting Jazz know they were on speaker phone. "I hacked into their security system, but there are no cameras in the rooms. It's taking me a little longer because, well, I'm a little overloaded right now, to be honest. And Wade won't let me have any help."

"You told me when I hired you that you didn't need a team, that you *were* the team."

"That was before I saw what Blake could do."

"I don't trust him yet...not for this."

"He has higher security clearance than you do, just as high as mine."

"It's a question of where his loyalties lie and why exactly he brought all this intel to us."

"I already told you I checked him out. His dad's looking for him—and not in a good way."

"Can you two please focus and stop bickering like an old married couple?" Jett asked. "We need intel, not lovers' quarrels."

Jett and Jazz smirked at each other as they listened to complete silence for about ten seconds. Then the quiet pounding rhythm of Max's typing resumed, and a throat cleared, which sounded like Wade.

"Do we have a room number?"

"No," Max said. "I'm not even sure he's out of surgery."

Jazz's grip on the front seat of the car tightened along with his insides. Room number or not, plan or not, Jazz was getting in that hospital. He was taking Mase home.

When someone patted his hand, Jazz jolted and looked up at Jett. With a nod, Jett opened the door and got out of the car. "Looks like we're going in blind," he said.

"Not blind," Max said. "We have movement. The man that Mase identified as Thor is leaving the waiting room and being escorted down a hall on the third floor. Get up there and follow him."

Without even disconnecting the call, Jazz jumped out of the car and ran for the hospital. Jett caught up with him just in time to slip into the elevator before the door closed. He had Jazz's phone to his ear.

"Can you see a room number?" Jett asked.

After a moment, he looked at Jazz and shook his head. As the elevator doors opened, they both looked around. Jazz hurried down the hall and around the nurse's station, frantically looking for a nurse leading a man down the hall, but then he saw a familiar face standing outside a hospital room, speaking with a doctor.

"I'm going to fucking kill him," Jazz said as he strode toward Finn.

"Who? Mase? Jazz, what the fuck, man?" Jett whispered as he hurried to catch up. "No, I don't know what's going on," Jett whispered into the phone.

Just as Jazz approached, the doctor stepped into the room and Finn followed. Jazz caught the door before it closed.

The doctor immediately started squeaking in Ukrainian, telling Jazz to get out, but everything melted away from him when he saw Mase unconscious on the bed. There were tubes and monitors.

The room spun at the thought of losing Mase, at the realization that he might still lose him.

"What's his status?" Jazz demanded as he grabbed the doctor by the collar of his lab coat.

The doctor gave him a mutinous look as he slid Jazz's fingers free of his lapels. "Who are you?"

"It's all right," Finn said. "This gentleman is his fiercest protector."

The doctor looked back and forth between Jazz and Finn, then also looked at Jett.

"I'll be in the hall," Jett said as he silently stepped out and let the door close.

"He is stable," the doctor said. "He lost a lot of blood, but he's stable. There was no irreparable damage, but he will need time to heal, yes?"

Jazz nodded but paid little attention to the end of the statement. *Stable*, he repeated to himself. *No irreparable damage.*

"Thank you, Doctor," Finn said.

"This is very unusual," the doctor said, his voice getting farther and farther away.

And even though they were behind him, Jazz didn't turn around. He couldn't take his eyes off Mase. *What if, what if, what if...*

His mind was full of them — the 'what ifs'. What if Jazz's back was the last thing Mase saw before he died? What if he'd died never knowing how much Jazz loved him? What if they could have had something amazing, and Jazz was just too scared to try, too scared that one day Mase would be the one to walk away from him because it was all too much?

"Mase." It was barely a whisper, but as soon as the word was out, Mase stirred.

Jazz waited for his eyes to flutter open, but they didn't. He grumbled something, then settled back into sleep. Jazz pulled up a chair and got comfortable.

Chapter Forty-Nine

Mase

His brain felt like it had been scrambled. Had he drunk too much the night before? When he tried to move, something tugged on his arm. Was he bound?

"We need to talk."

That British accent seemed familiar. Mase kept his eyes closed and tried to keep his breathing relaxed.

"Is he waking up?" the voice asked.

"No, probably just having a dream. His heart rate goes up and down with his dreams."

Jazz. He'd know that voice anywhere.

"You didn't tell me I was being guardian angel over him because you were in love with him."

"And you didn't tell me your code name was Thor."

Thor. Flashes started coming back to Mase.

"There are a lot of things about my op I can't tell you."

"We're duplicating efforts here."

"No. We're on the same team, both trying to gather intel for our respective countries."

"Same team? Fuck you. You said you'd make sure they had no reason to kill Mase."

"He wasn't supposed to get shot. Bagan and his men are harder to control than your compatriots thought, and so are Clement and his men."

"Well, that will no longer be a problem."

"What are you talking about?"

"The hit. They got approval from the Americans who are backing them. Thanks for the heads-up."

"I didn't have a heads-up. I was told after the fact to come do a sweep of Kozak's men. Fuck. Jazz, things are moving too fast. They're spiraling out of control."

"Well then, maybe we should work more as a team, like you said. Then we stand a chance of all getting out of this alive. Because right now, you and yours will be dealing with chaos and a huge fallout from trying to kill Lucien Barnard," Jazz said.

"They're not mine," Thor growled.

That's when it all came tumbling back. Sitting in that tiny room, waiting for any word that Jazz wasn't dead. The clock ticking like it was trying to move through molasses.

Mase gasped, blinking his eyes open. His vision was blurry, but he saw the outline of Jazz standing over him and tried to sit up.

"Shh." Jazz pushed his shoulders back until he was lying on the bed.

"Jazz."

"I'm here."

Mase shook his head, worried it was a dream. Jazz cupped his cheeks, stilling him. He put his gorgeous face so close that it filled Mase's whole scope of vision.

"I'm here," he said again. "And I'm not walking away this time."

"Then this is definitely a dream."

A quiet laugh burst from Jazz. "I have some things I need to tell you."

"First, tell me where I am and how I got here. Then tell me how you know Thor over there."

Jazz looked over his shoulder, then Thor stepped up. Mase remembered him from the compound.

"You're at the hospital. *Thor* brought you. You were shot."

"Sergiy. That bastard shot me."

"Yes, well, luckily, he didn't do a very good job," Thor said. "And with that, I'll step outside and relieve your friend Jett so he can get some coffee."

As soon as the door clicked shut, Jazz pressed his mouth to Mase's. Before he could think better of it, Mase wrapped his arms around whatever part of Jazz he could reach. Jazz stiffened and pulled back.

"Not a dream then," Mase said.

"I'm not walking away."

"Yet."

"I deserve that."

Mase closed his eyes, because even if Jazz did deserve it, he regretted saying it. He never wanted to hurt Jazz, especially not in retaliation for something he couldn't control.

"That night, after visiting the Congressman, I was going to come back to HC. I was going to talk to you, to apologize, to tell you I was seeing a therapist, but—"

"Wait. You're seeing a therapist?"

"Yes, but I got too cocky. I shouldn't have unbound you. I wasn't ready for that kind of touch, not yet. Maybe not ever, at least, not on my neck."

"Your neck? I thought it was your whole back."

Jazz pushed a breath out of his nose. "It is my back, but mostly because—"

"I don't need to know what that asshole did to you."

"My neck is the worst. The back of my neck is the worst spot."

Mase closed his eyes as regret filled him to bursting.

"But I didn't tell you that. My therapist told me I needed to be specific with you, but I wasn't. Being able to have anything with you had me wanting more, wanting everything."

"Like I said, I'll never get enough of you."

"I realized that my biggest fear is that you'll walk away from me. I think we both know that when I walk away, I'll always come back. But if you walk away..." Jazz shook his head then let it hang as he looked down at the sheets of the hospital bed. "If you walk away, I know that will be it."

"You realize how crazy that is, right?" Mase dipped his head down until Jazz looked at him.

"Mase, you're my first everything—my first love, my first real kiss, the first man who made me come, the first man I wanted to touch. Not the first man who touched me, but—"

"I am," Mase said. "I am the first man who touched you. Whatever happened before was not touch. That was cruelty and power and selfishness. I'm the first man who ever touched you to make you feel good—and I still want to be the last."

As Jazz moved to lay his head on his chest, Mase watched tears track down his cheeks.

"I'll never leave you, Jazzy. Please stop leaving me."

Not wanting to ruin things by touching some off-limits part of Jazz, Mase reached up and caressed Jazz's ear. He rubbed his thumb back and forth over the velvety soft skin of his lobe.

"I won't leave, not anymore. I realized there would be something worse than you walking away. If you died —"

Jazz's own words were cut off by a sob. Mase pursed his lips, trying to hold back his own tears.

"I guess we both learned that lesson," he said as arched up from his pillow to kiss the top of Jazz's head. "I thought you were in that explosion. I know, Jazz. I knew before that. You're it for me. You're all I want."

After a few moments, Jazz's breathing settled. He lifted his head and looked Mase in the eye. "Will you go to the therapist with me? She wants to meet you."

"I thought you were going to propose just then."

Jazz pushed on Mase's shoulder.

Mase hissed as it sent a throbbing pain through his whole body.

"Sorry," Jazz soothed as he pulled back.

Mase grabbed his wrist. "Don't go."

"I told you. I'm not leaving you, not ever again."

"Guess you'll have to quit your job, then."

Jazz snorted. "I said I wasn't leaving you as your boyfriend. I still have to work."

"Boyfriend," Mase said. "I like the sound of that."

E p i l o g u e

Jazz
One year later

Every time Jazz thought he was fucking everything up, things just got better. Maybe not better, but they moved forward, moved toward his end goal.

Like going to Mase the last year when he'd been injured. He'd thought it might end his career or at least compromise his cover. It ended up working out. Finn told the people he was working with that Lucien Bernard wasn't as impenetrable as they'd thought. He told them that Lucien was gay, that Andrew Mason had become his lover during their time in the States together.

They had dirt on him, and they had been using that to control him — or so they thought. But their time was almost up, and so was Jazz's time with the CIA. Like Mase, deep-cover work was wearing on him. When this case was over, they would take a break. They'd work behind the scenes for a while.

And every time he got the urge to run, Jazz called Marjorie or Sam or Mase. Sometimes he called Mase from the bathroom or from his bedroom, because having that door and wall between them helped. He still had his own room with a deadbolt, but he and Mase were able to live together. That settled Mase more than probably anything else, knowing that Jazz would be there, even if he was behind lock and key.

But the time between urges grew. Mostly because over time — and with a lot of prompting from Marjorie — he realized that setbacks were a measure of growth. They were proof that he was moving forward, even if it was one step forward and two steps back sometimes.

Then there were rare nights like this one where they had no place to be and nothing to work on, so they curled up on the sofa and watched movies.

"My mouth is still on fire," Mase said as he laid his head in Jazz's lap. "Remind me to temper your heavy hand with spices the next time you cook. What are we watching?"

Jazz smiled. He ran his fingers through the silky strands of Mase's hair as the movie started. As soon as Mase saw the opening credits, he groaned.

"Why do I always regret it when it's your choice?"

"You know I have a thing for Matthew McConaughey." Jazz tugged at Mase's hair until Mase turned to look up at him. Jazz smiled down at him.

"If I stay here, I'll be able to feel exactly how much of a *thing* you have for Matthew McConaughey."

"Don't worry, baby," Jazz said. "It's because he reminds me a little of you."

"Really? I thought you said I looked more like Charlie Hunnam."

"Your nose is like Charlie's. Your smile is all Matthew. And your body is better than both put together."

Mase's smile grew. "And you look like a tawny-skinned Orlando Bloom."

"Is that why you love *Pirates of the Caribbean*?"

"Maybe."

Mase slid his hand up Jazz's chest. When the pad of his thumb flicked Jazz's nipple, Mase laughed. There was no way he didn't feel the effect he had. Things still weren't where Jazz hoped they'd someday be, but they weren't where they'd been a year ago, either.

Progress. Effort. Sam had been right about that. Mase appreciated his effort more than the forward motion of the relationship. Watching Jazz put the work in made Mase feel loved—and everything Mase did made Jazz feel loved.

"Maybe we should delay the movie," Jazz suggested.

"No way. I'm going to lie right here while you watch all these sexy men take off their clothes and dance."

"I'd rather watch you take off your clothes."

"That can be arranged," Mase purred.

Jazz smiled.

"Right after the movie."

Jazz groaned.

There were a few things he'd discovered about Mase. The first was that Mase had more patience than Jazz did. The second was that if Jazz allowed Mase to touch him outside the bedroom, he was a lot more relaxed when Jazz tied him up in it. That worked better for both of them, because even though Jazz had started experimenting with penetrating himself, he was nowhere near ready for Mase to top him.

As the movie went on, Jazz realized that watching something sexy wasn't a good idea. Jazz got harder and harder. Mase kept chuckling and nuzzling his erection. And yet Jazz had no desire to push him off his lap. It was the sweetest torture.

When the movie finally ended, Jazz popped up off the sofa so fast that he almost knocked Mase to the floor.

"In a rush?" Mase teased.

Jazz was already pulling a tie from where it was stashed between the sofa cushions. They had silk ties all over the place. Most of their friends thought they were just two guys who were too lazy to pick them up. That worked out well for them and was probably why they didn't invest in silk rope like Mase had once suggested.

"I'll see you in the bedroom," Mase said as he sauntered down the hall, dropping his clothes as he went.

By the time Jazz got there, Mase was on his back, naked, with one wrist already bound. Jazz was around the bed within two heartbeats, buckling the other leather cuff. They didn't bind Mase's feet anymore, unless it was just for fun.

"I want you to show me," Mase said.

"Show you what?"

"What you do in your bedroom when I hear you moan?"

Jazz's cheeks burned. He'd been experimenting but hadn't realized he was that loud.

"What are you doing in there, Jazzy? Show me."

Even though he felt a little shy and embarrassed, it also made him proud. He was taking his body back. He was using it for pleasure.

Jazz pushed off the sweats he'd been wearing, then took the lube from the nightstand. He climbed on the bed, then straddled Mase's chest, facing his feet.

"Fuck," Mase groaned.

Jazz smiled when Mase almost bucked him off as he humped the air. Then he slid his palm down Mase's abdomen and down to his groin. With lubed fingers, he wrapped his fist around Mase's shaft, stroking up and down on a smooth glide.

"Your pink hole is winking at me," Mase whispered. "I want to taste you one day. Maybe you can sit just like this, and I can fuck you with my tongue."

Jazz whimpered and rolled his hips, pressing his erection into Mase's chest. He quickened his pace as he jacked Mase off. His hips rocked, his ass inching back as he did. As much as he wished Mase would just arch up and try to taste him, Jazz knew he wouldn't, even if his body begged for it. They were slowly getting to the point where they didn't have to discuss every new sex act in detail, but Mase was still hesitant.

Then he felt Mase's tongue on his balls. It was something he knew Jazz liked, so he felt comfortable trying it. Jazz pressed back farther and tilted his hips. He curled himself until he finally felt that wet rasp over that tight pucker.

His body jerked at the sharp pleasure of it. Mase groaned and his chains rattled as he yanked on his restraints. That sound now cranked up Jazz, because Mase did that when he wanted to touch, when he wanted more.

Something settled inside Jazz. He'd been worried that he'd never be able to let Mase near his ass. Even if he was never able to bottom for Mase, he still wanted that intimacy. He wanted to enjoy Mase's touch.

Mase lifted his hips off the bed. He pumped up into Jazz's hand hard and fast. Then his tongue did something that had a needy noise rising from Jazz's throat. He'd begun enjoying his own touch, but he had no clue that so much pleasure could be had from Mase tasting him.

He swiveled his hips, his breath catching each time that wet rasp moved over that little patch of sensitive skin.

"More," he demanded.

He wasn't sure what more really entailed or even if that was what he truly wanted, but the words came anyway...and Mase complied. He must have flexed his tongue between one thrust and another, because the next time Jazz rocked back, the tip pushed inside.

"Shit...Mase...*fuck*."

The hand Jazz had on Mase's hip for support dug into that taut flesh. Jazz gripped Mase's shaft so tightly that Mase grunted. The next time he pressed back, Mase got even deeper.

Mase was inside him. That thought made him shudder. Lightning burst up from his balls, shooting up his shaft as he started to come. He trembled and jerked. Then Mase was spurting between them as well, both their ejaculate landing on Mase's stomach, mixing.

Then Mase did something that struck Jazz as unbearably sweet but also funny. He pressed a chaste kiss at Jazz's opening. Jazz's chuckle turned into a laugh.

"What's so funny?"

"You literally just kissed my ass."

When Jazz swung himself around, Mase was smiling. "You're crazy."

"You still kissed my ass."

"I'd do it again, too."

"And I think I'll let you."

"I got to be the first man inside you." The sigh that left Mase was full of contentment.

Jazz didn't argue, because anything that happened before didn't count. There was only Mase.

Want to see more like this?
Here's a taster for you to enjoy!

Southern Awakenings:
From Bad to Worse
Gin Vane

Excerpt

Everett
Louisiana, 2018

"You know who you have to call, Everett."

Lead Detective Everett Kane sat at his desk with a single thought in his head, surrounded by files that looked like scrapbook memories. Because this Meyers case? Staging aside, it was Patrick Combs all over again.

Major Stapes leaned against the open office door, face unreadable in the light of dimmed fluorescents. "I'll be the first to admit I've no love for the bastard. And with how you all left things…well, there's a bigger picture now."

A hard laugh escaped Everett's throat. "He's the one who saw that in the first place. Back then."

The major nodded, but didn't look happy to agree. For all anyone ever said about "*that nutcase outsider*," not to mention the legitimate grief he gave the bosses back in the day, it'd be easy to turn a blind eye and avoid an uncomfortable sight. But Major Stapes had a reputation for giving credit where it was due. He was the one who'd hired the bastard back when. He knew what he was asking Everett to do—again.

The older man picked at peeling black letters that read *E. Kane, Lead Detective.* "Maybe so," Stapes hedged. "But it doesn't change the facts. Now that there's another body…do it now or do it tomorrow, but you're out of time. We need him."

Everett eyed the locked drawer of his desk. They both knew exactly who he meant, but Everett wasn't stupid enough to go saying the man's name aloud, even to the only boss who could halfway stand him. This case had conjured up enough old ghosts without adding *him* to the mix.

Everett shook his head. "I'm not workin' with him."

The major snorted, a paternal sound that made Everett feel like a kid complaining over chores. With his silver hair and well-lined face, Stapes often reminded Everett of his grandfather, though he wrangled small-town cops instead of stallions. He rapped his knuckles against the door. "Believe that's the second time you've tried to convince me of that, Detective."

Shit. Stapes was right about that too.

The fight fell out of Everett with a heavy sigh, leaving him hunched over the desk. He fixed weary eyes on the photo in front of him—a young woman in a State Rodeo T-shirt and a puddle of her own blood—cut up and dead in a way no person ought to be. One look at those photos and the petty wilted in his gut.

Yeah. There's that bigger picture to think on.

He tried to rub the tiredness from his eyes. "I'm not gettin' out of this, am I?"

Stapes' attention darted around the room—at the photos stapled over the walls, the files that littered every surface, the theories and timelines connected by string and too many cards to count. It made his point too well.

"Not this time."

The major turned on his heel, leaving Everett to stew in his half-lit office. The station lights had long ago been dimmed, which made sense. Everett's colleagues all had homes to be getting to. There'd been a time he had the same — a couple different homes, if he were honest.

He clicked his pen twice, then chucked it at the desk. Broken pieces of plastic scattered to corners unknown.

Fuckin' Harkan. Why'd Colt always have to be right?

Alone and accustomed to being so, he cracked the small window in his smaller office and blazed up a Camel filter. On a normal day, Everett was a strict only-with-coffee smoker. He was down to a pack a week when things stayed the right kind of average. But this one was peeling fast, half-gone from yesterday — a soft pack because *fuck it*, they weren't gonna last long enough to matter. Not when the State Rodeo was once again the scene of a murder. And *certainly* not now the name Colt Harkan was playing on a loop in his mind...

* * * *

Louisiana, 2009, nine years earlier

"I'm not workin' with him, Stapes. Guys who come off undercover...they ain't *right*."

"That's what I like about you, Kane. Got such heart."

Everett took the correction in stride. He slid into a chair with an easy smile, looking wry across the major's desk. A person would be hard-pressed not to give him the whole world when he turned on the charm like that — and Everett knew it. Just so damn likeable.

People couldn't help but say yes. Sometimes before they even realized what he'd asked.

Everett had always been a force-of-personality type, though he wouldn't say the overall package was terrible to look at. The title of Lead Detective kept him clean-shaven and clean-cut, his thick sheaf of wheat-colored hair cropped short and threaded with sun. When he looked in the mirror, his cornflower eyes saw how family life and the nine-to-five grind had dulled the edges of his expression, creased careworn lines he was still getting used to in the corners of his honest face. Everett wasn't as fit as he had been in his rodeo days, but he'd been known to joke in a western bar or three how time made grown-ups of them all. Eventually.

Everett kicked his leg up, bracing his shoe against the major's desk. He propped an arm on his knee, looked down his nose and tilted his head — every trick in the book to get Stapes to go his way. "You know what I mean, Major. Can't hardly tell what he was up to, there's so much black in his file. Looks more like sheet music than Times New Roman. Reads like arty poetry with three words to a page."

Stapes kept typing. "He's had more career in months than most do in decades, I'll give him that."

Everett grunted as he thumbed through the file in his hands. "How can you tell? Even his start date is redacted. And don't tell me it's some clerical error." He closed the rust-colored folder. "What's he doin' in Mason? Ain't we a little back-country for someone with this kind of weight in his file?"

When Everett looked up, the major had that look that meant *stop askin' and I won't have to lie to you.*

Stapes returned attention to his computer monitor. "He's owed some favors. He'll be comin' in rough, but we're the lucky ones here. I've done my calling around and even with those complaints from the brass, he's got the clearances. Might be the real deal."

It wasn't what Everett wanted to hear, but he knew that tone in the major's voice by now.

He grumbled, "Don't see why I gotta hold his hand any."

"Choose your training strategy as you see fit, Kane." Stapes chuckled from behind his big desk. "But he's your partner until he learns the ropes."

Everett stared at the patchwork file labeled *C. Harkan* and decided it was too thick to contain so little fact. But he let it thunk on the major's desk and leaned back in his chair, lacing hands behind his head like he couldn't be bothered. Seemed he was getting a partner after all. He asked, "When's Mr. Sunshine reporting for duty?"

A new voice at the door replied, "Ten minutes ago."

That low, even tone turned Everett's head quick, and he got his first look at Detective Colton Harkan.

Somehow, he looked exactly like his file—a few broad strokes to make the outline of a man. A body by default, formed out of assumption and habit. Like he'd shrugged into life one day and hadn't figured out why. At first glance, Everett was struck with the thought that a man with his background, running thick as thieves with all manner of rough, shouldn't look so quiet, so worn. So tired. Colt's dark eyes and darker hair gave him the look of a shadow, like a piece of thread left to twist in the wind and well, maybe Everett could see it now, on that second look.

Everett knew much about different kinds of dangerous. There was the obvious threat, clocked and taken out on approach.

And there's the one you never see comin'...

Everett's curiosity got the better of him as he held Colt's gaze, a worn-wood ochre that spoke of knowledge learned through pain. Wisdom, some might call it. Colt seemed the type to call it *necessary means*. He had an angular face that might've looked kinder with a smile, but it didn't seem to Everett those were muscles Colt flexed often—though the rest of him was in decent shape. Golden skin shone like he was hardly without a tan. The purple under his eyes matched a bad night's sleep or two days' drunk. Having had his share of both, Everett figured he wasn't in much position to judge and decided to extract the foot from his mouth as fast as possible.

He walked to the door, hand extended. "Everett Kane, Lead Detective. I'll be your—"

"I know who you are."

Colt's assessing eyes swept up and down Everett's frame, radiating how unimpressed he was with anything he was seeing. From Everett's khaki work slacks, blue button-up and cheap tie, even the pleasant smile plastered across his face, Everett knew himself to be the very picture of politeness.

None of it seemed to matter to the man in the doorway. He stepped to the side, angled around Everett and inclined his head to the man behind the desk. "Major."

With that, he left the office.

Everett's outstretched arm felt cold in the empty air, like the handshake he'd expected and had decidedly *not* received was some missed opportunity. His fingers itched as he pulled up short, anxious to get a read on the mystery he'd be working with. Could tell a lot about a man from a handshake. Maybe more from one passed by.

Everett's hands braced on his hips, thumbs digging into the leather of his belt. He watched through the major's window as Colt ambled to the only empty desk, set down a yellow legal pad like he'd been there for years, then left for whereabouts unknown.

Everett swiveled his head to the major, not caring the door was open or that the squad could probably hear him. "You've gotta be fuckin' *kidding* me, Stapes."

"Just a couple of months till he gets his feet."

"And if he don't?"

"Then I'll fire him — and you, if you don't start doin' what it is I pay you for."

Everett mumbled something about "Seniority my ass," that he was careful not to finish too loudly. Before the major could ask him to repeat it, he cut Stapes a sarcastic salute and stuffed his fists in his pockets, resigning himself to follow a man whose training would *clearly* include *Workplace Etiquette for Dummies*. If they made it through training at all.

* * * *

"So what's wrong with you, Harkan? Some kind of fuckin' asshole?"

The words were harsh, but Everett kept his tone light and it all landed softer than it might've otherwise. A little self-aware levity to fix whatever offended his new partner.

As far as Everett could tell, it had zero effect.

Colt hadn't looked his way since he stopped beside him at the coffee machine. The man stared straight ahead as he waited for the pot to fill, eyes fixed on the trickling stream of what he'd soon learn was underwhelming shop coffee. The silence stretched long enough that when Colt finally spoke, Everett almost didn't hear his baritone over the percolating machine.

"You're not my partner. You're my babysitter."

Colt snagged the coffee by the handle, flinching at the hiss of unlucky drops sizzling on the hotplate. He replaced the pot, then stared at Everett over his steaming white cup, a drawl like velvet over the steel of his words. "And I don't need one. Never have."

It wasn't a boast. It wasn't meant to start a fight— though it was clear if things got physical, Harkan wasn't worried over doing what needed done. Colt just…*said* it. Like it was obvious. Like a fact.

Ain't got no personality to him at all, Everett thought.

Unsure how to follow the major's orders with this man as his charge, Everett shrugged. "All right, Harkan. But I gotta give you the nickel tour anyhow, show you the ropes. So I can keep *my* job."

Colt blinked once in response.

To their right, a door opened and a redheaded woman breezed in, wearing a top too low for business casual and a skirt too tight for sitting. She looked up from the stack of files in her arms. Blue eyes landed on Everett and she smiled. "Detective Kane? Those files you were wantin'?"

She had the sweet affectation of a fine Southern lady, though she was doing her best with makeup, attire and attitude to disabuse the notion. Everett met her forward gaze and tilted his head at the door. Kelly would know what he meant.

"Leave 'em in my office, Kel. Take a look after lunch."

Kelly arched her auburn brow, but her curiosity was gone as soon as it came. She gave Colt an appreciative glance, and yeah, Everett supposed he should've guessed women would flock to this enigma he'd been saddled with. He had the exact kind of look that was honey to the fly—brooding, arrogant, unimpressed with life in general. But Everett had never been in so bad a mood he couldn't appreciate a beautiful woman, so as Kelly turned to leave, he let his gaze linger on a few points of those...*files* he planned to examine later.

When he faced Colt again, he hadn't expected what he found. The expression sat strangely on his placid face, but if Everett had to guess, it was something like a smile—full of implications he didn't much appreciate.

"What, Harkan?"

Colt's eyes fell to Everett's left hand. The ring on his fourth finger fairly burned with guilt. But when he leveled his anger on the man in front of him, ready to challenge the impending question, none followed. Colt only stared at the scratched golden band, then blinked back to Everett like it wasn't worth his trouble. He was just noticing. And telling without *telling* that yeah, he'd noticed.

Everett's jaw ticked as he inhaled sharp. His stance shifted to something ready for a fight. "Fuck you, man. Ain't a thing you need to be thinkin' over there."

Colt nodded over his coffee, obviously unconvinced. But when he flicked his eyes up to hold Everett's stare, those warm-wooded orbs seemed less empty, less sunk-in. More like a tracker on the trail. A predator in wait, contemplating the hunt. Everett was two seconds from decking him for something to do when Colt ignored all manner of space and checked into his shoulder, brushing past like Everett wasn't standing right there to follow Kelly out of the door.

"Let's wrap this tour up. Wanna get to something worth my time."

Not waiting for Everett to follow, Colt sipped his coffee and let the door slam. Everett massaged his shoulder, still tingling from the contact.

Fuckin'. Asshole.

About the Author

Rae has been secretly penning romances since high school. It started with short stories that grew into full-length novels. When she received her first Kindle and had thousands of books at her fingertips, she became a little distracted from writing. Then one day she read a book that she would have written a different way. She began writing again and hasn't stopped since.

When she's not writing, Rae can usually be found reading, walking along the beaches of Half Moon Bay, or taking her geriatric dog to the vet, yet again.

Rae loves to hear from readers. You can find her contact information, website details and author profile page at https://www.pride-publishing.com

PUBLISHING

Sign up for our newsletter and find out about all our romance book releases, eBook sales and promotions, sneak peeks and FREE romance books!

www.ingramcontent.com/pod-product-compliance
Lightning Source LLC
Chambersburg PA
CBHW030810260626
47169CB00001B/269